PRAISE FOR AH

"Nostalgia comes home to die in these fourteen stories, re-examining a horrifying decade without rose-colored glasses. The early days of the internet and the last gasp of a century on videotape all delivered in pulsing neon prose."
ANDREW F. SULLIVAN, AUTHOR OF *THE MARIGOLD* AND *THE HANDYMAN METHOD*

"Fans of *The Midnight Club*, *My Best Friend's Exorcism* and *The Pallbearer's Club* will love *AHH! That's What I Call Horror: An Anthology of '90s Horror*. This book is jam-packed with dial-up internet nostalgia, creepypasta-inspired monsters, occult rituals, Camaros, camcorders, weed, time travel, flannel shirts, Lisa Frank imagery, VHS weirdness, and a whole lot of nineties music."
CHRISTI NOGLE, AUTHOR OF *THE BEST OF OUR PAST, THE WORST OF OUR FUTURE*

"*AHH! That's What I Call Horror* is a thrilling ghost train ride through everything you can never forget about the '90s. In terms of nostalgia, it hits all the right spots—and for me, growing up away from the Anglo world, brought up several new curiosities—without being *about* the nostalgia so much as about the humanity. Beneath that bright, bubble-gum flavoured surface riddled with psychics and toy crazes and sitcoms and videogames, there's this overall question that I loved, so different from the usual "what's coming next?" of horror stories: "What happened there?". What happened to us then, in the chaos of a decade that for many of us, may as well have been the big bang that created everything our world revolves around today? How far did our obsessions, and gullibility, and fears, and desires, take us? And, ultimately, since nothing is ever wasted, what have those obsessions and fears turned into, since?

An absolutely wonderful read today, and no doubt one that'll only get better, more relevant, and more bittersweet over the following decades."

ALEX WOODROE, EIC OF TENEBROUS PRESS AND AUTHOR OF *WHISPERWOOD*

"*AHH! That's What I Call Horror* is an anthology that pulls on the most familiar and iconic elements of the '90s and draws it into a kaleidoscopic flurry of atmospheric stories that emphasize both the eerie and the uncanny. With witty characters, vintage backdrops, experimental formatting, and quirky but dark narratives, the stories breathe new life into pulp horror. It allows for a glimpse into the darkness of a time when I had just been born, but even so, these characters make me believe that I have known them all my life, have walked past them down the road, seen them watching me through the window across the street."

AI JIANG, AUTHOR OF *LINGHUN*

AHH! THAT'S WHAT I CALL HORROR

AN ANTHOLOGY OF '90S HORROR

Edited by
CHELSEA PUMPKINS

Copyright © 2023

All rights reserved.

No part of this book may be reproduced in any form or by any electronic or mechanical means, including information storage and retrieval systems, without written permission from the author, except for the use of brief quotations in a book review.

The story, all names, characters, and incidents portrayed in this production are fictitious. No identification with actual persons (living or deceased), places, buildings, and products is intended or should be inferred.

Editing by Chelsea Pumpkins.

Formatting by Carson Winter.

Cover art and design by Cassie Daley.

Interior art by P.L. McMillan and Jenny Kiefer.

All stories are owned by their respective authors.

*This one's for the goths, the geeks, the flannel skaters,
gel pen collectors, trapper keeper decorators,
the gamers playing ToeJam & Earl,
the latchkey kids, and valley girls.*

*For the ones whose screennames are too shameful to shout
and the kids painting their nails with sharpies and white-out.
For the Macarena dancers, the punks, the slackers,
Tamagotchi caretakers, and Lunchable snackers.
For fans who swooned over Scully and Mulder,
who watched Saved by the Bell and In Living Color.*

*For the teens in JNCO jeans hanging long and wide,
and the ones who were always kind enough to rewind.
For the peeps who can beatbox the dial-up connection,
I hope you totally dig this horror collection.*

CONTENTS

Foreword	ix
MADAME CRYSTAL S.E. Denton	1
THE HARVEST QUEEN Bridget D. Brave	23
WHO IN THE WORLD IS THE HAT MAN? Chelsea Pumpkins	37
BETWEEN THE BARBIE AND THE DEEP-BLUE RANGER Christopher O'Halloran	53
THE GRUNGE Caleb Stephens	63
NONA'S FIRST AND LAST ALBUM DROP Edith Lockwood	85
THE ONE WITH THE MYSTERIOUS PACKAGE C.B. Jones	103
CAUTION: CHOKING HAZARD Mathew Wend	121
RETURN TO GRAY SPRINGS: BLOCKBUSTER BLUES P.L. McMillan	137
ALIVE AND LIVING (PILOT) Carson Winter	177
THE END OF THE HORROR STORY Patrick Barb	207
THE FINAL AWAY GAME J.W. Donley	235
ABOUT A GIRL J.V. Gachs	251
THRESHOLD Damien B. Raphael	265

Acknowledgments	284
Contributors	286
Cover Artist	290
Story Illustrators	291
Content Warnings	292

FOREWORD

Watching *Saved by the Bell* while getting ready for school. Listening to terrible nu-metal on my CD player while waiting for the bus. Ejecting orange VHS tapes. Cutting thumb holes into my hoodie sleeves to make DIY gloves. Drawing a weird S on everything within reach. Smashing Power Rangers action figures together and making loud explosion noises. Dedicating hours of each day thinking about my Pokemon card collection. Wishing I had a dog like Wishbone. Saying "bad" to mean something's good. Failing to imagine what the neighbor from *Home Improvement* could possibly look like. Spelling "fat" with a ph. Telling people to talk to the hand. Describing everything as cool beans. Stockpiling Chuck E. Cheese tokens like a grandparent who survived the Depression. Binging Christopher Pike paperbacks like they were SpaghettiOs. Marathoning judge shows while sick from school. Pushing fruit-flavored ice out of triangle-shaped packets. Stressing out about my Tamagotchi getting sick. Squeezing cold pizza sauce on a circle of hard dough. Constantly craving Good Burger and orange pop. Fantasizing about one day drowning in green Nickelodeon slime.

These are the things that come to mind when I think about the '90s. Every decade is weird, but not every decade is as weird as the

1990s. We were in the final stretch of an entire millennium. Existing at the end of such a significant point in time does something to the brain. Everything is changing and heading down unpredictable paths. Life takes on a bizarre, almost artificial layer. What will people be obsessed over in the year 2999? I can't even begin to imagine, but I hope it's something embarrassing like chia pets and not something as soul-crushingly depressing like total and complete climate failure.

The stories in this anthology contain several purposes, but in the end they all share the same common objective: recapture a glimpse of the '90s. Do they succeed? Absolutely. Reading this anthology is like popping open a time capsule. Yet it also succeeds as an excellent horror anthology. The decade plays a big part in every story but never does it feel forced. Opening a book like this, one might fear an overwhelming dosage of references. Thankfully, the authors here are smart enough to avoid such traps—unlike myself, in retrospect, upon re-reading the first paragraph of this introduction. Any brand name drops actually make sense within the context of each contribution.

I'm not going to spoil these stories for you. You can probably guess some of the things you'll encounter while reading, just from the nature of the era the anthology is set. Yes, there are chat rooms. There are Blockbusters. There is grunge music. Okay, there is a *lot* of grunge music. But it works! Cobain would be proud.

Just as I am proud to now hand you over to 14 wonderful, entertaining writers. Take your time with this book. Absorb not only the stories but also the wonderful interior illustrations. And don't forget to have some fun with it. This anthology is a celebration of fun horror at its finest.

—Max Booth III
January 3, 2023

MADAME CRYSTAL

S.E. DENTON

The glass doors glide open, blasting sterilized AC into my face.

The atmosphere teems with harsh fluorescent lighting, flashing TV screens, and the galvanic hum of approximately 30,000 square feet of home electronics. Hootie and the Blowfish's "Only Wanna Be With You" rains down from the speakers.

Best Buy. A wonderland for the consumers, a personal hell for yours truly.

Six straight hours of this ahead for me. No freedom until 9:00 PM. And I'm *late*.

I cut through the CD section on the way to the break room to clock in and find Angela organizing CDs. Before I can backtrack out of the aisle, she spots me.

"Hi, Adam."

Our brief flash of eye contact makes my head swim. Her long curly hair is dyed a brazen Tori Amos red and she always smells like a Bath & Body Works store. She's busy scoping out the tracklist of a Joan Osborne album, so she only glances at me. I make a mental note to buy it later, even though I'm more of a Radiohead *The Bends* kind of person.

"Hi," I say, trying to keep my voice steady.

"How's your software thing going?"

For the past eight months I've been writing an encryption software called CypherQuest.

"Oh, you know. Not bad. I sold some copies on my website, so that's good."

"Awesome," she says, smiling in a way that makes my face turn hot. "Are you going to Jason's party tonight?"

Jason works in the movie section. He wants to be a director. He dubbed everyone copies of his last movie, *Zombie Babes*. I seriously doubt his future success. Plus, he's an asshole.

"Nah," I say. "I've got plans."

I don't tell her that my weekend plans are to fix bugs in CypherQuest.

"Yeah, I probably won't go either. I should stay home."

This is the longest conversation we've ever had. Despite the fact that I can feel my pulse in my throat and that I'm now five minutes late to clock in, I don't want it to end.

"How come?" I ask.

Angela replaces the Joan Osborne CD.

"My horoscope said that I should avoid crowds today."

"Oh?"

"Yeah." She picks up a misplaced Portishead CD and puts it in its correct location. "It might be bullshit, but my horoscopes always seem pretty accurate, so I dunno."

"What sign are you?" I ask her, even though I know nothing about signs.

"I'm a Pisces," she says. "You?"

"May."

"That's not a sign," Angela says, smirking. "May what?"

"May 16th."

"A Taurus," Angela says. "A bull."

"Yep. I'm a bull."

Angela smiles at me. "You're into astrology?"

"Yeah." Pretty much a lie. "Some things, I mean."

"Do you read your horoscope?"

"Most days. But not today."

I can't recall ever reading my horoscope, but I know that from now on, I'll be reading it every day. And learning everything I can about Pisces people.

Ross, the manager, rounds the corner, sees all of us huddled together, chatting.

"Adam, have you clocked in yet?"

His hair is gelled into pointy spikes. He's shorter than me, way older, and rounder. A perfectly-sculpted mustache covers his baby face. I know for a fact that he still lives with his mother. So do I, but I'm nineteen. Ross has to be at least thirty-five.

"Not yet...I was just..."

"We're organizing the CDs," Angela says.

"That's *your* job," Ross snaps. "Adam, clock in and go sell some goddamn computers."

I continue on my way back to the aisles of IBMs, Packard Bells, and Compaqs. I should be happy here, but among all the fluorescent lighting, cutting-edge tech, and Top 40 blaring on the overhead speakers, I feel depressed. This is what I get for dropping out of community college. My parents told me I had to get a job, and so I did. This is only temporary until my software business takes off, though. Only a matter of time before I'm the next Steve Jobs or Bill Gates. A fucking millionaire. Then people will be buying CypherQuest in Best Buys. In the meantime, all I have to do is collect a paycheck helping old people understand what a modem is or making Microsoft Word sound sexy to businessmen who prefer to create documents with typewriters. Depressing, but easy enough.

And, of course, there's Angela. She's the only part of this that is bearable.

It takes six attempts to connect to AOL, but finally I'm online.

I check my email, hoping for more orders, but it's empty. Just as well. I already have my hands full with the two orders I do have. I'm going to have to pull an all-nighter working on bugs as it is.

Downstairs, I can hear my parents watching TV. My stomach churns an undigested cheese-and-ham hot pocket and two glasses of Mountain Dew.

To procrastinate debugging CypherQuest, I do a quick search for horoscope sites. Several web pages turn up. Astrostar Astrology Experts, which charges money; Jenny's Horoscope Page that looks like a fourteen-year-old's creation; Heavenly Horoscopes, which is so obviously Christian; Angel Whispers Horoscope (same); and a few others. One in particular catches my eye: Madame Crystal. I click the link to the page.

It takes a few seconds to load, gradually revealing a twinkling celestial background and then the words "Madame Crystal" in bright pink curlicue font centered directly above a glowing crystal ball graphic. Below that: "Welcome! You're visitor number 6!"

Six? It must be a new website. I've had forty-seven visitors, and I thought that was weak.

There's another graphic of a stick figure with a flashing question mark above its head: "Ever wonder what the future holds? I will tell you! No gimmicks! Enter your email address and receive your FREE horoscope every day!"

I scroll down further, but there's no picture of Madame Crystal, only a text box for entering an email address. I try to imagine what she looks like, but all my mind conjures up is a mish mash of psychics I've seen on shows like "Unsolved Mysteries," and all of them had big glasses, bad makeup, and puffy hair. It's possible that Madame Crystal isn't even a woman. None of it seems very legit, but I don't want to mess with going through any more psychic websites, so I type in *geekboy75@aol.com*, enter in my birthday, and click the pink ENTER button.

A new screen with the same celestial background: "Madame Crystal has received your request. Check your email tomorrow for your *personalized* daily horoscope!"

That's that. I sign off, and go to work on CypherQuest.

I DON'T WAKE up until after noon on Saturday. My day starts off rocky. As I'm pouring milk onto my cereal, the whole goddamn carton slips from my grip. My bowl flips, scattering Cap'N Crunch all over the counter and half the milk spills on the floor. It takes me fifteen minutes to clean up the whole mess, wiping and sweeping everything up. By the time I'm done, I opt for some coffee and a pack of cold Pop-Tarts and go upstairs to check if I have any new orders.

"You've got mail!" blares from the computer speakers.

I click the mailbox icon, hoping for something exciting, like an email from some girl in a chat room or a response from one of the Silicon Valley jobs I randomly applied for in hopes that I'd get out of Tulsa. Instead, there's only my horoscope from Madame Crystal: *Your personalized horoscope! Open now!*

The email has no design to it at all—no colored background or fancy font. Only one sentence in Times New Roman: "Don't cry over spilled milk."

I blink a few times, making sure I read it right, then scoff. Coincidental. Cliche. But it also feels *weird*.

Maybe I'm reading too much into it. That's how horoscopes work, right? Vague enough so that whatever is said can fit anyone.

"Thanks, Madame Crystal," I say, and sign off.

AFTER PROGRAMMING all through Saturday night, I woke up Sunday afternoon with a stuffy head, chills, throbbing bones, and a burning throat. I call into work and barricade myself in my bedroom. As I stare up at my ceiling, shivering, I feel my body temperature rising, igniting my brain, enveloping me into the onset of a hellish fever dream. I don't remember much after that.

It isn't until Wednesday morning that I wake up feeling like a normal person again. Still congested and a bit weak, but decent. I snag a carton of orange juice from the fridge, offer an obligatory greeting to my mother who is reading some sort of prayer book at the kitchen table while the news blasts on the small TV on the counter.

"Are you feeling better?" she asks, not looking up from her book.

I love her—she's my mother. But she's also the woman who told me when I was in the sixth grade that demonic possession was possible for children who watched rated R movies, played violent video games, communed with Ouija boards, and listened to "grunge music" and "rapping," all of which I had done by age twelve.

I spent the first quarter of my teen years genuinely afraid of being possessed, going to church and bible study, and monitoring myself for any strange new sensations that could be a demon slipping into my skin. She constantly filled my head with fears.

At this point, we're practically strangers to one another. She has her bible and her church and her televangelist shows. I have my computer (I saved up for it and bought it myself), a CD collection of "disturbed" musicians, and my massive VHS collection of R-rated movies.

My relationship with my father is even worse.

I go back upstairs to my room and log on to AOL.

"You've got mail!"

Lots of mail. A newsletter from a programming club out in California. An email from my friend Charlie, who got a scholarship to Stanford (sparking the usual scorching bloom of envy in my heart), a few promotions for software and computer sales, and other crap.

And, of course, my missed daily horoscopes from Madame Crystal.

I start with Sunday's: *a germ is a seed that births a garden of disease.*

It's well written, but sort of weird. Also, like the milk horoscope, strangely parallel to my life having just recovered from the flu.

Monday's horoscope: *right now you are dreaming, and I'm there with you.*

I strain to recall anything from my fever dreams, but it's all a sickening blur.

Not wanting to waste more time thinking about it, I open yesterday's horoscope: *something big is on the horizon...*

It's all very weird. The germ thing, and the dream thing. I remind myself that I don't believe this shit, but there's a chill that starts at the back of my neck and slithers down my spine. I sip my juice from the carton and open today's horoscope.

There's only one word: *Kablooey.*

A chuckle works itself up my throat, although it's not exactly funny.

"Kablooey," I say. "Ka-bloo-ey..."

Downstairs, my mother screams.

Two days later, I'm watching firefighters dig through the eviscerated innards of the Alfred P. Murrah Federal Building on a 27" Sony TV in the home entertainment section of Best Buy. Pulverized concrete, twisted metal, the occasional children's shoe from the daycare center, rubble piled on top of bodies. My mother's cousin, Carol, is buried somewhere within that devastation. My mom has been on the phone every few hours with my great aunt Barbara, desperate for new details.

I don't recall exactly which of my mom's cousins Carol is, but the thought of anyone buried beneath tons of ruination makes my hands tremble inside the pockets of my khakis.

"Adam, change the channel," Ross, the manager, says to me. He somehow snuck up behind me without me noticing. "Sad shit doesn't sell TVs."

"This just happened *two* days ago, Ross," I say. "Less than two hours from here."

"We sell electronics," Ross says. "We have jobs to do."

His face sours as he watches the footage, before flicking his attention back to me.

"And what are you doing over here anyway?" he says. "Get back to your section."

I switch over to a boring golf tournament and head over to the computers. The images from the news recycles through my mind, along with one word:

Kablooey. Kablooey. *Kablooey*.

MY STOMACH TWISTS as I stare at the five unopened daily horoscopes from Madame Crystal. I haven't had the courage to open a single one since the bombing, but I also didn't want to delete them. Over the past few days, I convinced myself that it was a coincidence. That seemed more likely than a psychic predicting mayhem in cryptic emails.

I open Thursday's horoscope. It reads: *don't stop thinking about tomorrow*

As soon as I read the sentence a few times, my tension lessens. Seems like another cliche billboard slogan. No harm there.

Friday's: *don't stop it will soon be here*

It takes a moment for that one to sink in. What will soon be here? My stomach clenches, but only for a second, until I realize that it's connected with Thursday's horoscope.

I quickly open Saturday's: *it'll be better than before*

Madame Crystal is sending me fucking Fleetwood Mac lyrics. The same song Bill Clinton used for his inaugural campaign.

Sunday's horoscope completes the chorus: *yesterday's gone yesterday's gone*

Nervous laughter bubbles inside of me, but it doesn't reach my throat.

Before I lose my nerve, I double click to open today's horoscope and immediately see it's a completely different message than its predecessors.

It reads: *Here is the UNLUCKY # of the day...(drum roll)...#16!*

Sixteen?

Despite my sense of dread, I tell myself that the horoscope is meaningless. Sending song lyrics is harmless, as is assigning some number as "unlucky." Madame Crystal is either a poorly written computer program, a bored thirteen-year-old boy, or maybe a burnout hippie.

Regardless, none of this means anything. Nothing at all.

IT ISN'T until I'm eating my morning bowl of Cap'N Crunch that I catch a glimpse of the headline nestled up to the other more prominent headline about the Oklahoma City bombing. This one reads, matter-of-factly: *Unabomber Strikes Again.*

I scan the article. The day before, a mail bomb detonated at the offices of the California Forestry Association and killed Gilbert B. Murray, 47, the association's executive director. Federal agents believe him to be the 16th victim of the serial bomber known as the "Unabomber."

today's UNLUCKY number is...16!

"Oh shit," I say.

"Adam!" My mother stares at me from across the kitchen, holding a spoonful of strawberry jam. "What have I said—"

The cereal is already spurting up my throat. I manage to make it to the downstairs bathroom before a torrent of mushy Cap' N Crunch splatters into the toilet bowl.

I LOG ON TO AOL, again. My stomach still threatens to retaliate, although I'm pretty sure there isn't any more cereal left in me.

I type in www.madamecrystalhoroscopes.com.

Instead of the celestial background and crystal ball and curly, pink font, I get a stagnant white page reading "404 PAGE NOT FOUND." I check the web address for typos. Nope. Maybe it was only www.madamecrystal.com? I try that and get the same message.

In AOL search, I type in "daily horoscopes" and recreate my original path to Madame Crystal's site. I see in my history all the links I've clicked on, highlighted, remembering each website *distinctly*. The last one I looked at before finding Madame Crystal's was one called "Astro Secrets" promising to deliver wisdom from the cosmos. I scroll through all the results.

Nothing. Madame Crystal has vanished.

INSTEAD OF LETTING IT GO, I spend hours visiting astrology forums, looking for any mention of Madame Crystal. I visit several chat rooms and ask if anyone has ever signed up for her daily horoscopes or talked to her. Nothing turns up, which is odd.

Just about the time a headache begins to throb behind my left eye, an AOL messenger box appears:

MadameCrystal: hello!
MadameCrystal: ru looking 4 me?

I stare at the screen, dumbfounded. She must have seen one of my forum posts or was lurking in the chatrooms, although under a different user name. When I resurface seconds later from my shock, I check out Madame Crystal's AOL profile. No information there.

MadameCrystal: hello RU there?
geekboy75: Yes, I'm here.
MadameCrystal: hello adam!!!!

How does she know my name? I only have my screen name in my profile. I definitely didn't use my real name in the forums or chat rooms.

geekboy75: How do you know my name?
MadameCrystal: i'm MADAME CRYSTAL. i know all.
geekboy75: Right.

I think for a moment. Let my pulse slow back down before I type my next question.

geekboy75: What did you mean by "Kablooey" and "unlucky number 16"?
MadameCrystal: u already know
geekboy75: No, I don't know. Tell me.
MadameCrystal: i'm the messenger. ur the interpreter.
geekboy75: Where do you live?
MadameCrystal: everywhere
geekboy75: Do you know where I live?
MadameCrystal: yes
geekboy75: Where?
MadameCrystal: tulsa with your parents by the mall

They're fucking with me.

Is it one of my old programming acquaintances? Someone I pissed off somehow?

geekboy75: Hilarious. So I know you.
MadameCrystal: u don't know me
geekboy75: Whatever you say. I want to unsubscribe from your horoscopes.
MadameCrystal: LOL no u don't
geekboy75: Yes, I do.
MadameCrystal: bye bye adam

Before I can type anything else, Madame Crystal signs off.

ANGELA WALKS into the break room a few minutes after me and sits down at the same table to eat a small bag of Doritos and smoke a cigarette. In order to not let any awkward silence form, I ask her about horoscopes—if she gets hers off the internet.

"The newspaper," she says. "Also, my sister has a friend who's pretty psychic. Sometimes she'll give me tarot readings."

"Have you ever heard of a daily horoscope provider called Madame Crystal?"

I know she hasn't, because I was supposedly the sixth person to visit the website.

"Nope," she says, crunching on a chip. Her eyes are bright blue. Like swimming pools in July. "Why?"

"Well...I signed up for a daily horoscope on this website for Madame Crystal..." I pause, careful not to say too much. "And... things got really weird."

"How do you mean?"

"You'll think I'm crazy."

Angela sets down the bag of chips, and smiles.

"I love conversations that start with the words, 'you'll think I'm crazy.' Spill it."

I clobber together a messy summation of everything that's happened in the past few days—the eerie horoscopes, the Oklahoma City bombing, the sixteenth victim of the Unabomber. The online chats with a very clairvoyant Madame Crystal. Her abruptly missing website. Everything.

"I have no idea who this person is," I say, wondering if I've just killed all chances of ever asking Angela out on a date, even though I'm not sure I'd ever have the nerve to do so anyway.

"Aren't you, like, a hacker or something? Can't you figure out who the website belongs to?"

"That's not really my forte. I write software. And, besides, the website is gone, like I said."

"Maybe you should call the cops then."

"And tell them what?"

"That some creep is sending you messages about terrorist attacks. What if it's the Unabomber?"

"The email said 'Kablooey' and 'unlucky number sixteen.' That's hardly a confession. And she hasn't said anything threatening in her messages. Just weird, creepy stuff."

"Well, if she isn't actually psychic, then obviously she or he is a terrorist who knows you. Do you know any terrorists?"

"What? No. Why would I know terrorists?"

"I don't know," she says and stamps out her cigarette in the overcrowded ashtray. "What do you want me to say?"

I think for a moment. "Just tell me that I'm not crazy"

"Adam," she says. "I know a lot of crazy people. You're definitely not crazy."

She smiles at me, a genuine smile, and for the first time in days, things seem sane.

WHEN I GET HOME from work, I log on to AOL and wait for Madame Crystal. She must have been waiting for me, because she messages me within seconds.

MadameCrystal: hello adam. How was ur day?
geekboy75: Pretty shitty, thanks to you.
MadameCrystal: i only give horoscopes
geekboy75: foretelling horrible things that happen
MadameCrystal: it is a blessing and a CURSE

My stomach clenches. It's odd, but I swear I feel a presence. I tell myself it's only my wrecked nerves and imagination working together.

geekboy75: How do you know these things?
MadameCrystal: i'm a prophet.
geekboy75:If you know these things are going to happen, why don't you stop them?
MadameCrystal: there is no stopping them.
geekboy75:What do you mean? Why can't they be stopped?
MadameCrystal: *The LORD regretted that He had made human beings on the earth, and his heart was deeply troubled. So the LORD said, "I will wipe from the face of the earth the human race I have created—and with them the animals, the birds, and the creatures that move along the ground—for I regret that I have made them.*
geekboy75: Are you trying to tell me you're god?
MadameCrystal: LOL LOL LOL
geekboy75: Who are you?
MadameCrystal: do u want to STOP BAD THINGS, ADAM?
geekboy75: Who wouldn't?
MadameCrystal: DO U WANT TO?
geekboy75:Yes

A very long pause...

geekboy75: Hello?

MadameCrystal: ok, i will help u stop a BAD THING if u help me with a GOOD THING

MadameCrystal: i have written a secret letter and i want it delivered to my friend

geekboy75: Ok

MadameCrystal: i want to be a customer of your cipher program

geekboy75: How do you know about that?

MadameCrystal: i know about everything

geekboy75: Prove it. I'm going to think of a word in my mind. Type what it is.

The first thing that pops into my mind, for whatever reason, is the candy "Mentos."

MadameCrystal: MENTOS THE FRESHMAKER

This isn't happening. There's no way. I take a second to calm myself before typing.

geekboy75: Do it again. I'm thinking of an image.

I try to think of something happy, but instead I remember my estranged uncle's funeral in Florida when I was ten, and my mother telling me that it was Paul's own fault he was dead; that God gave Paul AIDS because he was gay. Something that felt like such a cruel belief to have, because he'd been such a kind, amazing person. My favorite uncle.

MadameCrystal: RIP uncle paul

Unbelievable. My lips go numb. My heart feels too big, slamming against my ribs.

geekboy75: Okay, you win.
MadameCrystal: give me the software
geekboy75: Fine. What is your address?
MadameCrystal: u r so funny
geekboy75: How am I supposed to give it to you? It's on a disk. You have to install it.
MadameCrystal: send it to john smith 556 county road 512 stonewall, alabama 36701 i will get it

I write down the address.

MadameCrystal: when i get it and send my secret message to my friend i will tell u about a BAD THING u can stop

Just like the night before, she signs off before I can type anything else. I stare at the address, wondering if it's Madame Crystal's or some relative of hers. When I put the address into the online White Pages nothing comes up. I search Stonewall, Alabama and locate it on a map, but there's no other information about it.

I tell myself that it's someone I know messing with me, but the logic has worn away, revealing something I can't even begin to comprehend. Somehow, I signed up to receive a daily horoscope from an actual psychic who is probably also psychotic. At least there's a physical address in reality tied to Madame Crystal. Demons don't have mailing addresses. Do they?

I SPEND the rest of the night fixing the bugs in CypherQuest, then put the program on a stack of disk drives for installation.

The next day, I send it off to Stonewall, Alabama. Then wait. And wait some more. All my spare time is spent on AOL, but not a single message from Madame Crystal. No daily horoscopes either.

April slipped into May. There were tornado outbreaks in the

Midwest. Some guy in California stole a tank and went on a rampage. Not to mention all the other things that happened in the world during those two and a half weeks. During this time, I tried to wrap my mind around why Madame Crystal wanted CypherQuest. How she even knew about CypherQuest. Was he or she a hacker? But that didn't explain how they knew I was thinking about poor Uncle Paul or Mentos. Those things were in my mind, not anywhere else. And what secret message are they writing? And to who?

Then, a few days shy of my twentieth birthday, I sign on to AOL after getting home from Best Buy and receive a message immediately.

MadameCrystal: hi adam!!!
geekboy75: Where have you been? Did you get the software?
MadameCrystal: yes and I have sent my secret message
geekboy75: To whom?
MadameCrystal: my secret
geekboy75: Fine. I haven't gotten any horoscopes.
MadameCrystal: i was waiting to give u this one
MadameCrystal: angela is going to die

My heart undergoes a painful spasm, and I'm certain I'm having a heart attack. Dizziness. Cold sweat. Wind in my ears.

geekboy75: How do you know about Angela?
MadameCrystal: angela will die
MadameCrystal: very bad
MadameCrystal: but u can stop it. u told me u wanted to stop a BAD THING
MadameCrystal: here is ur chance
geekboy75: How is she going to die?
MadameCrystal: she is downtown at the center of the universe. she will get shot there

The Center of the Universe is a freaky local attraction in downtown Tulsa. Fine during the day. A bit sketchy at night.

geekboy75: what time will she get shot?
MadameCrystal: 10:27

I look at the time. It's 9:30 and downtown is a good twenty-five minutes away from my place. If everything aligns, I can make it.

Without wasting a second more, I run out of the house, jump into my beat-up Civic and haul ass across the city, careful to not go over the speed limit. If I get pulled over, I could be too late. Bad mistake, because if I had been five minutes faster, I would have missed getting stuck in the most unforgivable Friday night traffic. I can't go forward, can't back up.

"C'mon, goddamn it!" I yell and smash my palm on the horn.

It's now 9:45.

After ten minutes, I get out of my car, walk along the median and get a glimpse of the cause: a Jeep and a pickup truck collided in the intersection. The person who was in the Jeep is lying in the middle of the intersection, blood and glass everywhere. The sight makes me woozy and I hurry back to my car.

9:57.

For a second, I almost jump out of the car again and run to the gas station on the corner to call the cops and tell them that a girl will be shot at the Center of the Universe downtown, but then sirens approach, and I can see the swirling lights up ahead.

10:01. 10:02. 10:03.

I'm never going to get out of this in time.

10:04. 10:05.

Slowly, the cars ahead of me start crawling forward. One of the cops is directing traffic around the accident. The body is covered, and blood and glass are still everywhere. The survivors are crying on the curb, scratched and shaken.

It all slides away in my rearview as I speed toward downtown.

I DON'T ARRIVE downtown until 10:25, two minutes before Angela is to be shot. A crappy industrial van is hogging the only street parking, so I don't bother. Since downtown Tulsa is mostly dead at night, I leave my car on the street and sprint to the pedestrian bridge over the railroad tracks.

"Angela!" I scream as I run. "Angela!"

I can see Angela in the distance, her auburn hair gleaming in the glow of a streetlamp, smoking a cigarette in a small group.

"Angela!"

She turns and sees me running toward her, squinting to identify who's calling her name.

I finally reach her, gasping.

"Adam?" she says, wild-eyed. "What the hell are you doing here?"

I struggle to catch my breath, even though I only ran a few petty yards.

"You're in danger!" I say "You have to–"

I don't finish my sentence.

Something explodes behind me.

IT WAS a miracle that neither Angela nor myself were killed or even seriously hurt, despite all the debris blasting past and more of it falling from the sky. Concrete. Glass and bricks. Parts of cars and metal and pipes. Broken office furniture and papers everywhere. The depth of the destruction is hard for my mind to process.

My car was taken out in the explosion, so I had to use a bystander's cellular to call my dad to pick me up. The police won't let anyone near the building, so all I can do is wait with all of the rubberneckers who are eavesdropping on all the reporters and cops.

A few feet away from me, a local reporter with usually sculpted blonde hair, is a mess, her eye makeup running, her blue eyes wild with fear as she faces a TV cameraman.

Her voice trembles as she speaks: "First responders are still working to assess what happened, but it is believed that a bomb went off shortly before 10:30 tonight. It is expected that the deaths will be minimal compared to the Oklahoma City Bombing, which took the lives of 168 people on April 19th, a month ago. The building was one of the tallest in the state, so the damage is severe, but luckily the First Place Tower housed offices, so there is hope that very few people were inside on a Friday night. However, it will take time to ascertain deaths. I can tell you right now that all of downtown has felt the impact of this explosion..."

A man with a bloody forehead is being interviewed by another local news reporter.

All I can think about is Madame Crystal. How she tricked me.

Was she trying to kill me? It seemed obvious that my death was her master plan, but Angela was where she said she'd be. And she knew about the bomb, just like she knew about the other acts of terrorism.

I can barely think over the ringing in my ears from the blast.

All I know is that it's a blessing to be alive.

MY DAD and I finally get home after one o' clock. My mother is devastated and hysterical, and I can't do much more than tell her that I survived and that I'll tell her all about it in the morning. For once my father acts like a human being, and comforts her, and gets her off to bed. I hurry upstairs and log on to AOL.

I expect Madame Crystal to pounce the moment I sign on, but nothing happens.

Minutes pass.

"Where the hell are you, you crazy bitch?"

There's a sudden commotion downstairs. Someone busting through the front door into the house. Seconds later, my mom screams. My dad yells. I stand up and start to head for my bedroom door, but my speakers suddenly blurt out, "You've got mail!"

I stop, turn around and click open my mailbox. A horoscope from Madame Crystal.

Footsteps pound up the stairs:

The fresh horoscope reads: *knock! knock!*

My bedroom door busts open, and I'm staring at several agents pointing guns at me.

I put my arms in the air.

"Adam Howard?" the lead agent with icy blue eyes and slicked back hair says.

"Yeah, that's me."

"The Adam Howard who wrote CypherQuest?"

"Yeah."

"You're under arrest for the bombing of the First Place Tower."

"What?" I say. "Me? I'm not a fucking terrorist!"

"You were downtown at the time of the blast tonight. Verified by your witness statement."

"Yeah, I was, but—"

"And we have your manifesto," another agent with a rusty mustache says.

I feel my face twitch. "*What* manifesto?"

"You sent us an encrypted message from an untraceable email weeks ago. Then today your software shows up in the mail. One of our agents put it together and we were able to decrypt it. Too late, I'm afraid."

"I didn't do any of that!" I yell. "I was framed!"

"You can tell that to your lawyer."

I try to point to my computer screen, show them Madame Crystal's email, but I'm cuffed and shoved out of my room, led down the stairs and out the front door. My mother is crying on the front lawn. My dad is pale, staring at me like I'm a monster.

This is where it ends. Just like that. My reputation. My future. My whole life.

Kablooey.

S.E. DENTON is a UX/UI designer by day and a horror writer by night. She lives in Los Angeles with her partner, cats, and too many books. She can be found on Twitter @infinitedent.

"Madame Crystal" is illustrated by Jenny Kiefer.

THE HARVEST QUEEN

BRIDGET D. BRAVE

Chloe Cline was the last girl in her class to get her period. It happened during the last week of school—right before Memorial Day weekend. This also happened to be graduation week for Sojourner's Rest Junior High, and Chloe's mom had picked out a pristine, white, Laura Ashley dress for the occasion. This meant Chloe spent the entirety of that sweaty graduation ceremony panicked that there would be a deep crimson stain on the back of her dress the moment she stood up to accept her diploma. Thankfully, her dress remained unmarred, although the fear kept her from attending the after-graduation dance. Best not to tempt fate, she thought as she scurried home to spend the rest of the evening in cut-off sweatpants. She'd be sweltering in the newly finished basement of her family home and watching Nick at Nite with a pint of mint chocolate chip ice cream within the hour. Her sister had rolled her eyes and called her "tragic" when she found out that Chloe skipped the final event of her junior high school career.

It didn't matter to Chloe. No one would have asked her to dance anyway.

She had hoped beyond hope that the summer between junior high and high school would have held some magical transformation. That she would have walked into the doors of Sojourner's Rest High School suddenly taller, prettier, more formed and womanly. Instead all she had to show for her ascension into womanhood was greasier skin and hair. Well, and now monthly cramps that got her excused from P.E.

It was during one of these benched days that she watched the Harvest Queen rehearsal for the first time. The whole town turned out for the spectacle of the ceremony: watching the best and most popular of the entire high school be crowned and then forever etched into the town's history. The glass case in the front of the high school prominently displayed each prior Queen's photo and crown; shining Chosen Ones, examples to the rest of the girls of who they should attempt to be. Chloe held her breath as the six finalist girls—the Homecoming Court—delicately climbed the stairs, smiling and waving to an invisible audience.

This year, one of her own neighbors was amongst the finalists. Amy Aubery, a first-generation FFoSR (Finer Families of Sojourner's Rest—the wealthiest and most well-placed in terms of housing and status). Her family had moved to the town right after Amy's mother had given birth to her and her brother. They were a rarity among twins in this area: fraternal. The fertile delta of Little Egypt, Illinois did not only refer to the crops, after all. Multiple births were common —both to human and animal mothers. But nearly all of those multiple births were of the identical variety. Split eggs that formed near perfect copies of one another. Fraternal twins were much stranger. She and her brother Andy had received nearly mythic status as children as a result. They were both golden blonde and beautiful. Amy had remained that way as she grew and developed.

Puberty was much less kind to Andy. As his sister grew elegant and stately, genetics had twisted him into more of a gawky bent branch of a male. His teeth were much too large, his knees too knobby. He was terrible at sports and awkward in appearance. Chloe had always felt sorry for him.

Amy now shone on the stage, as resplendent in her jean shorts and plaid tie-waist button up as she would be a week later in her white ball gown. Chloe already knew that she would be chosen. She met all the criteria.

The Harvest Queen was always a first-generation girl. She was always gorgeous, always involved in school activities, always had terrific grades. The rumor was that you had to be a virgin, but Heather Lane's ascension last year had made everyone question that. They'd all heard about what she did with Mike Delaney after junior prom. Even Chloe, who barely spoke to anyone, had heard the story. The Queens were always cheerleaders—the only sure way to instant popularity. They were never in band or choir, although show choir was acceptable. They all attended the First Non Denominational Church of the True Sojourner, but that was really true of everyone in town. Since Sojourner's Rest's founding in 1815, that church had been the primary place of worship.

Little Egypt was so named due to its similarity to the Nile delta region. The land was damp, swampy, and this made the soil rich. There was something that leant itself to comparison - from the mysterious pyramids left by the now-decamped Indigenous population to the sandy dunes of the river bottoms. Those who lived here chose to double down and named nearly everything some bastardization of Egyptian name or reference. Sojourner's Rest was from the story of the sojourner to Elgath, and the blessings of the sacrifice that traveler made. Like Elgath before, the land and the people of this area were blessed by bounty. Infertility was unheard of. The crops grew thick and green and to near-excess year after year. The people were healthy and long-lived. As a consequence, few ever left. Once your family established itself in Sojourner's Rest, there you remained for generations after.

That's why only girls born prior to arrival could be the Harvest Queen. This was a tradition linked to the tale of the Traveler: she had to be someone who had journeyed to these lands.

Chloe shivered with excitement despite her prior reservations about the Homecoming Dance. Her sister, Jennifer, had been tight-lipped about the tradition in years past. Every year she would return shortly before dawn to bathe and burn her clothes in the trash pile in the backyard, like every other teen girl in their neighborhood. Once Chloe had complained that she would never get to be Harvest Queen —their mother was raised here, after all. Jennifer had smiled a secretive wry smile in response.

PE was the final class of the day for Chloe, and she walked home alone still in her gym shorts. Regardless of her inability to participate, Coach Glass required that all girls still dress, or receive detention. Chloe didn't mind. If she was going to be on the rag, she'd rather stain those hideous purple shorts than her single pair of Guess jeans.

Her parents weren't home, but Jennifer had clearly caught a ride from someone, loud Soul Asylum already blasting from her bedroom. Chloe peeked in and found her sister sitting at the large pink plastic vanity that had been a gift for her 16th birthday. She was carefully applying blue eyeshadow beneath a fountain of bangs.

"What do you want, dorkwad?" she asked without looking away from her makeup application.

"Did you pick a dress for the dance?" Chloe asked, hanging onto the doorframe.

Her sister grinned and jerked her head in the direction of the closet, where a plastic bag marked Pristine Formals hung. "Go ahead and take a look. But if you get your grubby hands on the satin, I will drop you off the Meramec Bridge."

The plastic crinkled and gave way to a monstrosity of shimmery hot pink and black: fitted bodice with ruffled shoulders above a full-length ball gown. There were three hoop skirts tucked behind the dress, ready to add the necessary layers to make Jennifer Cline look like a full parade float. Chloe would never admit it, but she was so envious. Only upperclassmen wore the full formal gowns to the event. Freshmen like her were relegated to tea-length dresses that looked positively babyish by comparison. She wasn't relishing the idea of her scabby legs poking out from under a poofy knee-length skirt.

"I wish I had a princess dress. I'm going to look like a haunted doll."

"Your day will come," Jennifer replied as she blinked at herself in the mirror. "I wish I had bigger bangs. That bitch at Matrix cut my hair too short."

"I'm telling mom you said the B word."

"I'm telling mom you're a total narc. Now get out of my room."

Chloe clomped back downstairs. It was too early for anything she actually wanted to watch to be on, and if she started a movie now she'd just get interrupted by her parents arriving home and demanding she switch it to Inside Edition. With a huff, she decided to go outside.

Andy Aubery was dribbling in his driveway. He paused and made a shot toward the basketball hoop hanging over the garage door. It missed and bounced down the street, rolling to a stop in the mossy gutter in front of the Clines' house.

Chloe picked it up gingerly, trying not to get the muck on her hands and tossed it back to him. It went wide, landing on the lawn.

"Guess neither of us are making varsity," he said darkly.

Chloe let a laugh go before she could stop herself. She'd had limited interaction with the Aubreys since they'd gotten older. Amy and Jennifer had been friends as kids, but grew apart post-junior high. Andy's crush on Jennifer had remained obvious and embarrassing to everyone on the street, especially Jennifer. At least he'd stopped hanging around their driveway. That part always creeped Chloe out.

"Is Amy excited?" Chloe asked.

Andy scowled at her. "Should she be?"

Chloe felt her face go hot. "I would be."

Andy spat out a bitter laugh. "Of course you would. You pod people all think this is some kind of honor." He glanced up at the lit windows in the house behind him. "You know, not everyone wants to peak in high school. Especially not here."

"That's stupid. Being popular is everything here."

"Who wants everything to end when they're seventeen?" he asked sadly.

Chloe nearly asked him what he meant, but the sound of her own garage door squeaking open caught her attention. The Astro van pulled into the Cline's driveway. Mom was home. When she turned back to Andy, the boy ducked past the trees of the side yard, disappearing behind the house.

Friday afternoon felt charged with electricity, with school letting out at the halfway mark for the pep rally. Chloe bounced along the route home behind her sister, listening to Jennifer and her friends discuss the order of events of the evening.

"We'll finish our nails and then Mom said she'd set our hair while they dry. Dresses, makeup, then we can take our hair down. I'll tease yours first and you can help me get the back part of mine up and off my neck." Jennifer shot a look back over her shoulder at her sister. "Hey dorkwad, if you agree to zip us up, I'll tease your bangs for you, too."

Chloe couldn't control the giant smile that spread across her face. "Shut up, you will?"

"I'll do anything to keep you from looking like a fucking Amish person at our first joint event. But don't think this means you'll be hanging out with my friends at the dance. You're on your own."

"I'm meeting Andrea and Katie there."

Jennifer groaned. "Jesus H., is it too much to ask that you find cooler friends? It's like you're trying to be the biggest nerd who ever lived."

The insult didn't register. Chloe was too excited. She was going to a high school dance. She was going to watch the Harvest Queen have her first dance with her date. She was going to the Feast of the Lamb.

This was everything.

Four hours later, she was crammed into sparkly blue taffeta in the back of the Astro van, her dad going over the rules. "You can only stay out as late as your sister does. If she is home and you're not: grounded. No drinking, no drugs, and no boys. If I find out you've even been near any of those things: grounded. Do not get caught up in the dumb pranks some of the kids pull tonight. If I have to come fetch you from the police station: grounded." He handed her two folded $20s. "For the photos. Make sure you look presentable in them. Your mother will never let me hear the end of it if your photos are a mess."

Chloe shoved the bills into her new purse and clambered out of the van. Outside was a complete spectacle. A rented red carpet led the way into the gymnasium, which was now festooned with paper flowers and streamers. A banner proclaimed: "Sentimental Journey: Sojourner's Rest High School Homecoming Festival and Harvest Queen Ceremony, 1993." Upperclassmen were arriving in horse drawn carriages, hired limousines, and their parents' fanciest cars. Girls in gigantic formal dresses burst from the vehicles, rearranging the many layers of satin and lace, posing for photos with friends and waving and squealing at one another.

Inside, Chloe found Andrea already saving seats, waving excitedly at her until she was shoved in next to her. The lights were extinguished at 7:00 sharp, dozens of skirts rustling in the dark as an expectant hush fell over the crowd. A spotlight illuminated the walkway.

The Harvest Queen Court entered the gymnasium.

First was Shelly MacNamara, her perfect red curls coiffed into a bouffant. She wore a white satin dress with pearl accents, her numerous skirts swishing down the aisle. Shelly's father was the manager of the munitions plant, her family moving to the town when she was only five years old. Her escort, Mark Matheson, was red-faced and sweaty beneath the lights.

She was followed by Stacee Newby, a pretty brunette who was co-captain of the cheer squad. Stacee's parents were both doctors at the clinic in town. She had lived here since third grade. Her date was Daniel Haven, arguably the hottest guy in the entire high school. Chloe had heard her sister say that Daniel was sure to take over his father's car dealership, and definitely marry Stacee if she didn't make Harvest Queen.

The Harvest Queens never stayed after high school. Chloe had once asked why and her mother got a funny distant look in her eyes before mumbling something about college. It seemed odd that all of the Harvest Queens went away for college. Hardly anyone else did.

Best friends Denise Holcombe and Stefanie Davis followed in turn. They were escorted by the Fenton twin boys, who they had dated since sophomore year. Everyone joked that they would have a double wedding and end up raising families in a duplex. They seemed to do absolutely everything together. Chloe wondered if it would break the friendship apart if one made Harvest Queen over the other. Her sister had scoffed and said that no one in their right mind was voting for either of those "two skanks" for Queen.

Then Amy entered. Her blonde hair fell in perfect fat curls down her bare back, softly brushing her shoulders. She wore a strapless gown of dazzling white, studded with rhinestones that caught the light. Beside her was Clayton O'Neill, the captain of the football team and head lifeguard at the Sojourner's Rest community pool. Chloe put her hand on Andrea's arm to stop her from bouncing. Andrea's crush on Clayton had ruined more than one pool day and the girl couldn't keep herself still if he was within eyesight. Chloe missed the times before Andrea had noticed boys, back when they could still splash and dunk one another with abandon.

As Andrea stilled, a motion at the edge of the crowd caught her eye. It was Andy. He wasn't dressed for the event, instead in an oversized sweatshirt from the local coaster park and some grubby jeans. He was hugging himself with both arms and pacing slowly, his eyes never leaving his sister as she made her way up the stairs to her seat. Chloe felt a pang of pity for him. He clearly had not planned on coming to the dance, but even he couldn't miss this moment.

Katie followed Chloe's stare. "Oh gross," she whispered. "Why is he even here?"

"Why wouldn't he be?" Chloe asked, laughing.

Katie started to say something and then clamped a hand over her mouth. "Oh my gaaaawd. I almost forgot. This is your first full ceremony." She patted Chloe's arm. "It will all make sense, just try not to think about it. Remember: this is why we're all here."

Chloe was confused. She knew the Harvest Ceremony was a big deal, every family participated. Her mother had often referred to it as "The Compact." Just another in the list of weird rituals from their church. At least now that she's gotten her rag she could stop going to the Friday night blood anointing. She'd been so late that she was way taller than the rest of the girls and it was starting to get embarrassing. Chloe figured this was just another step in that whole "blood is the sign of life to the lifebringer," progression. The Church of the Jackal put heavy emphasis on the continuation of the bloodline. Exhausting bullshit rituals when you'd rather be at home in pajama pants.

The school orchestra played. The choir stepped into view. They began a strangely slow and rhythmic song. The girls on stage stood, one by one, as their names were called. Each came forward until they stood together, joining left hands in the center. They began to walk in a counterclockwise circle, their eyes staring at one member of the circle, then another. Stacee broke away first, her escort stepping forward to catch her right hand and pull her off to the side. Denise and Stephanie stepped away together, holding onto one another until the last moment.

"How do they know when to... stop?" Chloe whispered.

Andrea scooted closer, clearly proud to get to be The Expert. "So, I heard that it's like, you look into the others' eyes and you just... know. It's not you. You are spared."

"Spared?" Chloe said, a little too loud. The girls behind them made shushing noises. Chloe rolled her eyes. "Don't they want to be queen?"

"I mean," Andrea's voice was quiet. "Think about that in a few minutes. Ask yourself. Would you?"

Chloe suddenly felt very cold.

In the center of the stage, Shelly and Amy spun faster, their knuckles white from where their hands were joined. The song reached a strange crescendo and then dropped into silence. The only sound was the whisper of the skirts on stage and the fast breathing of the two girls as they turned and turned, until Mark rushed forward and caught Shelly by the waist. Shelly released Amy and fell into Mark's embrace. Chloe noticed she was crying.

Amy stilled, her eyes still turned toward the ceiling, her breath coming in noisy gasps. Clayton stepped back into the shadow, his hands falling limply at his sides.

The Harvest Queen stood before them. The crowd waited in breathless anticipation until the crown was placed upon her head. Then a riotous applause broke out. Amy continued to gasp and shake on stage.

"NO!" an anguished cry sounded from the edge of the audience. Chloe saw Andy fighting to get toward the stage. Several adults came over to grab him by the back of his sweatshirt. He fought against their grasp, nearly wiggling out of his clothes before they managed to subdue him. He was dragged into the hall beyond, his screams and howls echoing.

Before she could fully register what had just happened, Chloe was caught in the press of the crowd toward the doors beyond. Amy was already being escorted backstage. "Is he okay?" she asked, straining to look behind them.

Katie gave her a sympathetic look. "Don't worry about him. We need to get to the dance."

After the rest of the town had shuffled back to their cars, Chloe joined the other girls in the auditorium. Katie and Andrea took her by the hand, and she watched as her sister grasped the hands of two friends standing nearby. Solemn and entangled, they formed a large circle around the dance floor. In the center, the four members of the court not chosen were standing together. As she watched, the four began to sway and hummed a low tone. Around her, the other gathered girls joined in a companion tone, swaying opposite to the court's motions. This continued, the swaying becoming faster and more frantic as the humming grew in volume. It was so loud that Chloe wanted to clamp her hands over her ears, only her friends had such a tight grip on her fingers that she couldn't break free. Chloe felt drunk on the noise, her head spinning and stomach lurching as if the room spun in time with the hum. The song took on a life of its own, bringing with it inescapable visions of blood-soaked cloth falling to a dark and rusted earth, lush green springing forth. Chloe shook her head, trying to clear the hallucination. In the dark of the room beyond them, she felt watched by thousands of unseen eyes. In the back of her mind, someone was screaming. She thought it was Andy, then realized the voice was her own. The shrill shriek ended in a ragged sob, only to be replaced by a skittering noise she was near certain was in the room. It was thousands of legs, it was thousands of whispers, it was claws on the wood, it was the whisper of leaves scattered by the wind.

All at once, the noise and the movement stopped. Chloe's body returned to stillness, the whirling visions in her brain quieting, making her feel dizzy. The doors at the rear of the room opened. Amy was led in.

The girl was completely naked beneath a cape of roses, her crown still atop her head. She walked barefoot to the center of the room, the four members of her court parting to make a space for her. As she turned, Chloe saw that her face was tear-streaked, her mascara running in messy lines down her cheeks.

Denise and Stephanie then moved as one, removing the rose cloak from her shoulders. Amy stood in the dim light, her crown sparkling as her dress had before.

Shelly walked forward and took both of Amy's hands in her own. She smiled at Amy and mouthed, "it's okay." Amy nodded, her chin quivering. Shelly knelt before her.

Shelly then leaned forward and tore into Amy's thigh with her teeth. Amy let loose a scream. The other three girls on the court then pulsed forward, Denise and Stephanie biting on opposite shoulders, Stacee sinking her own teeth into Amy's side. Amy's scream became a hysterical wail as Stacee pulled back, ripping a large chunk of flesh away and spattering blood on the kneeling Shelly. Chloe looked wildly at her friends beside her. Katie was watching the proceedings with a fascinated grin. Andrea gave Chloe a sympathetic look and then pulled her toward the bloody scene.

Amy's cries stopped as the gathered crowd descended. Chloe was caught in the rush of frantic hands and warm wet blood, trying to twist her face away from what was happening. That's when she saw her sister standing beside her, her mouth a mess of gore. Jennifer lifted a hunk of quivering ragged something at her.

"C'mon, sis. Eat before the best parts are gone."

IN THE PRE-DAWN LIGHT, Chloe followed Jennifer through the side entrance to their house. She stood numbly as her sister stripped her dress and stockings off her, discarding them into a pile on the tile floor. She did not protest as her sister and mother shoved her into the scalding shower, nor when they scrubbed at her skin and hair the way they did when she was a much younger girl. After her sister had similarly been scrubbed clean, she was wrapped in a blanket and joined her family in the backyard, where they burned the formal dresses and tights. Her mother made soothing noises and offered a cup of tea, saying, "I know, baby, I know," at every gagging sound Chloe made. "I know, I'm sorry."

This was the deal you struck with Sojourner's Rest. The land was good to those who fed.

In the place where the Mississippi and Missouri rivers meet, there is a land where the ground is fertile, where the children grow strong easily and the adults grow old gracefully, both more so with each passing generation. Chloe had always wondered at the extreme luck of the people of her region, that they were able to live as they did for as long as they have.

Now she knew it wasn't luck at all.

BRIDGET D. BRAVE is now chilling in the dead center of the country with her husband and two cats. You can find her at beedeebrave just about everywhere.

"THE HARVEST QUEEN" is illustrated by P.L. McMillan.

WHO IN THE WORLD IS THE HAT MAN?

CHELSEA PUMPKINS

The blood recedes from your fingers and toes as Lindsay's words reverberate through your inner ear. "They call him *The Hat Man*."

Your heart flutters like a wounded moth, bouncing about your chest cavity before falling into your stomach.

You hear your name.

It's distant, garbled. As if coming from underwater.

A red swordtail peers from the porthole of a sunken pirate ship in the fish tank across the room. Bubbles gurgle out of a treasure chest. You hear the call of your name again, but you're entranced by a tetra fish as it dances with the plastic algae, swaying in the current.

"Hey!" Lindsay's voice—clear now, annoyed. "What's wrong with you?"

"Huh?" The dark basement comes back into focus. "Nothing. I'm fine," you reply.

"You sure? You're shaking," Rachel says, her face contorted in concern.

"What's the matter? You're not afraid of The Hat Man, are you?" Lindsay chides, wagging her flashlight beneath her chin. The beam reflects off her braces, casts sinister shadows onto her face. "You're not gonna call your mom again, are you?"

Muffled giggles tease from the dark behind Lindsay.

"Not gonna...call your *big brother*?"

"I said I'm *fine*, Lindsay!" Your speech is uneven. The trembling of your lips trips your words.

The giggles transform into snickers, growing in both volume and ridicule.

"Don't worry," Rachel whispers, reaching for your hand. "It's just a dumb story. Make-believe."

"I know," you say. "I'm fine." You swallow the burning coal in your throat and clutch the edge of your brother's G. I. Joe sleeping bag.

You hate G. I. Joe, and you loathe hand-me-downs. Next to the girls' 101 Dalmatians and My Little Pony bags, the faded army greens make you stick out even more. But Justin's sour scent lingers in its folds, and his smell is a refuge. You haven't felt safe since he moved out, to live with your uncle across the state. Since *he* started coming around.

Lindsay continues her story.

"He haunts your bedroom in the dark—a nightmare come to life."

She commands the room with her Eveready and her flair for dramatics.

"He sucks the breath from your lungs. He steals your thoughts. He takes your *soul*."

Her audience gasps on cue.

"And the next morning...you're nothing but a husk."

"Make-believe," you repeat, your voice softer than the polyester stuffing you're compulsively pulling from the torn seam of a faded fighter jet. You recite this mantra inside your head, through shrieks and laughter, through Bloody Mary and Truth or Dare, until, eventually, every girl in the basement has dozed off.

You're alone in the dark, willing yourself to believe The Hat Man is merely a sleepover story. Nothing more than an urban legend.

But the thing is, you've met The Hat Man. You *know* The Hat Man. You've awoken to the shadowed figure in your bedroom, night after night.

You thought it was Justin at first. You tried calling out to him, to ask why he was in your room, but your tongue lay dormant on the floor of your mouth.

Then you remembered Justin was gone. He'd left weeks ago.

Your pulse beat upon your eardrums in a quickening tempo. You strained to see in the dark (had the nightlight burned out?). You blinked away the blurry edges of sleep, and the silhouette was unmistakable. A wide-brimmed hat rested tall atop the tattered edges of a trench coat. He stood next to your vanity, towered above your chair, and his shape was reflected in the mirror.

The face of the shadow was featureless, but you could still feel his unrelenting stare. That ancient instinct burned into the synapses of prey that tells the body it's being watched. Hunted.

You tried to spring out of bed and run, but your legs were filled with lead. You laid cemented into your canopy bed, fighting against your body, begging it to get up.

But you couldn't even wiggle a toe.

The Hat Man held you in place and ensnared your gaze. You were trapped by the black hole gravity of his shadow—frozen in place, all kinetic energy drained from your limbs. He snatched your voice, inhaled your breath. You were suffocating.

Then, suddenly, you were free.

Air rushed into your lungs, your limbs were unshackled, and The Hat Man faded into the gray of the room as if he had never been there at all.

You ran from your bedroom into your mom's, and crawled under her comforter. She didn't even ask why, she just moved aside and let you wrap your arms around her soft, warm middle. You stayed awake until the ringlets of dawn curled around the window shade. The safety of daylight allowed you to close your eyes again.

That had only been the first time.

With the sleeping bag pulled up just below your eyes, tonight would be another sleepless night. You shiver, though you're not sure if it's from the chill in the air or the fear in your veins. You're keeping watch for The Hat Man. The red digital numbers tick by on Lindsay's clock radio, and you're grateful for the erratic rumbling of the furnace that startles you awake every time your eyelids grow heavy.

When the room begins to brighten with the soft morning sun, your breath slows and deepens. You've conditioned yourself for this, to claim the fleeting hours between dawn and the alarm. You drift off to sleep.

"You look exhausted, hon. Did you stay up too late?"

Your head is still foggy as you clamber into the backseat of Mom's station wagon. Your arms, overflowing with your sleeping bag, pillow, backpack, and slippers, rattle the beads on her seat covers.

"Did you at least have fun?" Mom asks.

You sigh. "I dunno, Mom."

She catches your eyes in the rearview mirror, and you can tell she's not going to drive off until you answer her.

"I got scared again," you confess.

"Oh, sweetie. Bad dreams?"

That's what Mom calls *him*—your 'bad dreams.' But last night, Lindsay gave *him* a name.

"I didn't see him," you say, "but I stayed up just in case."

"Why didn't you call me?" She shifts the car into gear. She's satisfied enough. You don't bother answering this last question. You shake your head at the memory of last time, when you woke up the whole house to ask to use the phone. You had fought to hold your tears in as Mom arrived in her pajamas. She had murmured "I'm so sorry" and "I'm sure you understand" to Lindsay's parents over and over as she shuffled you into her car.

Now she pulls away from the curb, lost in the bridge of a Sheryl Crow song.

Lindsay waves goodbye from the bay window. She wears the kind of smile only little girls learn—teeth hidden behind upturned lips—and her squinted eyes probe your poorly-guarded insecurities.

You close your eyes to catch a few Zs on the drive home.

That evening, while Mom is at her church group, you sign onto the computer. The static sound of the Internet connecting grates your nerves until the creak of a door opens, ushering you into the World Wide Web.

"You've got mail."

You hope it's from Justin (you always hope it's from Justin), but it's just another e-card from Grandma—a rabbit dancing beneath pink, glittery font. *Some bunny loves you.* Disappointed, you click on your bookmarks and navigate to Ask Jeeves. You type, "who is the hat man?" and click on the bright red *Ask* button.

You scroll through the first half of the results quickly, glazing over at the sleep experts' analyses. You've been through the tests before—questionnaires and sleep studies. Your mom even took you to a hypnotist. "To help you move on," she'd said. Every appointment is the same. They interrogate you and spit back useless hypotheses, as if something is wrong with you.

"It's just a recurring nightmare. A lucid dream, perhaps."

"Could be sleep paralysis. It's more common than you'd think."

"Sounds like a stress response. Have you felt stressed lately?"

It never helps. You're in danger. You're being stalked and watched, and, soon, you could be killed. But they just write prescriptions for exercise and melatonin, collect their co-pay, and check you off their schedule.

Then, on the screen, you see it. *Who is The Hat Man (or Hat Woman)?* You click the link and wait for your cursor to stop spinning. Paragraphs and images appear on the page like a mirage.

It's a collection of stories, just like your own, from all over the world. Figures in the dark—staring, terrorizing. The same cinder block that crushes your chest, the suffocated screams. There are drawings too—not all exact, but close enough. All of them feature the wide brim of a fedora.

The screen blurs as tears swell on the surface of your eyes. You're not alone. You knew it—The Hat Man is real.

You scroll this website for two hours, poring over every sentence. You save the images in a WordPerfect document, in case Mom can't pay the Internet bill again. You can't lose this evidence.

The garage door rattles and grinds—Mom's home. You click Save, close out of the document, and rush to turn the speaker off so she won't hear the AOL man bidding you goodbye. Mom gets upset when you fixate on The Hat Man.

Your alarm clock reads 3:16 AM, and you've been wired all night. At last, you hear the murmur of Mom's snoring—a recess bell that releases you into the quiet corners of the hibernating house.

You sneak back downstairs to the computer. It's too late to print off your pictures—the screech of the Epson printer would wake Mom up—but you can keep reading at least. Digital muscle memory pulls you through the familiar motions—screen name, password, *You've Got Mail*, bookmarks...Bingo.

You scroll down to where you left off and continue reading account after account of The Hat Man seen around the world.

[23:54] <UrbanKrow76>
When I opened my eyes The Hat Man was floating on my ceiling over my body. He had gigantic limbs with long, spindly fingers. His arms reached all the way to my bed, and those fingers wrapped around my throat. Tighter and tighter and tighter…

[02:07] <snafflin_coo_beasty>
There was a tall dark shadow of a man at the foot of my bed, with glowing red eyes. Then I smelled smoke. Lots of it. I started choking on it. My house was on fire and I was totally paralyzed. I couldn't even scream to wake up my kids. Never been more scared in my life. When I came to, I ran from room to room and everything was fine.

[15:37] <Mast3rBlast3r13>
I'll never forget it. He stood in the back corner of my room, still as a rock. I felt so heavy and tired, but for some reason I was sure if I fell back asleep I'd die that night. I was certain of it. I fought so hard to stay awake but eventually I drifted off. I'm still here after all. Not sure what to make of that.

The next one knocks the wind from your gut.

[22:22] <daHUNTRESS>
I always had the feeling The Hat Man was trying to communicate with me, so I reached out to a

medium I found in the yellow pages. I booked an appointment for her to come to my house for an overnight stay. She sat in my living room while I took a sleeping pill and fell asleep on the couch. I wasn't awake for any of it, but the medium claimed she made contact.

She said it had a feminine, almost protective, energy, but that didn't seem right to me. The Hat Man always leaves me feeling violated and empty. But, she insisted I was wrong. She wanted another session, but I wasn't buying what she was selling. Felt like a waste of money. I never called her back.

The Hat Man still visits from time to time, and I've never figured out just what he wants from me.

You run to the kitchen in your sock feet—electrified with hope. You pull the enormous yellow book from the phone stand and set it on the counter. You *flip, flip, flip* to the M's in the business section and glide your finger down the page until you find the word "medium".

There are six listings on the page. You fumble in the junk drawer for a pad and pen and copy the details for each of them, for safekeeping. You want to call right away, but that would be crazy. There's a pay phone by the gym at school—if you skip lunch you should be able to make some calls undetected. It's Salisbury steak day, starring a vile tray of viscid meat with fake grill marks. You wouldn't touch it anyway.

You put everything back where it belongs—book, pad, pen—covering your tracks. You sign off AOL, shut the computer down, and creep back to your bedroom.

You dump out the Smucker's jar of loose change from your

dresser onto your bedspread. You pluck all the quarters from the pile and zip them into the front pocket of your JanSport.

You won't sleep tonight; you can't. You're buzzing with anticipation. You sit in bed with your flashlight studying the names and numbers of the mediums. You close your eyes and repeat them back. Over and over, until the birds begin their morning melodies outside your window.

THE FIRST TWO mediums want nothing to do with you. "18 or older, sorry," they say. The third number is disconnected permanently. You hang up the receiver, dejected, as the quarter clanks through the terminal.

"Hello, this is Vera," a gooey voice answers the fourth attempt. "What do you need from me right now?"

"H-Hi," you stammer, and before you finish your sentence you hear her clucking on the other end of the line.

"Oh, deary, I can sense the heaviness within you. You must be very tired, yes?" Vera asks.

You nod, forgetting you're on the phone.

"I see," Vera responds. *How?* "Tell Vera what's been keeping you up."

You feel her warmth through the line and your shame evaporates. You tell her all about The Hat Man. About the first time, and the other times, and the doctors, and your research. You've added three quarters to the call already by the time she agrees to see you, to meet The Hat Man. The school bell clangs, signaling the end of lunch. You promise to call Vera back and schedule the session. She promises to help.

And she does.

You've planned Vera's visit diligently. You scheduled it during one of Mom's overnight business trips, and set up a web of fake sleepovers and 'last minute changes of plans' to ensure you'd be home alone.

The doorbell rings at 8:30 PM, sharp. Vera's here. You slide the door chain, crank the deadbolt, and let her in.

Her long gray hair is woven with a purple scarf in a thick braid, which lays alongside a single golden hoop earring. She wears a patchwork shawl that matches her quilted shoulder bag. Mauve lipstick outlines yellowed teeth and creases as she says, "Good evening, deary."

You mimic the hospitality of your Mom welcoming a vacuum salesman.

"Can I offer you some water?" you ask.

Vera smiles with her whole face, knowingly.

"Sure, deary. That would be splendid."

Over glasses of ice water, Vera explains how the night will play out. You watch beads of condensation race down the side of the glass while Vera talks about incantations and 'making contact', while assuring you'll be completely fine.

"You understand?" she asks.

"Yes."

She looks at you expectantly, her eyes squinting and brows raised. "Deary, I want to help you but I simply cannot set up the room until you compensate me for my visit."

Your face flushes. *Of course.* You combed every birthday card in your keepsake box for money to pay Vera. You pull the crumpled bills from your fanny pack and hand them to her.

"Very well," she says. "Shall we?"

Vera stands and moves towards the stairs that lead to your bedroom. You hesitate and fidget with the drawstring on your pants.

"I'm nervous I won't be able to fall asleep, with you watching and all," you say. *What if Mom comes home all of a sudden? What if The Hat Man hurts Vera? Hurts you? What if The Hat Man doesn't show up at all?*

"Oh sure, deary. That's no problem. Let Vera brew you a tea, to settle your nerves."

The scent wafts from the murky cup into your face—an astringent smell, reminiscent of the time you accidentally ate the bay leaf in Mom's stew.

Vera must have noticed the repulsion on your face. "This will keep you calm—help you fall asleep," she says. "And it'll make you more receptive to supernatural presences."

You look up from the cup, and meet her amber eyes. You don't want to be *more* receptive—you want to be rid of The Hat Man altogether. Vera must sense your discomfort. She wags her hand towards you, urging you to drink.

This has to be done tonight. It might be your only chance. You pinch your nose and gulp the herbal concoction down.

Upstairs you wriggle into bed, under the cloud of your comforter. You turn the switch on your lamp and pull your stuffed sheepdog, Norton, tight to your chest.

Vera has set up a card table and folding chair in front of your bed, facing your vanity where The Hat Man usually stands. The door and windows are shut. Candles are placed in each corner of the room and the flickering glow makes your eyelids heavy. Or maybe it's the tea. Vera reads from her notebook in a language you don't recognize, and you drift into the dark sea of sleep.

You dream of Justin. The two of you are playing in the backyard. You're both years younger. He's pushing you on the swings and you're yelling at him, between giggles, to slow down. He's laughing too, but not listening. He pushes you harder, and at the top of the swing's pendulum you feel yourself rise off the rubber seat.

"Justin!" you yell, "I'm serious! Slow down!"

Justin keeps laughing, louder now. He throws his entire body into the next push. You hear the clinking of the chains breaking free. You soar through the air in sheer panic.

You wake up with a start.

You can't move.

Sure enough, The Hat Man is back. There's an unfamiliar red hue to his shadow. You sense anger. *Maybe this was a terrible idea. Maybe this will make things worse.* Your heart rate quickens and your skin crawls with the legs of a thousand spiders.

"I see your eyes are open, deary," Vera says, towards you. "And I sense another presence in the room with us. Is this The Hat Man?"

Yes! You're screaming affirmatives inside your mind, but your body is shut down. You can't reply.

"I take it you can't reply," Vera says. "That's okay. Just try to stay with us so Vera can communicate with the other. Don't panic, don't fight it. The tea will keep you calm."

"Hello." She's not speaking to you anymore. "Please, show us a sign that you want to communicate."

A heavy moment of silence, as if all sound was sucked from the room. Your chest grows tighter, breaths shallower.

"We welcome you to communicate," Vera continues. "Simply move an object."

For the first time, you see The Hat Man move. His arm reaches from his side like creeping tendrils of a vine. He lifts your comb from the vanity. He brings it beneath the brim of his hat and mimes the act of drawing it through long, smooth hair.

Vera draws a quick breath. "Thank you, very good, Hat Man."

A draft ruffles the curtains.

"Oh," Vera says, "You are not a man. My sincerest apologies."

The candles flicker in unison.

"Madame, if you will, please tell me what your business is here, in this young girl's room."

The red-aura'd shadow glides over to Vera's table. Your mind is frenzied, flashing lights and warning bells. You're screaming, but silent.

Vera's hands are resting firmly on the table, but the pages in her notebook turn rapidly.

"Of course," Vera whispers.

You hear the scratches of a pencil against paper, but all you see is Vera gazing, unblinking, into the face of the hulking shadow in front of her.

"Deary, her name is Nina."

You strain to see the handwriting on the pages, but it's no use. You're still paralyzed.

"Nina Eldorado."

The scratching stops.

Vera gasps.

Suddenly, The Hat Man—Nina—bolts to your bedside.

"No, no," Vera says firmly. "That won't be necess—"

You're choking. Each breath burns your lungs and the smell of smoke and charred meat swarms your olfactory nerve. The shadow leans over you, blocking your entire view of the room.

"Nina, please, I assure you—"

The bedroom door flings open and a gust of freezing air rushes into the room, snuffing out the candles, ruffling Vera's notebook.

Nina leans closer to your face, hovering over your entire still body. You feel the brush of hair against your forehead, and it burns like the time your grandmother dropped her cigarette cherry on your arm.

Dark brown eyes emerge on the blank face that has haunted you night after night. They blink gently and envelop you in a sense of calm. You're light, warm, breathing easy—reminiscent of vacations to the lake where you'd float on your back in the summer sun. When your family was whole.

Nina nods, and with that subtle bow, you're released. You press yourself up, back against the wooden headboard, and sit face-to-face before Nina.

"I-I'm going to begin closing us off now," Vera declares from across the room.

Your eyes lock on Nina's—glistening and silky like your tiger eye gemstone.

Vera recites an incantation you can't understand, and you feel Nina start to evaporate. Her eyes begin to fade back into black. Nina lifts her arms and encircles you in an affectionate cocoon. You collapse into her embrace and weep.

You wrote down everything Vera told you that night.

Nina Eldorado was a young girl, an only child. Her father was a military captain and her mother was a renowned seamstress who designed intricate styles for California's most fashionable socialites.

On a visit to the city, their hotel caught fire in the middle of the night. The door to their suite was blocked by a wall of flame, and as it began to lick through the door jamb, her parents lowered Nina from the room's balcony in a harness made of bedsheets. By the time her feet reached the ground, flames were bursting from the balcony window. The plume of smoke and hot gasses carried a red fedora out of the room, one of her mother's pieces. Her parents didn't make it out. The hat was all she had left of them.

Nina was ruined with sadness. She was moved by the State to the Golden Gate Girls School, where she trudged through her days in a haze of despair. Before she turned eighteen, when she would be released into society, alone, she made up her mind to rid herself of the pain. During holiday break, when most of the students and staff left to stay with family, she lit two tall prayer candles in her dark room. She prayed to her parents and to her God for forgiveness, tipped the candles over onto the wooden floor, onto sheets soaked in turpentine, and laid beside them as fire engulfed the school.

Her body had left this world, but her spirit remained. Being trapped on this earth, invisible to the world, she vowed that no one should have to suffer as she did. She became a thief in the night—visiting sleeping sufferers and consuming their most tragic memories. She believed if she could hold their trauma for them, bear their weight alone, people left on this earth could live a life of happiness. She believed she could free them.

You've re-read this account a hundred times since last week, searching for the one missing piece of your puzzle. You close your notebook and bury it beneath your pillow. The clanging and splashing sounds from the kitchen tell you Mom is washing dishes. You plod downstairs and sit in your chair at the kitchen table behind her.

"Mom," you ask timidly, "why exactly did Justin move in with Uncle Roy?"

She freezes. Suds drip down her wrists over the sink of filmy water as you try desperately to read the back of her head. She lets out a breath through tight lips, the way you blow seeds off a dandelion, and turns the faucet off. "Sweetie. You know why he left."

She still has her back to you, rigid.

"Because...he needs discipline?" You repeat the talking points you were coached to say when your teachers and friends' parents asked.

Mom turns then. She comes to you and squats next to your chair. She rests her palms on your knees and looks into your eyes with tears in her own. "You know why," she repeats, her voice a dam holding back a wave of despair. "You know."

"I think The Hat Man visits me because of Justin," you say.

"What? Sweetie, we've been over th—"

"Did Justin hurt me, Mom?" you ask.

The sob bursts through her levees and she throws her arms around you, burying your face in the curves that have comforted you your whole life. Her perfume of geranium and sandalwood engulfs you. Her plush terry cloth robe caresses your cheek.

In an instant, your memories flood back.

The hurt, the confusion. The recollections, once obscured, wash not just over, but through you now.

And in their wake, you're free.

CHELSEA PUMPKINS IS a writer from Massachusetts with an aversion to happy endings. If she's not reading, writing, or watching something spooky, you may find her hiking in the White Mountains with her husband and sweet pitbull, Moose. Learn more about her work at chelseapumpkins.com and follow her on Twitter and Instagram at @ChelseaPumpkins.

"Who in the World is The Hat Man?" is illustrated by P.L. McMillan.

BETWEEN THE BARBIE AND THE DEEP-BLUE RANGER

CHRISTOPHER O'HALLORAN

I shouldn't do it. Mom says it's bad for you. That I'll choke. Or that I'll swallow it and it'll sit in my tummy like a ball of cement.

"She makes it look so cool, though," says Barbie, sitting against the wall. Her blue eyes stare dully at me and she's naked, like every Barbie, eventually. This one is my size, though. Something Nan bought for Tiffany, not realizing that thirteen-year-olds don't play with Barbies anymore, no matter how big.

Tiffany's bag of Big League Chew sits on her side table. Mom would kill her if she saw it in her room. Sitting out, the crumpled bag open to the air.

I look inside. The shredded, pink gum looks like the foam in the attic. It smells so good.

"It probably tastes so good, too," says Barbie.

My blue Power Ranger disagrees. Always the voice of reason.

"That's her gum, Joshua," he says. "If you ask Tiffany, I'm sure she'd give you some."

"Oh my god, that's so dumb." Barbie sighs, though she has no lungs. "She doesn't share. She *never* shares."

"She shared her Big Mac with us today," says Blue.

"Because she doesn't like the sauce," cries Barbie. "Mom should know that!"

They're propped against the wall, watching me decide.

"She won't notice if I take just a little bit," I say. "Right?"

Barbie's bright eyes glimmer. Her smile creaks as it widens imperceptibly.

"That's right," she says. "Just a few little strands."

"That's how it starts," says Blue.

Barbie's right, though. She'd never notice a few missing pieces. I just want the taste. It smells like the fair that comes through town every summer. So fresh.

I shake off my Sock'em Boppers and position my fingers up and at the opening of the bag. She'll notice if it's in a different position. I need to get in and get out without disturbing anything.

Easy...

My fingers dip in, the tips disappearing behind crinkled aluminum foil. I hold my breath, eyes wide. Ears primed for incoming footsteps. Last I checked, Tiffany was sitting at the top of the stairs whining into the cordless phone.

I feel gum, soft like an eraser and just as pink. Drool pools in my mouth. I suck it back and choke as it goes down the wrong pipe.

"Are you okay?" asks Blue.

My throat burns, saliva somehow turned acidic. I gotta keep it down. Don't want to alert Tiffany to my heist.

"He's fine," says Barbie.

I compose myself, then pull the few strands of gum up, up, up, like the claw games at the mall. Those claws always drop at the last minute, so my fingertips squeeze hard, squishing the gum between them.

Come on...

The side of my finger brushes the lip of the bag. I pull back quickly, trying to avoid tipping it, but I fail. It falls over, the bag landing sideways on the side table.

"She's going to know," says Blue. "I knew it. She's going to find out!"

"She's not," says Barbie. "We can put it back. She won't even notice. It's not like she pays attention to anything, anyway."

This is true. Right now, she's supposed to be babysitting me. *Supposed to be.* For all she knows, I'm drowning in the bath.

"Well, it's too late now," says Barbie. "Might as well grab some more."

I look at Blue, but he says nothing, so I grab a pinch in the other hand, too and stuff the mess into my mouth.

A faucet opens on my tongue, and my mouth fills with even more saliva. The sweetness makes my brain fire up, and for a second, all I can think of is pink, pink, pink. Sugary pink goodness.

Barbie doesn't even have to put the idea of seconds in my head. I'm so scared of the gum losing its flavour that I grab more—a handful this time—and cram it past my lips.

A strand slips past my tongue and down my throat.

No...

You can't swallow gum. It'll stick in your tummy for seven years. What do I do?

"That's enough," says Blue. "You've had enough. Now you're going to have to explain to Tiffany—"

"You buffoon," says Barbie. "She'll kick his ass."

My jaw aches. The ball fills my mouth, loose strands attaching to the larger mass like a growing tumour. I try to coax the strand up from my throat, but it sticks there at the top.

"If he gets ahead of it," says Blue, "shows his remorse—"

"She doesn't know remorse," says Barbie. "Tiffany devours remorse and shits fury. His best chance is to take the gum." The smile in her voice is a lot crueler than the one painted on her face.

The wad of gum slips along my tongue. Further back, floating along the river of my saliva.

"No!" Blue would throw his hands to his head in shock if he could move. "Take the gum?"

"She'll think she lost it."

"That's heinous," says Blue.

The wad stops. It falls to the back of my mouth and stops. My stomach heaves.

"*Tiffany* is heinous," says Barbie. "And besides, she has money. She's making money right now watching the kid and she's not even *watching the kid*. She can buy more gum."

I can't breathe. The wad of gum is lodged in my throat like a jawbreaker in the vacuum hose.

"Just because you can get away with something," says Blue, "doesn't mean you should do it. Honour means—"

I smack him, knocking him over. I don't mean to do it, but I'm panicking. I can't breathe and I really, really would like to. My arms go every which way, knocking Tiffany's pillow off her bed, pulling down the poster of Johnny Depp from *21 Jump Street*, and spilling the precious gum.

As if I'd be going back for seconds.

Help, I try to say, but the dolls can't move. They can't pat my back.

"Go to Tiffany, Joshua," urges Blue.

"No!" Barbie watches me with her calm eyes, even though her words sound like they're out of a beehive. "She'll punish him!"

"If he doesn't get help, he'll die."

Barbie goes silent. Thinking of a way out of this.

I don't want to go to Tiffany. I can't go to Tiffany.

The edge of my vision is starting to go all black. My lungs scream for air. The gum sits in my throat like hair in a clogged shower drain.

I turn and run toward the door, but my foot comes down on a Sock'em Bopper. The inflatable glove rolls my foot forward. Both my legs go out from under me.

I levitate. I'm soaring through the air like Aladdin on his flying carpet. Pale, yellow stars dot Tiffany's ceiling. Put up there when she was just a kid. They glow in the dark.

Will they glow when things go dark for me?

Then the magic carpet is gone, and I'm falling to the ground. I land on the Sock'em Bopper, and it pops with a huge BANG.

My back slams into the ground. A rush of vomit pushes out of my stomach and up my throat. It erupts in a geyser that quickly covers my face in bile and chewed-up, dinosaur-shaped chicken nuggets.

The huge mass of gum comes down on my forehead, bouncing off with a wet SPLAT.

I groan, my back on fire, my lungs on fire. I want to cry for my mommy, but she's gone and all I have is a cruel sister. Someone who'd skin me and turn me into a coat when she finds out I ate her gum and threw up in her bedroom.

At least I can breathe. Tiffany will be pissed, but less pissed than if she had to deal with my purple corpse.

It smells now. Sour, like what battery acid would taste like. The room has been sitting in the sun all day, baking, and now the smell hangs in the air like a swamp.

I go to leave.

"Wait!"

I turn back. Barbie looks at me, propped up against the wall. Smiling her beautiful smile. Naked and loving it.

"It smells like a pig's asshole. Don't leave me in here!"

Through watery eyes, I look at her. At Blue, face pressed into the corner where the wall meets the carpet. My Power Ranger, powerless.

I brought them along on this mission; I can't leave them behind.

With all the courage of a firefighter entering a burning building, I take a deep breath and return for my friends. I scoop them into my arms, turn tail, and slip in my vomit.

I drop to one knee with a squish and inhale involuntarily.

The smell turns my stomach. It's worse than when it goes into the toilet. It's mixed with all the dirt in the carpet, every teenage scent that's filled this room. Vanilla body spray, musty towels, and sweaty sheets a base for my throw-up to build on.

I escape on that one breath, stumbling with the two giant dolls beneath my arms. I cough, breathing in huge lungfuls of fresh air.

My knee is soaked. The vomit tingles there, acid chewing up my jeans. I need to wash it off. We head towards the bathroom.

And Tiffany.

She's perched at the top of the stairs. Her back is to me, pink crop top screaming. Her hair is in pig-tails like she's going out, but she's not allowed; she has to watch me.

"What did he say when you mentioned me?" Tiffany says into the cordless phone. "Did he seem like he missed me or what?"

I don't know who the heck she's talking to. She breaks up with her friends every week. A new one always comes into her life as the old one leaves. A friendship revolving door, like the ones at Sevenoaks Mall.

"He's such scum, anyway. I don't care that he's gorgeous...no, I don't care that he has a car. It *don't impress-a me much!*" Tiffany devolves into cackles, losing her mind at her own cleverness.

"Put this in her hair," says Barbie.

I look down.

In her hand, Barbie holds the giant mass of vomit-coated gum. It's stuck to her palm, grey-on-pink. It must have fallen onto it after bouncing off my forehead.

But she was so far away. It couldn't have—

"Put this. In her hair."

"W-why?"

"Yeah," says Blue, "why?"

"This is her fault," says Barbie, snake venom in her voice. "She wasn't watching you, and you almost died!"

She has a point.

"What do you think Mom and Dad would have done if they came home to you dead on her floor?"

"They'd be mad." I say.

"They'd punish her."

"I don't like this," says Blue. "I don't like this."

"She deserves it, Josh."

I peel the gum off Barbie's plastic hand. It's wet and soft. When I press my fingers, it squishes bile out of unseen pores. I can't remember it ever tasting good.

"It'll be funny," says Barbie.

It *will* be funny.

I glide toward Tiffany. I can't sneak up; she'll smell me. Smell the vomit on my knee, the stain on my forehead from where the gum landed. Puke is all over my chin.

I need to be quick.

I rush forward, making myself quick. Lightning-fast like Sonic the Hedgehog. I bounce from one side of the hall against the other, rattling the picture frames holding the family photos we took at Sears.

"Hang on a sec," Tiffany says to her friend of the week.

I'm two steps away, now one.

I wind my hand back, lips pursed in concentration. All the energy in my arm freezes for just the briefest moment before I slap my palm—and the gum—against her ear.

Tiffany reels.

"What are you dooooing?" she brays. Her mouth turns down, hand going to her ear. She winces.

Did I hurt her? It was only supposed to be a prank.

I squeeze Barbie and Blue under my arms and wait for advice. I can't move. Not without their instructions.

Tiffany's hand falls upon the gum tangled in the hair under her pigtail.

"What the fuck?"

I can't wait. I drop Blue and Barbie to the ground and try to sprint past Tiffany. The gap between her and the banister is narrow, but I think I can make it. I just need to be fast. Fast like a lightning bolt. Fast like Sonic.

Tiffany has always been fast. She reaches out to stop me, but I'm too quick. She only succeeds in smacking my foot.

Sending me off balance.

My head tumbles down where my feet should be. My body bounces. My arm smacks against the corner of a step.

I fly, becoming weightless. Aladdin on his magic carpet. Falling down like I'm on the Hellevator at the fair. Everything that was in my stomach is now on the floor of Tiffany's bedroom, but something flutters around in it regardless. Butterflies. A whole swarm of them.

WHAT DID HE DO? What did he do?

I paw at my hair, but my heart isn't in it. My heart is a block of ice, the cold spreading to the rest of my organs. Caressing my intestines. Freezing the half of a Big Mac my idiot mom got me.

I can't believe it. I didn't mean it.

Why did he do it?

"Josh?"

He's not moving. I look over the banister at his small, broken form.

"Josh, don't mess around."

Alexis squawks from the cordless phone, but I have more pressing matters.

A small, dark puddle starts to expand on the tiles around Josh's head.

My hands shoot to my mouth, but they're too slow to keep my gasp in my throat.

"*Tiff, just lock him in the bathroom or something, and if he threatens to tell—*"

I press the gummy 'end' button on the phone. The house falls silent. Downstairs, the clock on the mantle ticks each parent-free second away.

"You don't have many options," says a voice at my heel. "You're going to have to move fast."

I turn around, heart racing.

"Who's there?"

"Much as I hate to say it," says a man's voice, "she's right."

"Doesn't look like he's breathing."

It's impossible. As impossible as my kid brother laying at the bottom of the stairs with sharp bones stretching his skin at so many places.

The voice is coming from my Barbie. Three feet tall, smooth as the girls in *Tiger Beat*. She's on her naked belly, peering through the bars of the banister.

"You don't know first aid, do you?"

I spin. Did that sound come from Josh's Power Ranger?

"It won't do him any good, Dingus," says Barbie. "Kid's skull is leaking like a faucet."

"Are his eyes open?" asks the Power Ranger. "When people die in the movies, their eyes are always open, for some reason."

I've gone nuts. None of this is happening.

"Yeahhh," says Barbie. "They're open."

"Well...fuck."

"W-what do I do?" My voice feels small. Carried on only a whisper of air. It's all I can contain in my lungs.

"You have any power tools?" asks Barbie.

I try to talk, but the ringing in my head is so loud. My vision flutters.

"Focus!" snaps Barbie. "Power tools, do you got 'em?"

"I uh, I think so." I smack my mouth open and closed. "Dad has a hacksaw in the garage."

"That's not a power tool, sweetheart," says the Power Ranger.

"It'll do," says Barbie. "He'll be easier to move in pieces."

CHRISTOPHER O'HALLORAN IS A MILK-SLINGING, Canadian actor-turned-author with work published or forthcoming from No Sleep Podcast, Tales to Terrify, The Dread Machine, and others. His novelettes are in anthologies Howls from Hell and Bloodlines: Four Tales of Familial Fear. He is Reviews Editor-in-Chief, Social Media Co-Manager, and Discord Mod for the most active horror book club on the web, HOWL Society. Follow him on Twitter @BurgleInfernal or visit COauthor.ca for stories, reviews, and updates on upcoming novels.

"Between the Barbie and the Deep-Blue Ranger" is illustrated by P.L. McMillan.

THE GRUNGE

CALEB STEPHENS

*"Don't you kill me
I'm doing just fine
Laying out my noose
And knotting the line"*

Soundwave, "Stitches"

Valley Oaks Cemetery: Gray Springs, CA
October 14, 1995
5:45 pm

Most Friday nights, the kids in Gray Springs can be seen down at Crystal Cove, tossing back lukewarm bottles of Mad Dog 20/20, or gathered around a keg in the field behind Lance Foster's house, drinking beer from Red Solo cups. Tonight, they'll all be heading to Gray Springs High School for Homecoming, the girls decked out in the finest gowns JCPenney has to offer, the guys in their rented cummerbunds and tuxes. Everyone who's anyone will be there, which is exactly why Patrick and I won't.

I mean, sure, we're nobodies, but that's not the real reason we're ditching. Scott Stark's grave is a popular place. Normally, there are a few die-hards from school milling around, roach clips at the ready, sharing long-lost Soundwave concert stories in between bong rips. With the dance going on, there's a good chance we'll be left alone, which is perfect.

We need to focus.

We have a rock god to resurrect.

I KNOW exactly where I was the first time I heard Scott Stark's trademark growl shred a set of stereo speakers. It was on a fishing trip up to Lake Chabot with Uncle Will. Dad had just cut bait on me and Mom, and she'd convinced Uncle Will I needed some male bonding time or some shit like that. Anyway, I'd been complaining about it, how pissed I was at Dad for leaving us, how unfair it all felt, when Uncle Will popped a Soundwave cassette in the stereo deck and hit play.

The music swallowed me. The gritty wall of distortion, Scott's voice cutting through the guitars like sonic fire, stripping paint. It was such a release for me.

I couldn't get enough.

The next day I blew my allowance on every Soundwave record I could get my hands on, every EP, from *Sawtooth* to *The Calling*. Their music felt so personal, like Scott had somehow cracked open my skull and fished the lyrics straight from my brain. So, a couple of years later, when Uncle Will told me that Scott frickin' Stark, lead singer of Soundwave, was from Gray Springs, that he grew up here, I nearly shit my pants.

"Seriously?"

"Yep. Nice guy. I even jammed with him a few times. Crazy as hell, though. He was a couple years behind me in school."

It was the last thing Uncle Will ever said to me. He had a heart attack a week later. That's what Mom told me, anyway. It's total bullshit. Uncle Will was the definition of health. He crushed marathons like beer cans. She still won't tell me. Anytime I bring it up, she drowns the question in a vodka bottle. All I know is losing Uncle Will royally screwed her up. It was like the lights were on in her eyes one day, and then—*whoosh!*—he died, and out they went.

That was six years ago. I was nine. No lights since.

"Okay, yep, that looks great," Patrick says, fiddling with the camcorder. "Oh, shit, hang on. I gotta fix the light setting." He's staring at me through the lens of his Sony VX1000, looking like a deranged Steven Spielberg with his black eyeliner, Tripp pants, and shin-high combat boots. (Patrick O'Halloran is my best friend, by the way. He's goth as shit, and I love him for it.)

He waves a finger. "Almost got it."

I glance around. "Dude, can you hurry it up a little? I'm not super pumped to be caught desecrating my hero's grave."

Patrick clicks more buttons, adjusts the aperture. "Relax, Colin.

Everyone's at"—he lowers his voice and tosses up a set of air quotes—"the big dance."

I can't help but laugh. That's the thing about Patrick: he looks like the kind of kid who might murder you in your sleep, the kind who walks around looking like a white version of Candyman with a hook hidden in the folds of his trench coat. But he's nothing like that. He just loves heavy metal and horror movies. *Especially* horror movies. *Cannibal Holocaust. Hellraiser. Alien.* Anything that gets his blood pumping.

It's why we're here. There's this amateur horror short-film competition coming up at UC Berkeley with a full-ride scholarship on the line for first place. Patrick is convinced it's his ticket out of Gray Springs, that if he doesn't win, he'll be stuck behind the wheel of a Royal Crest Dairy truck, delivering milk for the rest of his life like his dad; which, to him, is a fate worse than death.

"There we go," he says. "You ready?"

I nod.

"Okay, camera speed...action."

I raise the grimoire, which is honestly pretty freaky-looking—ancient and stained, with a pentagram and a bunch of weird symbols stenciled on the front in blood-red ink—and flip it open to the resurrection spell. The pages are brittle, the text so faded, I can barely decipher the words. I clear my throat, and my voice slides out in a slow drawl.

"Spirit of trees, servants of earth, come to me. I invoke thee, Beelzebub and Saasiyah. I command thee, upon the dark wings of Asimon to restore your servant, Scott Stark. I summon you by stealth and blood and..." I trail off, look back at Patrick. "Dude, do I really have to cut myself? I mean, isn't that a little overkill?"

The recording light winks off, and Patrick covers the microphone. "Dammit, yes, of course, you do, Colin. This shit has to look real. And, besides, you told me you would. You promised."

"Okay, okay," I say, waving at him to continue. "Jesus, chill out."

The red light on the camcorder blinks back to life, and I slip the knife from my pocket. It's Swiss Army, circa 1989, the last thing Dad gave me before he bailed, which means it's extra dull as I work the blade into my palm. I make a show of cutting myself, then squeeze a thin trickle of blood into the middle of the salt circle we poured over Scott's grave.

Patrick flashes me devil horns from behind the video camera, sticks out his tongue.

I raise the book and continue to read.

"I summon you by stealth and blood and shadow, oh great Aluka. I have made thy mark and command thee raise Scott Stark to life once more." I thrust my chin back for effect, hold the grimoire directly over my head like I expect a bolt of lightning to rip down from the sky and set it on fire.

"Rise, oh, god of grunge, oh, master of rock! Rise and reclaim thy metal throne!"

"Aaand cut!" Patrick says. "That was *sick*, dude. Great job!"

I press my palm to my lips and suck the blood from my lifeline. "You want to do another take? Make sure we got it?"

"Yeah, maybe one more with—"

A rumble cuts him off. He steadies the camera and shoots me a quick *what the fuck* look.

I shrug.

Another rumble hits, the earth trembling, shifting beneath our feet. Plumes of dirt shoot into the air, a fissure racing between my legs toward Scott's tombstone...which sheers in half with an ear-splitting *crack!*

I gawk at it open-mouthed, turn to Patrick. "Are you seeing this?"

My words hang there unanswered as the salt circle disintegrates, collapsing in on itself until we're left staring at a black hole punched straight down into the earth.

A hole from which a hand rises.

Followed by another.

They sink into the grass and pull higher.

"Holy shit," Patrick stammers.

My eyes are cranked so wide they're on fire, my voice lodged in the small, tight space behind my Adam's apple.

Somehow, Patrick is filming again.

A face appears. Two cobalt eyes, and a blonde-whisker chin. I recognize the mud-caked hair and aquiline nose. The square jaw. It's plastered over the walls of my room in the shape of posters, over a dozen shirts in my closet—at Redding, howling from the center stage of Pink Pop.

I'm staring at a dead man. I'm staring at Scott Stark.

THE CAMERA WHINES.

Scott grinds his thumb and forefinger into the bridge of his nose with a groan.

It feels like someone kicked the air from my lungs.

He squints up, rubs his temples. "Hey, can one of you help me out here?"

Neither of us moves.

"Guys, c'mon. My head is killing me."

Without thinking, I step forward, feeling as though I'm floating, feeling like my feet are hovering a foot off the ground.

This isn't happening.

Scott takes my hand. It's like gripping a block of ice.

It's happening. Yep, definitely fucking happening.

He scrambles out of the grave and crumples to his knees, spitting clods of dirt from his mouth, coughing up black liquid like his lungs are full of tar, which, who knows, they probably are. Oh, and he's half-naked, his burial jacket hanging off his torso in shreds, his slacks shredded, revealing legs that are all rangy tendon, and bulging joints.

He stands and looks at Patrick, who's got the camcorder pointed straight at his crotch.

Scott's lips twist into a snarl. "Hey, what the hell, man? Is that thing on? Are you filming me?"

Patrick punches the camcorder's power button, nearly dropping it. "Oh…sorry. My bad. We were just, uh, yeah, making a film and—"

Scott raises a finger and plants a fist to his mouth. Then he's back to yacking, expelling more black goo into the grass.

Patrick gags. "*Gross.*"

Scott glances at him in a wince, his forehead bleeding sweat, his skin shining like wet cement. "So, who are you two clowns, anyway?"

Patrick steps forward and offers his hand. "Yeah, hi. I'm Patrick. Patrick O'Halloran and this is my best friend, Colin Hayes."

Scott crosses his arms. "How did I get here?"

"What's the last thing you remember?" I ask.

His brow collapses. "Just these...flashes. I was in a hotel or some shit, with Shane and Dave." He jabs his palm into his ear a few times, looking like he just came in from a swim. "Oh, and some girls we met at the show. I remember my arm burning...and then nothing."

I know the story. Everyone does. The overdose happened in Detroit, the band partying their balls off after a rager at the Fillmore, the last concert they ever performed. The Statler Hotel. July 14th, 1991. Three members of Soundwave woke up the next morning. Scott didn't. He was twenty-seven.

"I'm sorry, man," I say. "You're dead."

His face hardens. "'Dead'? What do you mean I'm *dead*?"

I point at his tombstone, and he turns. When he looks back, his eyes are wet with fear. "What's the year?"

"It's 1995."

It's like I've decked him. He sits down hard, ass-first, legs wide, head in hands.

"Oh, *shit.*" He curls his fingers into his hair. "Ohshit, ohshit, ohshit. I fucked up, didn't I?"

"Yeah you did," Patrick says.

I elbow him. "*Dude.*"

He shrugs. "What?"

I roll my eyes and kneel next to Scott, set a hand on his shoulder. His skin is as cold as a metal pole on a February morning. I'm pretty sure I'm seconds away from catching a case of first-degree frostbite.

"Hey," I say, "why don't you come with us? We'll get you some clothes and fill you in. A lot's happened since you died."

After a moment, he peers out between the gaps in his fingers and nods.

Big Jim's Thirsty Jug Gas-N-Go
Main Street & 56th Avenue
6:37 pm

Patrick is standing in the grease-spattered parking lot of the Gas-N-Go, waiting for his mom to arrive with a change of clothes (for the film, of course) while I post watch near the dumpster, ready to shoo away anyone who tries to use the bathroom. Scott's inside, cleaning up and grumbling to himself about how crazy this all is, how he can't be dead, something like that. I'm thinking the same, but more so freaking out about how many people called the cops on the corpse in the tattered suit and the two kids hauling ass out of the graveyard.

I'm half-expecting to see a parade of blue and red lights roaring down the street when Patrick's mom pulls up in her battered Volvo station wagon and cranks down the window. Her face is all soft curves, pure bread dough, punctuated by two warm, chocolate-chip colored eyes. She's the kind of mom who doesn't care that her son looks like he fell out of a Halloween catalog and is low-key obsessed with death. To her, he's just Patrick, and that's enough.

"Here you go, sweetheart," she says, handing him a paper sack. "You going to be done soon? I'll have dinner ready in about an hour."

"Nah, we still have a ways to go, Mom," Patrick replies. "You and Dad go ahead and eat without me."

"How about you, Colin? You hungry?"

I'm starving, and she makes a mean lasagna. "No, I'm good, Mrs. O'Halloran. Thanks, though."

"Okay, well you boys be safe out here, and Patrick, don't be home too late. I'll save you some leftovers."

The car rattles off, and Patrick saunters over, bag in hand, stopping midway to peel it open. His lips unglue as he does, his eyebrows shooting up beneath his bangs. "Dude, *no*."

"What?" I ask.

He reaches in and retrieves a crisp white button-down shirt, pinching it at the collar like he's holding a sewer rat. The patch on the breast reads, *Hi, I'm Christopher O'Halloran, Your Friendly Royal Crest Delivery Man!*

He gives the shirt a shake. "What the shit, man? I can't give *this* to Scott."

"You don't have a choice," I say, taking it from him along with the bag. I head for the bathroom and Scott answers on the second knock, the door opening an inch. I raise the sack. "Here you go."

"Thank god," Scott says, snatching it. Behind him, puddles of brown water are pooled all over the floor and sink, the mirror smeared with mud. It looks like a bomb went off. He slams the door and emerges a few minutes later with his hands spread wide.

"Seriously, guys? This is the best you could do? A milkman?"

Patrick hangs his head. "Sorry, my mom screwed up. I told her to bring some of my dad's clothes and—"

The rev of an engine swallows his voice, the squeal of tires.

"Well look who it is, Pattycake and Gays!"

I cringe at the sound of Lance Foster's voice: Colin Hayes. Colin *Gays*. Hilarious.

He's parked behind us near the entrance to the Gas-N-Go in his cherry-red Chevy Camaro along with one of his goons, Matt Smith. They both have white tuxedos on, their necks stamped in navy blue bow ties, looking like a pair of dim-witted James Bonds.

Lance grins. "Shouldn't you two be at home, jerking each other off by now?"

"Shouldn't you?" Patrick replies.

Lance spouts an overbaked laugh. "No, Patrick. That's what girls are for, but you wouldn't know anything about that, would you?" His gaze falls on Scott. "Who's the creeper? Your dad?"

"Fuck off," Scott growls.

"Yeah, okay, milkman. What are you gonna do, pour me a glass of one percent?"

Matt cracks up and pounds the dash, seal-barking like Lance just said the funniest thing ever.

"I don't need this shit," Scott says, heading for the road.

Lance watches him go with a smirk. "Uh oh, Pattycake, your dad looks pretty pissed off. You better go feed him a bottle."

I feel Patrick bristle next to me and tug his arm. "C'mon. Let's go."

By the time I drag him away, Scott is gone.

Castle Pines Subdivision
Somewhere along Ash Street
6:45 pm

We catch up with Scott a few minutes later. He's shambling down the sidewalk, looking like a Royal Crest zombie in his uniform, which I guess he is, his right foot dragging behind, slowing him down.

"Hey," Patrick shouts. "Wait up. Where are you going?"

"Don't know yet," he replies over his shoulder. "Maybe hitch a ride up to Seattle and see if my dad is still alive. Check-in with a few guys from the band."

"You can't," I say. "You don't have enough time."

He stops, turns. "Why not?"

"Because you only have until midnight before you...you know..." I wrap an invisible noose around my neck and give it a tug.

His lips twitch, and he limps toward me. "And just who told you that?"

"The guy at the pawnshop. The one who sold me the spellbook."

He brings his face an inch from mine. His breath smells like formaldehyde as it slips past his rotting teeth. "You better be fucking with me."

I raise my hands. "I'm not. I *swear*. I never thought this shit would work. Neither of us did. Right, Patrick?"

He nods.

Scott's face crumples, and he scratches an ear. "Well shit. What time is it?"

Patrick glances at his watch. "A little before seven."

My breath quickens. "Um, Scott."

He gives me a dazed look. "What?"

"Your ear."

It comes off in his hand, his eyes widening as he brings it in front of his face. "Oh," he says, giving it a gentle wobble. "Well, that sucks."

"Seriously? Cobain, too?" Scott asks.

I nod. "Yeah, with a shotgun."

"Poor bastard."

We've been sitting on the curb for a solid twenty minutes, filling him in on all he's missed since he died: Rodney King and OJ Simpson, the Oklahoma City bombing. The internet. He hasn't stopped staring at his ear the entire time, cupping it in his palm and stroking it like it's a puppy.

"And you said computers talk to each other now? Like Skynet or some shit?"

I crack a knuckle. "Well, not quite like that. The internet is mostly for porn."

"*So* much porn," Patrick adds. "But it takes forever to download, trust me."

Scott runs a hand over his face. "Did Soundwave…did they find someone else? Another singer?"

I shake my head. "No. They tried, but they couldn't replace you."

"No one could," Patrick echoes.

"Then I screwed them, too. Goddamn."

I move to clap him on the back, to tell him how sorry I am, when I hear the familiar roar of an engine, the bass-heavy thump of a woofer on full blast: The Notorious B.I.G.'s "Juicy."

"Hey, milkman, catch!"

I spot the carton flying through the air and duck. Scott must see it too, because he's ducking with me, leaning low and to the side.

Patrick doesn't.

It smashes into his chest in a geyser of white, milk exploding skyward, soaking his face and neck, drenching his spiked hair. The camcorder.

The Camaro blows past in a howl of laughter, the brake lights flashing halfway down the block, the car turning into a driveway.

"Son of a bitch!" Patrick shouts, spitting milk into the gutter. Except it isn't milk at all, I realize. It smells *way* too sour, the consistency *way* too thick.

It's buttermilk.

Patrick curses and wipes the video camera, frantically dabbing at the lens, the viewfinder. He worked two summers at Wal-Mart to buy it, hauling sacks of hot garbage to the dumpsters, cleaning diarrhea stains off toilet lids. It's like watching someone trying to save a newborn; I keep waiting for him to slap the thing and scream for it to, *breathe, goddammit, breathe!*

He takes a nervous breath and presses the power button. Nothing happens. He tries again to the same result.

A storm cloud ripples over his face. "That's it!"

Before I can stop him, he's up and running down the street, headed straight for the Camaro, his trench coat flying out behind him like he's a death-metal superhero.

Only he isn't. Lance will totally kick his ass.

I catch up with him near the driveway and grab his wrist.

"Let go," he says, whirling around.

"Screw these guys, man! They suck. Let's just get out of here."

His lips tighten. "No, Colin, don't you get it? They'll never stop this shit unless we do something. They'll never leave us alone." He jerks from my grip, and marches onto the lawn, uncurling both middle fingers. "Hey, Lance! Fuck you."

Lance turns, and I notice the girl perched in the doorframe behind him, the one holding the flowers he brought her. The one I've had a crush on since the eighth grade.

Jesus.
I grind a hand over my face and groan.
I know exactly where we are.

Amani Jones' House
741 Ash Street
7:15 pm

Oh. My. God.

It's all I can think. Amani is beyond gorgeous, her dark skin striking against her creme-colored gown, her brown eyes glowing beneath the porchlight. Why she's with an asshole like Lance is beyond me. Sure she's pretty and all, but she's so much more than that. She's the best basketball player in Gray Springs by a mile, including the guys, and it's not even close. She's funny and kind and a killer actress in the school plays. I pretty much wilt anytime she looks at me.

It's what she's doing now, looking at me, as her father shoulders outside and strides toward Patrick. He's a good six inches taller than Lance, all muscle with biceps that stretch the sleeves of his blue Izod polo: Gray Spring's Fire Chief, Mr. Jones, is not a man to fuck with.

"What did you say?" he asks, his voice so deep it sounds like it's welling up from some ancient spring.

Patrick takes a step back, the anger melting from his face. "I, uh—nothing, sir."

"Who are these boys, Lance?" he asks, glaring at Scott now, a deep line creasing his forehead.

Lance shrugs, a look of ignorance splashed across his face. "Beats me, Mr. Jones. They go to school with us, but I don't know them. They were throwing rocks at my car a minute ago."

Matt nods from the Camaro. "It's true, sir. I think they're high."

Anger pools in my chest. "No, we aren't! They're the ones who—"

Mr. Jones spins on me, his finger out and stabbing. "You will get off my property immediately, gentlemen. And you will leave my daughter and her friends alone, or I will call the police. Am I making myself clear?"

Scott straightens, flashes him a mock salute. His eyes are yellow, swimming loose in their sockets. "Yes, sir. Copy that, sir."

Patrick drifts back toward us with his shoulders slumped, his camera still dripping buttermilk. "Fine, let's go."

"Where?" I mutter, glancing at Amani, who's frowning at me now.

"I don't know about you guys," Scott says. "But I could use a drink,"

Outside The Cork and Bottle Liquor Store
Johnson Square
8:10 pm

Scott takes a swig of the forty he bought after bumming twenty bucks from Patrick. "So, is that guy always like that?"

"Worse," I say.

Patrick grumbles next to me, still polishing the camcorder, muttering for it to work. I can smell the buttermilk with every swipe.

Scott takes another drink, belches. "You know, I wasn't so different from you two at one point. An outcast. A loser,—"

"Ouch, harsh," Patrick says.

"—everyone giving me shit because I was different or whatever. I had no clue what I wanted to do with my life. It wasn't until I found music that I felt semi-normal."

"How'd that happen?" I ask. I'm only half-listening, my mind still on Amani, thinking about the look she gave me. *Ugh.*

"My neighbor played guitar. He had a PRS. Super nice guy. He invited me over a few times, taught me some chords. I think he felt sorry for me or something."

I stiffen. I know the guitar. It's been sitting in our garage, stuffed behind the deep freezer for the last six years. Mom couldn't bear to sell it. "Wait. What was his name?"

Scott looks at me, the skin beneath his eyes drooping like puddles of melted wax. "Will Summerall. Why?"

The name hits me like a brick to the face. I can't speak for a second. When I do, it's in a whisper. "He's my uncle."

Scott flashes me a grin. His front incisor is missing. One of his cuspids. "No shit. Your uncle is Will? How's he doing?"

And just like that, my astonishment is gone. I hang my head. "He died a few years before you did."

Scott lets out a long, slow whistle. "No way, how?"

"I don't know. My mom said it was a heart attack, but that was a lie. He was too young, too healthy. I just know it was something bad."

"Damn. Sorry, kid."

We all sit in silence a moment, even Patrick, who's taken a break from cleaning the camcorder to listen.

Scott grips my shoulder. "Listen, your uncle, he made all the difference for me. Soundwave wouldn't exist without him. He even wrote the riff to 'Stitches.'"

"Seriously?" I ask, a note of wonder creeping back into my voice.

"Yeah. I tried to get him in the band more than once, but he was into theater. Stage plays. That kind of thing. He didn't have time for both. He was damn good, too. I saw him perform a few times. The guy was incredible. I can't believe he's dead."

"Me either," I mumble.

He brings the forty to his lips, swishes the beer around his mouth. "You know, I can't even taste this shit?" He rears back and launches the forty in a high arc, the bottle shattering in a piss-yellow spray of malt liquor and glass beneath the streetlight.

"Awesome," Patrick says.

Scott stands and brushes his slacks. "Look, if I only have a few hours left, I'm sure as hell not letting Will Summerall's nephew"—he glances at Patrick—"or his friend, take any more shit from that douchebag."

Patrick's eyes spark to life. "What do you have in mind?"

Scott waves at his camcorder. "Well, that asshole fucked up your video camera, didn't he?"

Patrick nods, and I feel myself doing the same, rising to my feet.

"Then what say we fuck up something he loves?"

A grin curves over Patrick's chin. "Oh, yeah. Totally. Let's do it."

Gray Springs High School
Home of the Fighting Skeeters
11:17 pm

If there's one thing Gray Springs doesn't have a lot of, it's money. *Beverly Hills 90210* we are not. It makes spotting Lance's ride easy work. The Camaro is parked near the bus loop, the paint gleaming like a jolly rancher beneath the sodium vapor lights.

I can't wait to ruin it.

For as long as I can remember, Lance has wrecked my life. Spitballs in class and wedgies in the locker room. Swirlies in toilets clogged with yellow water. He's nut-checked me more times than I can count. Even worse, he's spread lies, started rumors that I'm gay, which I'm not. He's done the same to Patrick, who I'm pretty sure is. It's beyond messed up. Patrick should be able to be himself, to like whoever he wants, but he can't. Not with assholes like Lance Foster around.

Screw you, Lance.

I launch an egg and watch it splatter over the hood with a satisfying thud. Patrick throws his and smiles as egg yolk fireworks across the windshield. Then we're all slinging eggs rapid-fire, pelting the fender and body, the doors and the tires—*thunk! thunk! thunk!*—turning the car into a glistening mess of yolk and egg white.

A head pops up from the backseat. Another. Matt Smith and some girl with a ribbon of lipstick smeared halfway across her cheek.

Matt fumbles at the latch and tumbles out of the car, jerking his underwear up—tighty whities. *Figures.* The girl follows, ducking behind him like we're carrying revolvers instead of a couple dozen of Ocean Mart's Grade A finest.

"Oh, you three are dead," Matt says. "Wait until—"

Patrick's egg hits him square in the mouth. I fire one into his chest, Scott another into his groin.

"Bullseye!" Scott spouts with a laugh.

Matt folds like an accordion, clutching his jewels. Then he's spinning around and hauling ass toward the entrance, flashing a pale slice of butt cheek as he tries to hike up his pants. "Lance is gonna kill you guys! You're so screwed!"

I watch him go, and then wave at the girl, who I recognize as Evelyn Freeling, one of the varsity cheerleaders; she's in my trigonometry class and has breath that smells like bubblegum.

"Sorry about that," I say. "We didn't mean to scare you."

"It's okay," she says, her gaze now resting on Scott, her eyes narrowing. "Hey, isn't that...?"

"Yeah," Patrick says. "It's him."

Her nose scrunches up. "But isn't he...*dead*?"

"Yup," I answer, glancing at the gymnasium doors, where students are streaming outside and racing in our direction. "Just like we're about to be."

I move to run, to haul ass out of the parking lot before Lance turns my face into a pound of ground beef. Scott's hand lands on my shoulder and stops me. He shakes his head, the tip of his nose missing now, a piece of his chin. "You gotta make a stand. Patrick was right. He'll never leave you guys alone if you don't." His jaw hardens. "Don't worry, though. I've got your back."

Goddammit. He's right of course, but it doesn't change the fact we're all about to get our asses kicked.

I take a deep breath and spin around.

Several members of the football team are the first to arrive, followed by a pack of skaters clad in flannels and chinos. A few band kids push into the mix, and I lose track from there, a sea of tuxedos and gowns pressing in around us, forming a circle, voices rippling through the crowd.

"Oh my god, look at his car."

"Whoa, Lance is gonna be so pissed, bro."

"Yeah, he's gonna lose his shit."

Threads of sweat drip down my neck, my cheeks.

"What. The. FUCK?"

The sound of Lance's voice is enough to make me want to piss myself. He pushes through the wall of bodies, his eyes glued to his car, breathing so hard I can practically see the steam jetting from his nostrils.

An egg splatters across the front of his jacket.

"That's for breaking my camcorder, asshole," Patrick says.

Lance's face buckles into a snarl. "I'm going to murder you, O'Halloran."

He's about to lunge when a hand cups his arm, Amani tugging him back.

"Lance, please, don't hurt them."

"Let go of me," he orders.

She doesn't. She pulls harder, instead. "Let's just go wash your car, okay?"

"God, don't be such a bitch, Amani! I said let go."

I have no idea if Lance means to do it, or if it's an accident, but as he rips free, the back of his hand smacks her cheek and sends her whirling to the asphalt.

I don't even realize I'm moving toward him, that my fingers have already balled into a fist.

"Don't touch her, asshole!"

He turns, and I force everything I have into the punch—all the years of taking his shit, every name he's ever called me—and drive my fist straight into his chin.

His head snaps back. A collective gasp runs through the crowd. He wobbles, takes a dizzy, sideways step.

For a moment, I think it's enough.

It's not.

He massages his jaw, and his eyes turn to slits. "That was stupid, Gays."

He launches a vicious haymaker, one I barely manage to duck. There's a moist crunch followed by a brittle sucking sound, and I look up to find Lance's fist lodged in Scott's chest, buried to the wrist.

Scott dips his head with a wicked grin. "So was that."

He digs his fingers into the lapels of Lance's tux and rips him forward with a cough, a sound that rattles deep in his chest, a phlegmy buzz like an ignition sputtering. It grows from there, crawling up his throat until I can feel it in my lungs.

His jaw falls open.

A cloud of flies burst from his mouth and burrow into Lance's hair, swarm over his face and neck and ears. For a moment, it looks like his skin is alive, like it's transformed into a writhing black mass.

"Get them off me! Get them off!" Lance yanks his fist, which won't dislodge from Scott's chest, Scott still clutching Lance's jacket, talking now, speaking to Lance in a growl.

"If you *ever* fuck with these two again, or anyone for that matter, I'm coming for you, dick. I'll find you and drag you to hell with me, got it?"

Lance nods, his eyes brimming with tears, flies seeping from his hair and winding down his cheeks, crawling beneath the collar of his shirt.

Scott shoves Lance back. "Get out of here then."

There's a moist, ripping sound, Scott's arm tearing loose in a fountain of black sludge, his detached fist still clutching Lance's tux, who, at that point, screams like a ten-year-old.

It's not just him. Everywhere, people are shrieking and sprinting away, in-between cars, wheeling toward the high school, running for the street.

The only one who isn't is Amani.

She's shaking, clutching her knee, scooting backward across the blacktop, her eyes still plastered on Scott like he might vomit a swarm of flies at her next.

I rush over and kneel down, offer my hand. Even as terrified as she is now, I still can't help but notice how beautiful she is.

"Don't freak out, okay. You're safe. I promise."

"What is that...thing?" she says as I help her up.

"A friend, believe it or not. Here, c'mon." We walk together slowly, Amani hobbling next to me, hissing with every step until we reach the bench.

She sits and says, "Sorry, I think I rolled my ankle when Lance... you know. God, he's such a jerk." She folds her hands in her lap. "Thanks for what you did back there."

I feel my face heat up. "I—it was no problem."

She opens her mouth to say something else, then shuts it, her gaze back on the parking lot. She frowns. "I don't think your friend is doing so hot."

I turn and spot Scott limping away between a Ford Bronco and black Chevy Impala, clutching his chest, the milkman uniform stained black beneath his missing arm.

"I'd better go help him." I start forward, stop. "Amani?"

"Yeah?"

"Would you maybe want to hang out sometime? I mean, it's cool if you don't want to."

She smooths her dress, smiles. "Sure, I'd like that."

I struggle to suppress the grin tugging at my lips as I turn and sprint across the blacktop toward Scott. Patrick is already there when I reach him, steadying Scott on one side. I slide in on the other, and we work our way up the hill at the edge of the parking lot toward the old oak overlooking the city below.

"I used to come up here and write lyrics sometimes," Scott says, collapsing against the tree. "Just to get away from everything, you know? I always loved this view."

I stare at the horizon. On a clear day, you can see the ocean from here, but right now, all I can make out are the city lights and a sweeping stretch of black sky. A police siren wails in the distance.

Scott chuckles. "Sounds like the cavalry is on the way. Thanks for letting me crash your party tonight, fellas. It was fun."

I glance at my watch: 11:57 p.m. My throat constricts. "There's gotta be...I don't know, something we can do for you?"

Scott shakes his head and rubs a patch of skin from the hollow of his throat. "Nah, man. You already have. I never got to say goodbye to this place. Gray Springs is a shithole, sure, but I had a lot of good times in this town, made a lot of memories." He looks at me. "You did good tonight. Will would be proud."

"Thanks." I don't want him to go. It's only been a few hours, but for some reason, it feels like I'm losing Uncle Will all over again.

He nods at Patrick. "And keep on filming. I've got a good feeling about you. I think you'll go far." His lips are flaking now, his remaining ear. He raises his fist and gives both of us knuckle bumps. "Wish I'd had more friends like you guys when I was alive." He blinks, his eyes turning gelatinous, leaking down his face. "Take care of each other, yeah?"

Patrick's voice cracks. "We will."

A smile curls across what's left of Scott's face, something like peace settling over his disintegrating features. And then he's gone, turning to ash—his remaining ear, his nose, his cheekbones, and chin, what's left of his hair and eyes and teeth—everything blackening until it collapses inward in a waterfall of dust.

We sit together in silence, staring down at the city lights, neither of us moving for what feels like hours. After a while, Patrick pulls the camcorder into his lap. "Think anyone will ever believe any of this?"

"Lance will," I say with a laugh.

"Yeah, for sure. It's just, man, I wish we could have finished the film. It would have been epic."

I shrug. "Maybe we still can? Let me see that thing."

He hands it over, and I run my hands over the smooth black plastic.

"Maybe it's dried out by now?"

Patrick shakes his head. "Nah, I've tried. It's wrecked."

"You sure about that? Stranger things have happened tonight." I bring my thumb to the power button, keep it there. "Ready?"

Patrick gives me a half-grin. "Go for it."

I click the button and the video camera whirs to life.

CALEB STEPHENS IS a dark fiction author writing from somewhere deep in the Colorado mountains. His short stories have appeared in multiple publications and podcasts, including Chilling Tales for Dark Nights, Tales to Terrify, MetaStellar, The Dread Machine, Nocturnal Transmissions, and more. His fiction collection If Only a Heart and Other Tales of Terror is forthcoming in fall of 2022 and includes the short story "The Wallpaper Man", which was recently adapted to film by Falconer Film & Media. You can join his newsletter and learn more at www.calebstephensauthor.com and follow him on Twitter @cstephensauthor.

"The Grunge" is illustrated by Jenny Kiefer.

NONA'S FIRST AND LAST ALBUM DROP

EDITH LOCKWOOD

My first regret? That I have but one life to lose fighting The Man.

My second regret? Wearing fishnet stockings in the woods.

"Son of a bitch." I snap the twig, but the damage is already done.

Stacy puts a hand on her hip and looks me up and down with the flashlight beam. Her black jeans and oversized flannel shirt are much more suited to espionage. "Actually, it makes them look better."

"Looks hella cool, actually." Heather plucks the straps of her practical overalls. "But I strive for functionality in my clothing."

I poke a finger into the hole and make it a little wider. Perfect. I don't think it's a stretch to say I could basically be Courtney Love.

All three of us pause for a moment, while the leaves rustle and cicadas chirp in the summer night, because we had to wait until after eight for the sun to set. It's too hot, really. It's suffocating, like the smell inside a gym bag.

Heather and Stacy look a little uncertain. They need a speech from their fearless leader, a.k.a. me. "Okay. Gather round, girls. Ladies. My sisters in our unholy and yet divine mission to right the wrongs done to us by The Man."

Stacy and Heather come closer until we're in a huddle like some jock football players. Even up close, I can barely see their faces. The only light comes buzzing from the parking lot at the edge of the woods. Beyond that, the brick radio station looms, with a spindly tower behind it. This close, I swear I can feel the radio waves in my teeth.

I clear my throat. "Here's the 411. The Man, in his infinite cruelty and greed and obsession with mass consumerism, has taken our voices. He has stolen our moment in the spotlight, by reneging on our—"

"What does renege mean?" asks Stacy.

"Betray! He has betrayed us by breaking a promise to play our song on the radio. He has declared war against us with unequivocal violence. And he expects us to surrender!"

"As if!" says Heather.

"Never!" says Stacy.

"Heather?"

Heather snaps to attention. "Yes ma'am."

"Your mission, should you choose to accept it, is to pick the lock."

Heather jangles her bag of lock picks. "Beeyotch, what do you think these are, beanie babies?"

"Stacy?"

"O captain, my captain?"

"You're the lookout. Meanwhile, I..." I slip a cassette out of my front pocket. It's labeled with masking tape: TOP SECRET DIAPHANOUS SHADOWS EP HIGHLY CLASSIFIED. "My job is to get this on the airwaves, one way or another."

We all put our hands in a circle.

"One—two—three!"

"Fuck Silver Station!"

I wasn't always a hardcore rocker. In fact, this might surprise you, but I was a total goody-two-shoes for basically my whole life. Like, I stole a pack of rainbow zebra gum from the convenience store when I was five, and my mom made me go back inside and pay the clerk with my allowance and read an apology I'd written in crayon. I was so scarred from the experience I stayed on the straight and narrow.

Until about six months ago.

That's when I learned life is like a box of chocolates. Not! Actually, it's shit. Nobody cares about you. They lie and say they love you, then stab you in the back as soon as you let your guard down. There's no room for a goody-two-shoes in a world like that. You gotta be hardcore. I threw out my Lisa Frank folders (can you believe I still had them as a freshman? Kill me!) and dyed my hair black (most of it, because it's super hard to get the back of my neck). I started listening to Rage Against the Machine and Nirvana and Radiohead–all majorly hardcore. When they scream, I scream. It's like tapping into this primal well of rage inside me.

Music says all the things I can't say.

That's the point, right? To go beyond words. Like yeah, I write lyrics and stuff, and at the risk of being arrogant, they're kind of all that and a bag of chips. But that's not the whole story. Music expresses the pain and anguish in our souls that can't be expressed in mere words.

Except now my pain has to be corporatized, sanitized, and monetized. Easily digested, compressed to three minutes. My pain is only good enough if it appeals to a mass consumer audience.

Do you get why I fucking hate Silver Station?

The lockpicks scratch at the door. "Um, Heather?" I say. "Not to be a buzzkill or anything, but we've, like, been standing out here for six minutes." We're huddled under the awning where I'm pretty sure the one CCTV camera can't see us.

"I've almost got it, I swear." Heather sticks her tongue out and avoids all eye contact.

Stacy sighs. "Maybe we should go home."

"Go home? And what, watch Blossom and listen to the Spice Girls?"

"You know I like that song." Stacy starts humming Wannabe.

I elbow her. "Oh my god you did not just. The Spice Girls are not hardcore."

Stacy rubs her arm. "They have some really good songs."

"About what? What do any of their songs say? What do they mean? What are they trying to communicate? How can you listen to that kind of meaningless drivel?"

"At least I don't watch Star Trek."

"I don't watch Star Trek anymore!"

"Booyah!" says Heather. The lock tumblers click into place and the back door of the radio station swings open. It's dark inside, except for the red glow of emergency exit lights on linoleum. Cool air conditioning beckons me inside, to take a deep breath.

"Weird." Heather leans inside and looks both ways. "Isn't Midnight Mike here doing the late show?"

"Should be." I take a step inside. "Dude, did anybody bring a flashlight?"

"Ask and you shall receive." Heather unzips her fanny pack, pulls out a heavy Maglite and slaps it into my palm.

"Cool beans."

"That's my dad's. He'll kill me if I lose it, so don't lose it. Not until I lose my virginity, anyway."

Stacy snorts. "Nona won't lose it. She's used to holding stuff that big in her hand." Heather giggles and her laughter bounces up and down the dark hallway.

"Shut up! No, I'm not!"

"Didn't you say you had a boyfriend? Mr. M?"

"Don't talk about him. Like, ever. Especially when we're on a divine mission."

"So, he's not your boyfriend anymore?"

"No! And he never was! And I'm never having a boyfriend again!"

"Again? So, he was your boyfriend," says Heather.

"He's not—"

"Take a chill pill," says Stacy. "It was just a question, not an interrogation." She hangs outside the door.

"Are you coming?"

"Umm…"

Something rustles in the woods behind us. Is it a bear? Just peachy, I'll end up eaten by a bear before even getting inside the building.

"Enter now or forever hold your beliefs," I hiss.

"Sorry." Stacy fumbles with the pager clipped to her belt loop. "Um, my mom just sent me a message."

"Oh, you are such a liar."

"4321, see? That means I'm about to be grounded. Gotta bounce!" She closes the door and Heather and I are alone in the darkness.

"Total Spice Girl move," whispers Heather.

"110 percent. You won't abandon me, right?"

"I'm always good to go. So, let's?"

We hurry down the hallway, and I'm not really sure, but maybe there's footsteps behind us? It's probably just Heather's Doc Martens stomping away. Although, this sounds less like the "clomp clomp" of a teacher coming to class down the hall, and more like, I don't know, a cockroach? Kind of skittering, with long pauses in between. It's probably just a rat, now that I think about it. At least it's not a bear.

"Which way is the studio?" Heather says. "How big can a radio station possibly be? Why are there so many offices?" We pass room after room. Turns out we don't actually need the Maglite, because we're navigating by the red emergency lights. And maybe advertising our presence with the flashlight isn't a real brain-genius move.

At least I don't hear anything behind us anymore. But why does that make my stomach sink, like when Mr. M said we couldn't see each other anymore?

Something inside me screams "Run! Go home, and blast Beastie Boys until Dad stomps up the stairs and threatens to throw your boombox out the second-floor window." The thought of Dad yelling how I've ruined my life because I dyed my hair actually fills me with warm fuzzies, and I want to dip more than ever.

There is totally nothing behind me. Watch. I'm going to prove it.

Flashlight time.

O.M.G.

He's a totally normal guy in a suit, baggy pants and long jacket, and a fat striped tie that comes down to his fly. There's enough gel in his hair that the corkscrew curl on his forehead could open a wine bottle. He's anywhere between...I don't know. I suck at guessing the ages of anyone out of high school. Maybe he's 30? 50? Is there a difference?

"Motherfucker!" shouts Heather.

"Can I help you?" he says, like we just walked into Ponderosa.

I try a more tactful approach than Heather. "Maybe. But you look like the walking embodiment of mass consumerism." I shrug, to create an air of indifference and nonchalance, and cover up my pounding heart. What am I scared of, his choice in neckwear?

He smiles, but it's more like his mouth just stretches to reveal his teeth. "Try me."

"Okay." I whip out my cassette tape, which has our best songs. "Midnight Mike promised to play our EP. I'm Nona, the lead singer of Diaphanous Shadows. The A side is You know what you did (to me) and the B side is Yes I mean you."

"I am Midnight Mike."

"What? But he has glasses, and a beard, and…" And didn't look like a total creepazoid. His eyes are doing this weird thing where the eyelids blink like camera shutters. Maybe he has astigmatism. Does astigmatism cause weird blinking?

"I'm wearing contacts and I shaved. Follow me."

"Um, okay."

"Psst." Heather nudges me. "Are you sure about this?"

"I mean, it sounds like he's gonna take care of it, right? He'll take us to the booth, we play the cassette, we become famous hardcore grunge rockstars, badda-bing, badda-boom."

"What if he's, like, Ted Bundy?" Heather doesn't even bother to lower her voice. "Do you trust him?"

"Fuck no, I don't trust any guys. But if he pulls any funny business…" I slap my palm with the Maglite for emphasis. "You know I got up to brown belt in karate."

"Is that like black belt?"

"It's close, it's really close. Come on!" We hurry to catch up with Midnight Mike as he turns a corner into more darkness. Ooh, spooky, another hallway that smells of ammonia cleaning products and a dying air conditioner. Why doesn't this guy turn on the lights? Probably embarrassed of the suit. His suit is about as snazzy as a movie theater carpet.

He stops suddenly and gestures to a door on the left. "The booth is in here."

"In there?" Heather looks at the blank door suspiciously.

"In there." He nods. Up close, I can see he's got some sort of earpiece, like the guys in Men in Black. It spirals from his ear and down his neck. What a weird-ass cell phone.

"Just wait outside for me," I tell Heather. "I'll be back soon."

"I…" Heather glances behind us, looking for the exit sign. "I gotta be honest, Nona. I'm wigging out a little here."

"Fine! Then leave!"

Her eyes widen. "I don't want to leave you…"

"But clearly you do. Peace out, girl scout." It's the most devastating insult I can muster, and it leaves Heather rocking on her heels.

I follow Midnight Mike into the room and he flicks on the light, revealing a broadcast booth. "The tape deck is over there." He points, but it's more like raising a hand with hidden ropes and pulleys. What is with this guy? He's probably on drugs, maybe smack. I think that's heroin. Don't tell anybody, but I'm straight edge.

I walk over to the player and pop the top. It's brand-spanking-new and shiny, covered in about a million buttons. "Whoa. Where did you get this?"

"Silver Station bought it when they acquired us."

"Huh. I guess mass consumerism is good for one thing. Money. Money is the one thing." I pop open the tape deck. "Just like this?"

He nods. "Just like that."

The tape player clamps down on my hand. "What the—" I try to pull my hand out but it's stuck. Blood dribbles down my wrist. After a second, the pain hits like a power chord. "What the hell! Your tape deck is fucked up! Get me out of this!"

Midnight Mike—or whatever the hell he is—stares at me blankly. He's waiting for something.

I blink back the tears. Tears are not hardcore. Oh god, Heather was right. He is like Ted Bundy. Or that other one, BTK. The wire from his ear, it's actually going into his neck, into a lump under the skin like my grandmother's chemotherapy port. What the fuck? Is he like the Borg?

This is how Captain Picard must have felt in Season 2 Episode 16 "Q Who."

Try to be like Captain Picard.

I raise my chin. "What are you going to do to me?"

Midnight Mike meets my eyes, but his are dead gray static. "I'm going to acquire you."

He might as well have said assimilate.

Is my life flashing before my eyes right now? Only two weeks ago I was...

Me and Heather and Stacy and a bunch of other peeps are sitting around the long picnic-style table during lunch period. No one sits on it the way they're supposed to. I like to straddle the bench like First Officer Riker on the USS Enterprise.

I fiddle with the radio on the table. Mr. Messing is definitely watching, leaning against the painted cinder-block walls of our lunch-room prison with a smirk on his face. Ugh, he's so cute in his purple sweater vest.

I clap my hands once. "Please! Ladies and gentlemen, calm yourselves. Quiet down. There's nothing to fear. You need only bask in the wondrous glory that is Diaphanous Shadows." I sneak a quick glance at Mr. Messing. His eyes meet mine, but his face is blank. What's he thinking?

"What is this, fireside chats?" says Matthew. We just learned about FDR in US History II.

"Literally no one gets that joke, but we still know you're a nerd for telling it."

"Says the girl who had to run home after daylight savings to check up her VCR timer for Next Generation because she was paranoid she would miss it."

"Dude! That's so not true."

Stacy glances at the clock and starts to stand up. "The bell is going to ring in one minute. I forgot my algebra book in my locker."

I yank on her wallet chain to get her to sit back down. "Any second now. They're going to play our song on the radio."

"Your song?" says Peter.

"Weren't you listening? It's our band Diaphanous—"

"Do you know how hard it is for a local band to make it onto the radio?" says Mr. Messing. He must have snuck up behind me. "Especially with Silver Station buying up all the local radio stations, after The Telecommunications Act deregulated ownerships."

A pall falls over the lunch table. Why does he have to be such a buzzkill?

Mr. Messing shakes his head. "Just watch. In ten years, there won't be any privately owned radio stations. They'll all be owned by one corporation, and they'll all play the same music."

"No!" I put a hand over my goosebumps. "That will never happen. Music is about freedom of expression. How can you corporatize that?"

Mr. Messing smirks. "They will."

God, he's such a know-it-all. I hate how smart he is. I give Mr. Messing my best ten-thousand watt smile, outlined with black lipstick. "Well guess what? Midnight Mike listened to the EP at the radio station and he loved it. Said he would play it today at 12:39, right after Heart-Shaped Box—"

The song plays out and it's over. The space between the music breathes. It's so wide I could fall into it like a canyon. The moment stretches endlessly, waiting for the opening power chord of "You Know What You Did (To Me)." Today, we're on the radio. Tomorrow? A year from now? I don't think Warped Tour is too much to hope for.

But the opening power chord never comes. Instead, a smooth male voice says, "Thank you for listening to WYKM 35.4. Now a word from our new owners, Silver Station. We'll be back after these few messages."

The bell rings and people groan, then start to scatter, fearing the dreaded late bell.

"What happened?" Stacy shakes her head sadly.

"Those bastards." Heather punches her palm.

"That sucks, dude," says Peter. "You know, tonight they're replaying the season finale of Star Trek at 7 on UPN. That'll cheer you up. All good things…"

"Come to an end." Yeah, I know. Life is pain. Why was I so stupid to expect anything different?

Mr. Messing jerks his head towards the doors. "Out. You're going to be late."

Heather, Stacy, and Peter slink out. I reach for the radio, but Mr. Messing grabs my hand first and stops me. "It's too bad," he says. "But I did tell you. It's hard to make it onto the radio."

"Yeah?" I look up at him.

"Especially at your skill level. Oh, don't look so upset. It's true. You've only been playing for what, six months?"

"My guitar teacher says I'm really good. I'm a natural."

"Well, of course he does, you're paying him."

Has my guitar teacher been lying to me? Do I really suck?

Mr. Messing tilts his head. It makes my stomach drop. God, what is wrong with me?

"You look better as a blonde," he says.

"I don't give a shit—"

"Watch it. I'm still your teacher. Ah, don't be a crybaby now."

Tears roll down my face. It's so not hardcore. All I want to do is go home and hide under my blankets and scream into my pillow. It wouldn't be the first time.

The bell rings. He hands me a hall pass to get out of being late. That's nice of him. "Get to class, Nancy."

"Nona. My name is Nona now."

He pretends not to hear. Instead, the radio man says, "Thanks for sticking with us at Silver Station."

Thanks for sticking with us at Silver Station.

Thanks for sticking with us at Silver Station.

By the time I'm out of the lunchroom, crumpling the late pass in my hand and wiping mascara from my cheeks, I've decided.

I'm gonna stick it to Silver Station, all right.

I THOUGHT I was going to stick it to Silver Station. Mr. Messing was right. I am a big crybaby. I'm not hardcore at all. I don't really have black hair and my real name is Nancy and the No Fear "tattoo" on my arm was drawn with a gel pen during 8th period geometry. And I'm saying things like "please let me go" and "I wanna go home," which are totally not hardcore at all.

"Of course," says Midnight Mike. "As soon as we're done."

"But what are you doing? It hurts!"

"Not anymore."

He's right. It doesn't hurt but it's still scary as shit. Why am I going numb everywhere? My teeth are buzzing.

"What are you? What's going on?"

"You're being acquired."

"What does that fucking mean!" My spit lands on his cheek and he doesn't flinch.

He raises a hand towards my ear, and in it is a telephone cord with a jack on the end. Except it wriggles and jack knifes like it's alive and I've got this terrible feeling he's going to slip it inside my ear, like in those books with the kids who change into animals I got at the bookfair every year.

I'll never get to go to another book fair.

"Don't look so upset," he says, just like Mr. Messing.

Don't look so upset.

Don't look so upset.

"I hate you!" I forgot the Maglite was even in my hand until it bounces off Midnight Mike's skull. That gives me a second to rip my hand out of the tape deck and grab the wire by his ear and pull. The wire wriggles in my hand for a second before I chuck it across the room and it slithers into a gap between the trim and laminate floor. Midnight Mike drops and his head cracks on the floor, blood pooling. No, it's not blood, but tiny little telephone cords, all squiggling and writhing away from his skull. Away from his skull towards me, up my pant leg.

I have to get out of here. I open the door. Run down the hall. I can't fucking see where I'm going, it's dark. Where's the flashlight? Oh god, I can feel them climbing up my leg, the worms, the telephone cord worms. They're on my neck. No, that's my hair. Isn't it? There—a door! Lock it! Lock it!

I'm in another recording booth. A steaming cup of coffee sits on the desk, but no one's in sight. The door knob rattles behind me and I jump out of my skin. A telephone cord worm is trying to squeeze under the gap.

"Open the door, Nancy," says Midnight Mike, calmly like he's asking me to keep listening.

"What the fuck! I thought you were dead!"

"Of course not. Please excuse the interruption in our regularly scheduled programming."

"What the fuck are you!"

"Acquired. You'll understand, once you've been acquired, too."

"Fuck off you wormy Borg bastard!" Another telephone cord worm creeps under the gap and I stomp it until it stops moving. How long can I keep this up? The door is particle board.

Maybe he has the same thought. The doorknob stops shaking and I hear footsteps walking away. Probably going to get something heavy to bash the door in.

Shit, shit, shit. There's no way out. No windows. What fuckass fire marshal okayed this building?

I'm going to die here. I'm fifteen years old and I'm going to die in a radio booth that smells like burnt coffee with a hint of body odor and Old Spice. I never even got my driver's license. Or got to go to prom. Or make it on the radio. I'm going to die.

No, even worse. I'll be acquired.

No tears this time. Just certainty. Certainty that I'm going to die, and my life never amounted to anything.

I sit down at the desk. He'll be back any second.

The LIVE sign shines above me, like clouds parting and heaven's light falling on me. It's a sign all right, from God.

I should tell them to call 9-1-1. There's a crazy Ted Bundy made of worms trying to break down the door and turn me into a Borg.

Oh yeah, that will go over well. They'll come and send me to the funny farm. And we're twenty minutes from civilization. I'll be "acquired" by then.

But that's not the real reason I don't scream for help on the airwaves. When am I ever going to get this chance again?

I'll play my EP. Talk about a swan song. I laugh. Damn, that's a good joke. I wish someone was here to hear it.

I lean forward and tap the mic. "Hello? Yeah. This is, uh, Nona. I'm filling in for Midnight Mike. Intern program. Um." I clear my throat. "This is, uh, a hot new EP from a local band. Di—diaphanous..."

I pull the cassette out of my pocket, along with a handful of ribbon. The casing must have cracked when I was fighting with Mike, and now its guts are uselessly pooled in my hand.

Perfect. What a perfect end to my meaningless, disappointment of a life.

The door handle rattles again. Mike—no, he's not Mike anymore. The radio man is back to silence me. To only broadcast approved messages, mass-produced crowd-pleasing hits. My time is up. Speak now, or forever hold your peace.

I grab the microphone. "Okay, change of plans. This is talk radio, now. Late night confessions and shout-outs. Guess what? My name isn't Nona. It's Nancy. And my hair isn't black, either. And honestly? I hate fishnet stockings. They rip on everything. They are such a waste of money. And I'm always worried I'm going to poke my eye out on this spikey collar I'm wearing."

Music is about expressing yourself, without words. But these words come so easily, when there's nothing left to fear. I glance at the smeared "no fear" pen tattoo on my arm and smile. What do I care what people think, when I'm about to be acquired? The freedom is intoxicating. Music says what we can't say, but at the end of my life, there's nothing I can't say.

"I don't really like Radiohead. They only have that one good song. And my first CD wasn't Cake, it was Backstreet Boys. And I think I'm pretty awesome at playing the guitar. Oh, and guess what? I love Star Trek. Yup. Live long and prosper, beeotches."

The doorframe splinters.

"I love you, Mom. I love you, Dad. Keep kicking cancer's ass, Grandma. And…" I take a deep breath and release the last secret, the thing I said so many times in my songs, over and over, not knowing if anyone was really listening.

"Mr. Messing took my virginity and then dumped me when I told Heather because he said I couldn't keep a secret. Well guess what, local listeners? He's 32 and lives with his parents. That's right. He made me swear not to tell anybody. Guess what, Mr. Messing, I'm telling everyone."

The doorframe breaks. I pick up the coffee cup and hurl it and miss. It shatters against the wall, next to a very annoyed-looking police officer.

She crosses her arms. "Are you done?"

"Are you with them?" No sign of a cord down her neck, or in her ear.

"With Middle Township Police Department? Yeah, I'm with them. You're supposed to be under arrest."

"Supposed to be?"

"We got a call about somebody breaking into the radio station." She dangles a fanny pack of lockpicks. "Are these yours?"

"Actually, no. Um, this is a weird question, but…" But did you notice the corpse of Midnight Mike covered in telephone cord worms? Why do I ask? Oh, no reason. "Have you seen Midnight Mike?"

"Who?"

"I think he was in the other studio. Down that hall?"

"There's no one else here."

I let out a long, deep breath. Okay, I'm just losing my mind. I can live with that.

She sighs too and uncrosses her arms. "How about you come down to the station and make a report about Mr. Messing."

"I don't want him to get in trouble."

"It's a little late for that."

"He'll get fired. He'll be so mad. He'll hate me forever. Is he going to go to jail?"

"He deserves to."

"But it's my fault. I kissed him first." This is your fault, you know, he said. I knew you were a bit of a slut.

She shakes her head. "You'll understand when you're older."

I hate it when parental units say shit like that. "Whatever. Are you gonna arrest me or not?"

"I tried to, but you were too fast, and escaped out the back door. I never even saw your face." She jerks her head towards the hallway. "Go on. Get out of here, you little hooligan."

Running home through the woods at top speed, I tear my fishnet stockings to shreds.

MR. MESSING ENDED UP RESIGNING. I think it was "quit or else you're fired." I feel bad, but when I went to his house to apologize, his mom told me he didn't want to see me. Everyone tells me it's not my fault. Most everyone. Some people call me a slut. Heather calls those people dickwads.

My right hand is pretty fucked up from the tape player. Mom's taking me to a specialist next week, but I doubt I'll ever be a great guitar player now. It's a tragedy, honestly. Like if Slash got his hand stuck in a blender.

Mom's taking me to a therapist, too, who's always asking me how I feel. Okay, I guess? It's over, isn't it? She keeps telling me, "You might not feel okay someday and that's okay." Mom keeps telling me she's sorry. Why is everyone acting like I'm a ticking time bomb?

There are more important things to deal with, like the slow death of artistic expression via radiowave. Midnight Mike never showed up for work again, but the rumor is he's a junkie who probably OD'd somewhere and they haven't found his body yet. I definitely wasn't dumb enough to tell the therapist about the telephone cord worms and almost being "acquired," but she did say it's not uncommon for people to hallucinate under extreme stress.

Sure. Okay.

Those Silver Station bastards keep buying up more stations, but it's like nobody even cares. Did you know it's not that hard to be a ham radio operator? And stick an antenna in your backyard? And set up your own pirate radio station, where you play all the music made by people who aren't famous, who aren't part of the corporation, who are just trying to say something?

This is Nona's Pirate Ship Radio signing off. Don't be a poser, and thanks for listening.

EDITH LOCKWOOD enjoys transforming her anxiety and intrusive thoughts into bittersweet stories, several of which have been published in The Dread Machine. When not writing, she can be found playing with knitting needles and/or dangerous chemicals, and occasionally writing cryptic micropoetry on Twitter @Edith-Lockwood13.

"Nona's First and Last Album Drop" is illustrated by P.L. McMillan.

THE ONE WITH THE MYSTERIOUS PACKAGE

C.B. JONES

Bryce finds the package as soon as he gets home from school. Cardboard-brown and a little smaller than a shoebox, it lies in wait on the middle of his bed. Addressed to him in a black Sharpie scrawl with familiar handwriting, his first thought is the package must be from Sabrina. Some sort of surprise. The thought is only fleeting, however. Looking closer at the shaky script, he realizes it doesn't have her trademark loops and curls. Still familiar though. Where has he seen it before?

Slicing open the packing tape and folding back the cardboard flaps, he's greeted with a few index cards resting atop some bubble wrap.

In that same familiar handwriting, the first card reads:

Shhhh!

Don't Tell Anyone.

The second card says:

Believe me.

The third:

Place your index finger on the circle and wait.

:)

By the time he's finished with the third card, he's hit with a sudden realization. The little notes, the address on the box, the handwriting: it's his own.

DOWNSTAIRS, he asks his mom, "Where did that package come from?"

"The mailbox," she says, giving him a look. "What was it?"

"Oh, just more college recruitment stuff. Some place I've never heard of," he says, thinking of the index card's instructions.

"Still have your heart set on MIT?" she asks, her smile eager and stretching.

"Yeah, just gotta wait to hear about some of these other scholarships. Already got the three. But I could probably get a full ride in-state."

Mom cocks her head, gives him that look that says, "are you outta your damn head?" But she doesn't say anything because she knows it's a touchy subject. They've been here before.

And Bryce is already darting back upstairs, before it can start up again, before he can get pissed off, before he can be reminded of it all, how maybe she's kinda right.

WHAT'S in the box isn't college recruitment brochures, what's in the box below the index cards and the bubble wrap and tangle of charging cords is a . . . Bryce doesn't know what. It's some sort of contraption, a rectangular electronic device of sorts that reminds him of a Game Boy. It's a little longer and wider than a deck of cards, but thinner. On one side of the object, his reflection fills a screen of black glass. On the back, is textured plastic and a couple of openings. An oval and a circle. In the oval is something that looks like a camera lens. In the circle is shiny black plastic.

Place your index finger on the circle and wait.

Bryce does so. The faintest of impulses jolts the pad of his fingertip and the black glass sparks to life in a brilliant glow. There's a background of pink and purple swirls looking like a Lisa Frank sunset. At the top of the screen is today's date and a listing of the current temperature. Below that are rows of symbols that remind him of the family computer downstairs in the living room, the Compaq with Windows 95.

Icons. That's what the little symbols are called. And if it wasn't obvious enough by their artistic rendering, each little icon is accompanied by text. There's a calculator, a camera, a phone, a map. Something that says messages.

Intuitively, Bryce presses the phone icon with his finger and it responds like the touchscreen of an ATM, bringing up a dial pad. He enters his home phone number, presses the green phone button. Raising the rectangle to his head as if it were a conch shell, he hears ringing. Elsewhere in the house, the phones begin to ring.

He hangs up before anyone can answer.

The bizarre contraption is entertaining for a little while, but only just so. It reminds him of a more advanced Sega Game Gear, or something. Even with all the device's bells and whistles, Bryce eventually runs out of things to do.

The calculator is rudimentary. Not something super advanced that he could ever use on his homework; he'll have to continue to use his TI-82 for that. A program called "Browser" reminds him of the internet on his friend Steve's computer. Steve has real internet, none of that AOL crap, has shown Bryce some pretty wild stuff on that thing late at night. But Bryce doesn't know what to type in to go to any sort of website, so he just lets it lie.

The coolest feature so far has to be the camera. It takes pictures that save digital copies onto the device itself. No waiting for development and a helluva lot better quality than a Polaroid. There's a button that switches the lens so that it's pointed directly at Bryce's mug. He makes a goofy face and snaps a pic.

And after that, Bryce is done. No longer creeped out by the handwriting–more curious than anything–Bryce tucks the contraption under his pillow and pushes the box it came in beneath his bed.

But before he can move on to other things, the device vibrates and chirps at him. He places his fingertip on the circle. It blinks to life, greets him with a message.

It's a simple question, really. One that Bryce will be asked multiple times. It appears in an off-gray box accompanied by an unfamiliar number.

The message reads: **Having fun?**

Bryce can see a little keyboard appear below the message. The whole interface reminds him of a chat room.

Bryce types back: **Who are you?**

Somebody who knows you better.

Better than what?

Better than you know yourself.

Bryce's fingertip shakes over the screen. Knees weak and a shock of sweat flooding his armpits, he sits on the bed, grips his knees. After steadying himself, he looks out his window, scans the yard and street in front of his house, looking for someone that could be watching.

There's nobody there, just his brother's Blazer parked by the curb.

The One with the Mysterious Package

The phone buzzes again.

You think you know better, but you don't.

Buzz.

She ain't the one.

Buzz.

You'll see ;-)

That final message, Bryce thinks he knows what's going on, thinks he knows who sent the package.

While his mom and dad have been the type to express reservations about the seriousness of he and Sabrina's relationship at their age, they're generally the "let it ride" type. They want what's best for Bryce, or at least what they think is best. Mom and Dad will push to a certain point and then leave it at that, maybe a comment here or a look there. Because maybe they learned their lesson the first time around. Maybe they're just happy that Bryce is doing as well as he is. They know it could be worse.

They would never stoop to these manipulative games. Not like they're exactly tech savvy, either. The only time Dad interacts with a computer is when he stares off slack-jawed at the flying toaster screensaver during dinner. How would they get a hold of some sort of phone/computer prototype anyways?

No, there's only one person who's given Bryce much shit about being with Sabrina since the very beginning. There's only one person who's worked a spell at the Nakamura computer distribution center before being fired for pissing dirty. This person likes to say he didn't know it was possible for a dude to be pussy-whipped before he had even gotten any. This person constantly tells Bryce that he was thinking with the wrong head and that he should live it up his senior year, that being tied down was the last thing he could possibly want. And what about the future for God's sake?

His older brother, Brandon. That's who it is. Has to be. Bryce must follow up on this hunch. Before heading downstairs, he tucks the index cards into his front pocket.

Out the front door and looping back toward the basement's exterior entrance, Bryce can hear the muffled machine-gun riffs of Metallica blasting through the door. He knocks as a courtesy before barging on in. Not like his brother's gonna be able to hear him.

Within the basement den there's the trademark smell of reefer, a funk of sweat, and vanilla incense. Bryce lets his eyes adjust, sees his brother's hair peeking out over the thrift store recliner, a halo of smoke enveloping his head, an ember glowing near his fingertips.

Brandon stares at a TV frozen on the PAUSE screen of his Sega Saturn, polygonal Virtua Fighters frozen mid-punch. The boombox has transitioned from propulsive hard rock to some acoustic power ballad, the Metallica guy singing how nothing else matters.

Bryce reaches out and taps his brother's shoulder. Brandon jumps with a start, arms flailing, spliff tumbling. He stands, facing Bryce eye-to eye. It's almost like looking at a mirror—in fact, once their growth spurts aligned they had been mistaken for twins—that's not it though. No. It's more like looking in a funhouse mirror that shows you what you'll look like after a series of poor decisions. Dropping out of college and living in your parents' basement, working third shift at the tire factory, how your eyes look tired and your smile turns bitter.

"Jesus! You ever hear of knocking, dickwad?"

"I did."

"Well, knock louder next time. I'm tryin' to rock, here. What do ya need?" he says, leaning to pick up the dropped joint.

"You trying to fuck with me? I got your box."

"Box?"

"Good job on the handwriting, too."

"What you talkin' bout, Willis?"

Bryce slides a card over. Brandon studies it like a smirking Sherlock.

"Put your finger on the circle and wait—what is this? You're writing yourself notes on pleasing your girl? Is that what you do? Just shove your finger in there and wait? Bro, if this is how you're finger-banging..." he trails off, laughing.

Pleasing your girl. The words stick in Bryce's head. A vague memory comes over him, a sense of deja vu. He's been here before, asking his brother for pointers on doing things the right way with regards to pleasing Sabrina. Bryce had wanted to do right by her as inexperienced as they both had been. But he can't place the memory.

"So, I'm guessing the promise ring you gave her is paying off? You're getting to third base, at least."

"Man, shut up."

"I'm just saying. What's that ring mean, anyway? That you're promising to get married as virgins?"

"We're just saving ourselves for each other. And it's like a deeper commitment."

"I thought that's what engagement rings were for? Look, are you seriously thinking about ditching MIT for this chick? Cuz no offense, I don't think she's getting in."

"I'd be an idiot to not take a full-ride in-state."

"Dude. I *know* you're getting scholarships. And Mom and Dad have all the leftover money from my fuck-up they said they would contribute. Not like I'm gonna need it. It was conditional, y'know? You have *got* to take them up on this."

"Look, I dunno what I'm gonna do. And don't you say shit about Sabrina," Bryce says. He's not going through with this again, how any time this comes up it's Sabrina who's at fault when it's always been his decision.

Brandon just shrugs and takes a toke of the joint. "It's your life, bro. We all know you're destined for great things. I blew my chance. Just don't wanna see you blow yours." As Bryce leaves, Brandon shouts, "Come back anytime you need some pointers."

WITH HIS BROTHER a dead end (in more ways than one), Bryce is adrift. He can't stop thinking of that message.

She ain't the one.

How can that be? They've never had any real fights. He's never felt this way about anyone before. What could go wrong?

There have been times when he waits for her in the courtyard at school and she comes out of her 7th period class, laughing and talking to that annoying Kyle Gardner. Sometimes, Bryce sees them and feels the briefest pangs of jealousy, but these feelings fade when Sabrina notices him from across the courtyard, rushes over to him like he's just stepped off a plane from a long trip.

Still. Things can go bad.

There's nothing left for Bryce to do now except take a drive and try and clear his head. He jumps into his little blue Ford Ranger, taking the contraption with him. The windows are down, and he listens to the radio, cruising the neighborhoods, feeling the warm spring air.

The songs both torment and pacify him. He hears meaning in every lyric, like the DJ designed the playlist just for him. Soon he finds himself up the street from Sabrina's house, spies her red Pontiac Grand Prix in the driveway. He pulls over to the curb, cradles the device in his lap—and not sure if this is going to even work—dials her number. The connection is better than any Motorola bag phone he's ever used.

"Hey," she says.

Her voice is as clear as a bell and upon hearing it, a fizzy warmth shoots down the small of his back. "Hey, just seeing what you're up to."

"Just vegging out to this Real World marathon. Supposed to be writing an essay, but I gotta see what these crazy kids are up to. How about you?"

"Nothing much. Just chilling." Bryce feels relaxed now. It's reassuring to know that at any point during this conversation he could walk right up to her front door and find her lounging on the couch in her den.

"You wanna meet up later? Mom says we're skipping church this evening, but you could come over here. As long as we're just in the den and all."

Bryce pauses a moment before saying yes. He hates himself for coming over here, for not trusting. Tries to rationalize it by telling himself he has to test out the phone function on the device.

Later, he'll find himself here again and again, parked up the street with her voice in his ear. From this vantage point he'll watch and wait. He knows it's not fair but he can't stop himself: waiting for her bedroom light to flicker out, waiting to see if she ever leaves.

THE MESSAGES RETURN.

Having fun yet?

Bryce types back, **What do you want?**

What's best.

But I'm happy, Bryce responds.

For now. . . Look at this.

It takes Bryce a while to figure out what comes next. There's an image of sorts that's been sent to him through the messaging program. When he blows it up to full size, he sees something that looks like another type of computer program, a digital document or something, images and borders and text. There's a circular photo of a woman in the middle, flanked by a banner of the Chicago skyline. Squares that read, "Friends" and "Message."

Below the picture is a name, as if it wasn't clear from the get-go. Even with the slightly softer and more mature face, there was never any doubt as to who that was. The hair, the smile, the eyes. The name reads Sabrina Albright, which just so happens to be Bryce's last name. Below that it reads "Lives in Chicago, Illinois" and "Single."

Bryce paces the room, gripping the device, his heart racing. He finds himself muttering, "No, no, no."

With tremoring hands he manages to type, **WHAT THE FUCK IS THIS? WHO ARE YOU?**

You mean you don't know? You're a smart boy...

Bryce is greeted with more images. They're all of the older Sabrina. Still beautiful. In one, she walks towards a golden sunset. Her back is to the camera, and she's holding hands with two young children, a boy and a girl. Another, she sits at an outdoor cafe, a drink in her hand and a smile on her face. In a final pic, she's in mid-embrace with another man, staring into his eyes.

FUCK YOU, Bryce types. **You're lying. This isn't real. Who put you up to this?**

You'll see.

UNHERALDED TECHNOLOGY and pictures from the future. Bryce can only conclude that time travel is involved somehow, as wild as that sounds. This is clearly some type of warning from his future, an opportunity to change everything, prevent him from heartache and pain.

I'm not gonna let *it happen.*

He thinks now that he knows what the future holds, he can change it. Is that what the anonymous sender's goal is? To be on the lookout for cracks in the relationship and fix them before they fissure beyond repair? Or are they wanting him to throw in the towel because this particular movie only ends one way?

He's reminded of that one movie, the one Sabrina had wanted to rent because it had pretty-boy Brad Pitt in it. The one about time travel. She had ended up hating it. Thought the story was weird and confusing. Didn't like how Brad was a crazy person in it (even if he did show his butt).

Bryce, however, sci-fi and math nerd that he is, loved it. The one thing he took away from it was this: your destiny was inevitable. Even in the face of time travel, no matter what you did to change the future, you only ended up cementing your fate in ways you couldn't foresee.

Bryce picks up the device, looks at the photos from the future. She still looks gorgeous. Somehow, even more so. Sitting in the dark

The One with the Mysterious Package

of his room, the glow of the phone illuminating his face, he's already pining for the woman she will become.

Lunch breaks at school were open campus affairs that allowed for a brief respite from class. Oftentimes, Bryce and Sabrina wouldn't even bother to get food because it cut into their time to idle their car at the city park where they would cuddle in each other's arms, the taste of her spearmint kiss and the smell of her Tommy Girl perfume providing all the sustenance he would ever need.

Today it only makes him sad. He's distant, thinking about how this will only end in tears and heartbreak, miles down the road. Whether he seeks his dream and goes off to MIT without Sabrina or stays in-state and goes to college with her, the result is the same.

They park under their usual tree out beyond the old baseball stadium and near the county fairgrounds. Kids make laps around the looped drive that snakes through the park like they always do. Bryce makes note of a black Lincoln town car creeping past.

Sabrina senses him tense. "What's wrong?"

"Nothing" he says.

"Ok," she sighs. After a stretch of silence she says, "I think you should go to MIT."

He looks over at her, eyes narrowed.

"One of the best math and physics and engineering programs in the country? In-state has nothing on it. It's a once in a lifetime shot. We can do the long-distance thing, totally make it work. They've got this internet stuff with email and everything. We could write each other every day and not even have to wait."

If you only knew, Bryce thinks.

"And like it's only a few months between breaks. We can take turns visiting each other's campuses."

"It's gonna be too much. I'd rather be with you. I can get the same degree more or less. Some things are more important." *Like love,* he thinks, but he doesn't say it out loud. It seems like too much of a line from a movie or TV show, like something a naive kid would say.

"Babe, it's your dream."

"You know you want me to stay with you. You're just saying all this so you're off the hook for changing my mind. If I choose to go you're still gonna be heartbroken. Either that or you don't really care where I go and you're content to just let us drift apart."

"Babe, that's—"

"I don't really wanna talk about it anymore."

Bryce jerks the car into R, almost strikes the black Lincoln. It crawls forward and idles, doesn't honk or anything, tinted windows shining back at them.

In Bryce's pocket, the device vibrates. In front of them, the car peels out, speeds away.

Once they get back to school, he discreetly glances at the message. The same number as before.

Looking good, it says.

IT ONLY MAKES sense that the time traveler is here now, communicating with him in the present. The messenger could be anyone. Bryce is especially skeptical of men in uniforms. Easy disguises. He looks for black cars, winces any time he sees them glinting in the sun. On the way home from school one day he spots a drifter hanging out in an alley a few blocks from his house. The drifter wears a trench coat, a hood pulled low over his head. Bryce makes a loop around the block, white knuckling the steering wheel, but when he pulls back around the guy is gone.

Later, a different number sends him a message. It's just a line of blue text, accompanied by the instruction to **CHECK THIS OUT!**

Bryce's finger touches the blue text and the phone computer takes him to a video screen.

Bryce has seen porn before. In his brother's basement room,

mostly. Where half the guys had mustaches and the women had big hair and his brother pointed out what Bryce would later learn was the clitoris and told him that was what the women peed from and to avoid touching it.

What Bryce sees now, though, he's astounded. His heart jackhammers in his chest, skin tingling with a lusty anticipation.

Over the next week he finds himself coming home early and locking himself up in his room, zoning out to an endless supply of salacious videos, hours gone like anesthesia, until he stumbles from his bedroom sore and chafed and waiting until after dinner when he can go back and do it again. He has half-hearted phone conversations with Sabrina while staring at the phone, saying "yeah" and "huh" and "I dunno" while he watches pounding flesh and writhing bodies.

He gets his first C in a long time on his Calc midterm. There's just not enough hours in the day to study when he's got this kind of stuff to watch, when he's the only one in the world he knows of that has the access.

This is how it happens. She already senses something.

When he meets up with Sabrina at their usual spot in the courtyard, sees her walking a little too close to Kyle Gardner, laughing a little harder than usual, he knows he's gotta get his shit together.

Any time he feels the urge to retreat to his bedroom and zone out to the screen, he forces himself to take a cold shower. He runs a lap around the block. He calls Sabrina. The urges grow weaker by the day, and despite a barrage of texts, links he no longer clicks, he kicks the habit.

SLOWLY, he realizes. Slowly, he knows. This messenger from the future with the porn, the distractions, the warnings, they're throwing up every obstacle they can, trying to sway Bryce from continuing this very serious relationship with Sabrina.

Maybe the future turns out bad, sure. But now Bryce *knows* the future. He can change it.

He resolves to turn the tables. After all, he's got a magical device from the future. He's got the advantage.

When Sabrina's Grand Prix is on the fritz, just clicking whenever she turns the key, Bryce is there. He knows she doesn't have the money after buying a prom dress, and her folks are in no hurry to spot her. There's been no recent babysitting gigs, either. And while he's never been a car person before, he goes down the rabbit hole of videos and information provided to him by the device.

Soon, he's in her front driveway with his dad's sockets and pliers, switching out the alternator. Her vehicle starts and runs like it always did. She gives him one of the best hugs he's ever gotten. He swells with something like pride and warmth, swears he can feel this deep love radiating off of her.

It's not just car repair that he finds on the device. There's instructions of a different sort. He thinks of his brother saying, *Come back anytime you need some lessons.* Dumbass.

And so, with a pile of sleeping bags in the back of his little Ford Ranger, they park behind the abandoned farmhouse way out in the sticks. They've gone here plenty of times to make out and fool around. It's one of their favorite places, out here underneath the night sky.

Tonight, "Crash" by Dave Matthews Band is playing on repeat from the truck's speakers, and things heat up until Bryce puts his newfound cunnilingus skills to good use.

"I love you," she says, out of breath and holding him tight. "I love you, I love you, I love you."

Like hell anybody's taking this from me, Bryce thinks.

YOU ABSOLUTE DUMBASS, the message reads. **What are you thinking?**

I'm changing it, Bryce types. **She's the one.**

You're doing the same shit you've always done. It doesn't end like you think. That stuff you're feeling? It's not real.

Shut up.

It will fade with time. You end up alone and sad, with the best years of your life behind you, trying to pick up the pieces. Full of regret.

We're meant to be together.

I didn't want to have to do this. You give me no choice.

"I THINK I'M READY," Sabrina says in Bryce's ear.

They're at their usual spot, surrounded by burgeoning farmland and lying underneath an overcast sky, clothes still on for the moment.

"Are . . . are you sure? What about the promise ring?"

"I'm . . . I just don't want to wait any longer. Why wait, y'know? What does it change? Do you not want to?"

"Oh, I do. Believe me." He kisses her, smiles. "I'm ready if you are."

From out in the field there's an explosion of headlights, tearing through the dirt toward them, rutting up young crops. Bryce shields his eyes, squints. He can't see the vehicle through the blinding lights, but he knows without a doubt it's a black Lincoln town car.

And stepping out is a figure about his height, about his build. A fun house future mirror version of himself.

"Brandon?" he asks.

"No, but not the first time I've been mistaken for him," the figure says, stepping to the side of the headlights, revealing himself. He's holding a shotgun in one hand, a suitcase in the other.

"Is that..." Sabrina trails off.

"I don't..."

"Time to break this up," the man says, setting the suitcase down and drawing a bead with the shotgun.

Sabrina screams and Bryce yells, "Wait!"

"Don't worry. It's not a fatal round. I obviously can't kill my past self. Paradox, y'know?"

The engine idles in the silent dark, Bryce trying to figure out the implications of all of this, Sabrina whimpering by his side.

"Why go through all of this, though? The phone, the messages?"

The older Bryce shrugs. "It's how I remember it. Ya gotta admit, I almost had you."

"We're not leaving each other." Bryce pulls her closer to him.

"You have to. It's how it goes. In this thread, anyway. You'd be surprised how easy it is you're able to forget. You two stay together, you'll end up hating each other. Is that what you want?"

Bryce looks at Sabrina. "It's not gonna happen. I won't *let* it."

"Look, it's clear I'm not gonna convince you. I tried to give you a choice." Older Bryce leans down and lifts the lid of the suitcase, revealing a complex array of technical components. He presses some buttons on a keypad and an emerald light spews from the center of the suitcase's open maw. An oscillating hum emanates and the light widens into a black void.

"What the—" Bryce says, sees his older self take aim again.

He shoves Sabrina back and leaps forward, hearing the blast before its force pounds him in the chest, knocking him back to the ground. His diaphragm momentarily paralyzed, he struggles to breathe. Chest burning, the night sky rolls on above, indifferent. His older self peers down at him with a canister in his fist. Jets of spray pound into his face. Bryce's eyes burn and flood with tears and he chokes and gags. Rolls onto his hands and knees.

Sounds of a struggle. Sabrina screaming, her feet kicking up the dirt. Bryce can only look through a veil of tears and snot, too far away on his hands and knees to stop anything. Her scream fades into the night, her body disappearing into the void.

"What the fuck did you do?" he cries up at his older self.

"Don't worry. It hurts a while, but you'll forget in time. Like completely forget. It's some sort of side effect. A failsafe measure to keep the path going. Like I just had a flashback right now." The older Bryce gives a theatrical shudder. "But rest assured she's perfectly fine.

It's a big mystery for a while, and you're a suspect for a while, but you have your story, and a lot of it will check out. The rock salt injury, the vehicle tracks, the shotgun shell. All evidence that points to a kidnapping. And when she turns up twenty years from now, completely unaged, it's quite the conundrum, but it's all we've got."

Bryce grips the dirt underneath his fingers, screams.

A cyclone of memories fills his head, handfuls of them thrown at the wall. Possible lives lived. Possible lives gone. Possible lives not forgotten. How Sabrina's scream slowly faded like a cartoon character that falls off a cliff. How it haunts his dreams and waking hours until he slowly forgets and can't figure out why.

There's another life where he attends college with her and they have an apartment together and get married their junior year and how later, after graduation and the first child, they slowly drift apart. And even after the second child there's a brief respite, a mirage that things might get better, until he finds the texts on her phone.

The next series of memories are flashbulbs, subliminal frames in a film reel that he can barely make out. Seeing her from the windshield of his car as she leaves the stranger's house, her taillights fading down the unfamiliar street. There's the noose hanging from the rafters in the garage, the swirling red and blue lights.

The kids were safe and sound in their beds. They were safe and sound.

Right?

But that was then. Or much later. Or before or who even cares anymore?

Because this is now, the only now that Bryce has ever known.

Bryce rises to his feet, fistfuls of dirt in his hands. He throws it into his older self's face. It must not have been a memory from before, because it takes him off guard. Older Bryce fires the shotgun blindly, the rock salt spray going over Bryce's head. Bryce runs headlong toward the void.

In a frantic scream, Older Bryce yells after him, "The threads! You'll fuck it all up! Paradox! A complete unraveling! It can't happen this way!"

Bryce stands at the precipice, hesitates. There's no way he can be stopped now. He looks back at the bitter man he's become.

"Is that *girl* worth the material unraveling of the known universe? The death of time and space?"

But Bryce doesn't care. The love of his young life is down that wormhole. The sky above starts to crack open. He steps in and lets the void take him.

C.B. Jones is a horror author living somewhere in the middle of America. His debut novel The Rules of the Road was released in 2021. He really hopes you'll take a gamble on it and check it out.

"The One With the Mysterious Package" is illustrated by P.L. McMillan.

CAUTION: CHOKING HAZARD

MATHEW WEND

"Where's the playlist?" demanded Sarah. She had asked this at the last three Christmas season preparation meetings, met with rebuffs each time. With an hour of play, it always got old and every year the worst tracks were hotly contested.

"She's on there again."

"God damn it! All I want for Christmas is spew," she said, mimicking vomiting in the wastebasket. That got some giggles from the new employees, but the lifers overpowered them with a groan. Every holiday was a heated staff debate between those who thought the playlist was the worst thing ever and those who thought the customers were the worst.

"Hopefully this is the last season. Mariah can't stick around forever." Sarah's manager was a lifer, and one of the few good ones. Steve could make and take jokes, where others were too chicken to show emotion. He smiled. He was nice. He stood out like a sore thumb from the other long-term staff that needed a chill pill.

"Any other questions? Remember, Tickle Me Elmo is a laugh a minute and the Cabbage Patch Doll can eat any food you put in its mouth. Both sell themselves and supplies are low. Push NERF, LEGO, Mighty Max, and for the girls, Polly Pocket. Sell as much of the other toys on the floor as possible. We have Mighty Max and Polly Pocket to run through, as well as the last LEGO Ice Planet. Let's burn through that backstock please." The room was a smattering of side-talk but no voiced questions, so he dismissed them to start the evening shift.

Over the scraping of chairs, Sarah approached Katelyn, a seasonal hire. "Hey Kitty Kat, you excited to sell some bomb toys?"

"As if," she laughed. "Cannot wait to see the floor chaos."

Katelyn was fresh out of high school and had landed her first job at Bon Marche for the holiday season. Sarah saw how green the kid was and wanted to prepare her for the throngs of shoppers who would soon be the needed sales for the holiday.

"You are going to hate Mariah by Christmas," Sarah said.

"As if, again. That song is so fun and happy! Maybe you just need someone to want you for Christmas." She gave a laugh and walked through the doors to the sale floor.

Maybe she's going to be okay at this, Sarah thought.

Caution: Choking Hazard

"Excuse me, miss," said a customer, tapping on Katelyn's shoulder roughly.

She jumped, eyes wide. "I'm so sorry," she said looking up and immediately noticing a furrowed, angry brow. "I must have gotten lost in my work, how can I help you?" She attempted to assuage the anger she saw percolating from the middle-aged mother in front of her. She had zoned out to the repetition of the Christmas music. Wham's "Last Christmas," currently.

"I'm sure," she said in a tone that announced she would be speaking to the manager later. "I'm looking for the Spice Girls clothing section. I was told it was here."

"Oh gosh, I am so sorry about that! This is Toys. You must have taken a left at Appliances instead of a right. If you'd like, I can help guide you—"

"No, it was your coworker's directions. I'll find it myself. But while we're here, I want one tickled Elmo and the garden path doll that eats food. And make it quick, I'm very busy."

"I'm truly sorry, ma'am, but we're out of the Cabbage Patch and Tic—"

"No, I see them right there," she barked, pointing at the large glass display in the center of the section. Children milled about it, pawing at the glass with their greasy hands, ignoring the signs saying do not touch.

"Unfortunately, those are only display models. We do have a new shipment coming in—"

"Then I'll take them at fifty percent off, thank you. No need for packaging. Thank you and go make yourself useful."

"I'm sorry ma'am, but I'm not allowed to do that."

"Then please go get your manager so I can talk to an adult around here who is able to make grown-up decisions. You kids have no respect for your elders—" she paused, making a pointed effort to stare at the name badge, "kate-uh-lyn," she hammered on each syllable.

Katelyn gave a sigh and walked away from the conflict. She rounded the corner to look for a manager, and Sarah slid in stride next to her.

"This lady has me buggin' but you're handling her so well," Sarah whispered as they walked. "I saw it all, so let me tell Steve. Two witnesses are better than one."

Steve would be in Appliances. No one could outperform him there, and he loved breaking sales records. One year he sold a family a second fridge for their living room just for the Super Bowl. If either woman cared about retail careers, they may have considered him a hero.

He was talking to a mother who had far more patience than her husband who stood off to the side, two kids running around his ankles. He shouted at them from time to time when they got too far away. He dripped exhaustion.

"That guy is the actual sale right there. Steve is so good at this," Sarah leaned in, the two of them standing a few meters away. "He keeps Mom interested until Dad loses patience. Once Dad breaks, he'll spend anything to get home and watch the end of the second half. He's a pro."

Steve shot a look that told them to bugger off for two more minutes before interrupting. But his plea for time was cut off by a knifing scream from across the store.

Sarah quickly pushed Katelyn in the direction of the scream "You go, I'll tell him what's happening and see you right there." The new hire took off at a sprint, her Converse slapping against the tile as Sarah ran to explain to her boss and send him after security.

KATELYN ROUNDED the corner to Toys and found her horrible customer trapped in the central glass display case. "How in the fuck,"

she wondered loudly, but ran up to the edge and shouted at the woman to check on how she was doing. Not well, she surmised.

In one hand, she clutched a Tickle Me Elmo doll, which giggled and spasmed through her torment. In the other was a hungry Cabbage Patch Doll. It ate, machinating slowly inch by inch closer to her scalp. Its mouth was full of her hair, tiny plastic teeth chomping permed curls deeper and deeper down its dolly throat. Rivulets of blood dribbled down from the woman's scalp as she did her best to rip the toy away from her.

"I don't know how to open it," Katelyn shouted toward Sarah as she came running through the aisles.

Sarah scrambled to the register that held the keys for the display, digging through rubber bands and paperclips in search of the small keyring. She glanced at the struggling customer. "That tickles," she could hear the doll mock, wriggling all the while against her still-greedy clutches.

Katelyn climbed the edge of the display, carefully timing her leap into the chaotic abyss. She was fully aware of the group of people outside the terrarium. Splashes of blood smeared the glass like a Magic Eye design and all she wished for was to be on a boat at sea.

"Please get this demon off me," screamed the indignant customer as Katelyn reached for the Cabbage Patch doll.

Katelyn grabbed the back of the doll, pushing aside the gearing that dragged the hair deep into the mouth. Mercifully the chewing slowed, and she pulled the hair from the doll's belly. The woman sat in her enclosure crying while the customers outside began to cheer at the success.

"That's mine," the woman said through sobs, reaching dumbly for the doll even as Katelyn pulled hair from its mouth.

Sarah ran up with keys, eyes beaming praise at her understudy. She opened the panel of the enclosure to let both inhabitants out, customer and service employee. Security showed up to escort the unruly customer away at Steve's guidance, and the staff started breaking the crowd up.

With the crowd walking away from the display case, Sarah and

Katelyn paused in each other's gaze, stunned silence settling over them. They breathed and exchanged an unsaid shock of the evening. A calm was settling.

Above the thrum of Mariah Carey and the fading crowd, a mechanical noise came from the display case, echoing a tinny cry unprompted. Elmo, spasming in the corner of the display, laughing and giggling out an electronic, "Oh boy, that tickles." Then the toy went silent.

THE REST OF THE NIGHT, Toys attempted to control the disorder. Much of the area was taped off, and the two dolls were stowed under a register. Katelyn was tasked with fixing the bookcase and display to the best of her abilities. Rubber gloves, bleach, and a disintegrating rag scrubbed away at the glass until it neared spotless. Sarah stayed close by, helping customers and fielding far too many questions from inquisitive busybodies. Their only saving grace was the end to the Christmas playlist, which made way for announcements and security business.

It was the third bucket of bleach that did Sarah in. Chunks of hair, skin still coagulating at the roots, hung with purpose off the plastic rim. She walked through the back hallways that connected various departments to empty it into a mopping station. She fell into a folding chair, letting the exhaustion of the unbelievable fight fade from her ever so slightly. Never in her life did she expect slinging building blocks to ten-year-olds would lead to a night like this.

With one gloved hand, she pulled the hair from the bucket—trying her best to ignore the wad of flesh at its apex—looked away from the globule of the woman's head fat and chucked it into the trash of the janitor's station nearby.

"So I hear you had a fucked up night."

Sarah looked up to see Katelyn, the two breaking into laughter until Katelyn started crying. The two hugged.

"It's not much, but Steve was really proud of how you handled yourself," Sarah said, patting her coworker on the back. "This is, honestly, one of the wildest stories you'll be able to tell in your life. Be proud, kiddo."

"As if," Katelyn laughed through her tears.

"It's true. Why don't we finish up? I'll help, then we can grab a drink. Zimas in the parking lot on me?"

"Booyah."

Closing came, with all-calls over the intercom asking customers to make their final purchases. Toys was a ghost town, rows of playthings without anyone to bring them home. Countless eyes stared empty from their plastic and cardboard cages. The two returned through aisles of LEGO and Barbie and MightyMax to the scene of their pain: the display case.

Dark crimson hues stopped both of them in their tracks.

"Holy shit," Sarah gasped. "I don't remember this much blood from her. This is wild."

Katelyn started hyperventilating. The display case was splattered with blood on almost every inch of glass. Worse, it was on the floor and trailing through the department now.

"This isn't right," Katelyn searched for breath and found none. "I cleaned out that case. None of this should be here."

"I know you did," Sarah said.

"No, I cleaned this. I was done. This is new. This is—this is fresh. This is blood that—"

"It has to be someone playing a game," said Sarah with a nervous laugh.

It was matched by an electronic giggle across the toy section, by the Hot Wheels. "Oh boy," came Elmo's voice.

"Did you move the dolls over there?" Katelyn asked.

"Why would I?" Sarah replied, nervously glancing at her underling and then snapping back to the direction of the doll.

"This isn't funny, asshole," she directed down the aisle with belied bravado. "We had a horrible day. Stop making it worse. I'm writing you up for this."

Silence met them.

"This has to be the worst prank ever," Sarah said, starting toward the joyful toy.

"What are you doing?" Katelyn was scared, every syllable forced out. "Why are you going that way?"

"They're just toys, Kate."

They walked down aisles slowly tracking the blood down halls of metal stanchions displaying the latest sales. Peering around each corner, they developed a silent communication that as much helped them forward as it shared their belief of the ridiculousness they felt they faced.

A giggle came again just one row up. It said GI JOE - MODELS - NERF on its end cap. Sarah peeked around the corner and turned toward Katelyn, vomit pouring from her throat. Katelyn jumped away as quickly as she could.

SARAH LOOKED BACK down the aisle. There laid what was left of the rabid customer from earlier. Her hair was gone, skull gazing directly at Sarah like a cloudy, unblinking eye. Blood smeared across the floor from a deep gash down the length of her flayed chest. Trails of her insides splattered across the floor around the far end of the aisle.

"We need to call security," Katelyn begged, knowing the closest phone was back at the start of their investigation.

"Do you want me to go all-call someone?" Sarah asked, head between her legs.

"Absolutely do not leave me right now," Katelyn said, tremors running through her muscles. "Should we go together?"

"This is so uncool," Sarah said, grabbing a large NERF gun with a rotating barrel and chain feed of twenty darts off the shelf, stepping like a princess over the giblets of her former customer. She swallowed spittle as much as fear, then checked the action on her toy weapon.

"What are you doing?"

"Got a better idea?" Sarah asked with a shrug.

Katelyn followed her stalwart leader across the muck, trying not to look down as she gained footing. She grabbed a bow and arrow with ten-inch darts and an extra ammo pack for good measure. Under the harsh glare of the retail lights, the two doubled back to the central kiosk.

THEY WERE NOT the first to the checkout counter. Blood and viscera covered the desk and the phone lay shattered on the floor. The trail of blood led down the hall toward Appliances.

"We need to find Steve," Sarah said, her hand wavering in a point toward the blood trail.

"You seriously want to go toward this bullshit?"

"Not even a little bit. But how can we leave him?"

"How do we stop these things?" asked Katelyn, staring incredulously. "With plastic weapons? Against haunted toys?"

Sarah stared at her new coworker for a second. "You think the toys did this?"

"You don't?"

"Obviously not. It must have been some rabid customer that ripped her apart. The holidays are wild. I told you that... right?"

"We both heard Elmo's giggles," Katelyn said with a fierce resolve. "Just before we found the body. If you have a better explanation, I'm all ears."

Sarah started walking toward Appliances. "I've done too many holidays for this. I'm getting Steve."

Katelyn sighed and followed.

THE BLOOD SPLATTERS faded around the escalators, which whirred steadily in the otherwise silent mall. "Maybe we should just call for him?" whispered Katelyn.

"Steve!" shouted Sarah, her words echoing across the clothes-lined department. She turned to her coworker. "How is it so quiet here? We didn't close that long ago, right? Where's security? Who's in this department?"

"It's so weird," said Katelyn, poking at a clothing rack to see what lay in its center. "We weren't in the back hallway that long, right?"

"Is someone up there?" came a voice from the floor below.

The voice was unknown to them, so they took no chances. Katelyn pointed to the center of the racks she had just investigated, and the two quietly slipped into the ring of clothes. They hid between pants with legs as big as the waists if measurements were to be believed. In silence, they sat watching the escalator roll forever upward.

"I'm coming up there," shouted a male voice, moving upward to the floor slowly.

First Sarah saw black hair and then a face she did not recognize. A hand followed by the rising stairs, holding a pistol at the ready. Her breath caught. She peeked through pants to the next rack over, scarcely making out Katelyn. Her coworker was equally frozen in fear at the sight of a gunman now in front of them.

"Hello?" he shouted as he reached the top of the escalator, scanning the floor with his gun at the ready. "Show yourself please."

The women furtively stared at each other. Katelyn nodded toward the armed man, eyes pleading to Sarah to show themselves.

Sarah shook her head sternly—no.

"If you can hear me, I'm police. I'm not on the job right now, but I am armed. You can see my badge here." He pulled out a wallet and waved it wantonly. "I'm just trying to get innocent people out right now. Please show yourself." His barrel scanned the floor.

The two glanced from him to one another, fear and doubt exchanging freely between their looks. Katelyn again nodded toward the cop, more assertive this time. She reached to separate the JNCO hiding her but a scritching sound from above stopped her in her tracks.

The strange sound came from the ceiling tiles above the escalators, moving slowly toward the cop. It was staccato, something dragging a few inches at a time, and continued for what felt like minutes until stopping directly above the maw of the escalators. At a creepingly slow speed, the ceiling tile started to slide.

"I'm armed and have a gun trained on you," he shouted, pistol pointed at the gap. He took a few steps back. "Come down and we can talk things through."

The tile stopped moving, leaving a sliver of darkness visible. Two small toys fell from the hole, flopping to the ground like the plastic they were. Small flakes of plastic skittered across the floor as their fragile machinations shattered from the fall. The cop jumped and then trained his gun back toward the ceiling tiles.

"This is my last warning. Come down or I'll be forced to escalate," he shouted.

The aggressiveness froze the two women.

Katelyn noticed movement by the officer's feet first. The Cabbage Patch Doll shifted ever so slightly. She would have believed it was an illusion had she not seen all the bloodshed earlier. It stuttered and spasmed in slow motion toward the officer inch by inch, and the absurdity brought forth a nervous laugh-scream mixture that she forced back into her throat. This was a toy, not a threat. It was impossible even as she watched it move forward again.

Inch by inch, it crept forward, reaching for the cop's foot. The officer backed up, as he focused above, unaware that he stepped toward the toy.

The Cabbage Patch Doll stretched its jaws, opening an abyss of darkness that swallowed his foot and then his ankle. Blood and sinew splattered across the faux marble floor as it reticulated inch by inch up his leg. The officer looked down and screamed as the toy worked through the fatness of his calf, rendering flesh to food in a most unhappy meal. He tottered and fell, and the doll chewed up to his kneecap.

The officer screamed and fired at the toy, bullets passing meaninglessly through plastic.

Sarah mustered everything in herself and charged to help. "Waste of shelf space," she shouted, "Come eat these!" She ran from her denim cover and fired her NERF gun blindly. The first dart missed the Cabbage Patch Doll but got its attention.

It disengaged its machine-formed jaws and spun to face her. The second dart hit the unmoving Tickle Me Elmo in errant fire, creating a deep cut in its midsection. The doll laid, somehow, in two from the sponge bullet.

Sarah looked back and shouted for Katelyn to run, when a force slammed into the back of her knees, knocking her down. "Does that tickle?" came a modulated laugh.

The small red demonic toy was only feet away, slumped over and giggling incessantly. She scooted away but the freakish Christmas gift's beady eyes drew close. She stared down its giggling, and then she felt the bite of the Cabbage Patch toy from behind.

The vegetative doll's bite chomped toward her skull. Its jaws closed in on her scalp and the skin started to pull taut and then rip slowly apart from her head. She felt the flesh slowly tear and separate from her skull, flushing her with intense pain. She pleaded for the biting to stop but it remained unsated.

Sarah stared at her coworker's jean shelter, pleading for help. In a denim explosion, her friend came forth and ran at the Cabbage Patch Doll, swinging her leg with karate kid strength.

Katelyn's foot connected and was enveloped, as though she was kicking a bag of Gak. Inward it sank, unreposed and undaunted. The toy's body suckled around her ankle, mouth awkwardly agape and releasing Sarah's hair.

Katelyn forcefully pulled her foot from the plaything and ran toward Toys. The Cabbage Patch Doll shirked away, if toys could, freeing further from Sarah's skeletal buffet.

The Cabbage Patch Doll showed its full life and turned toward Katelyn's retreat, thin strands of Sarah's hair dangling from the corners of its mouth. Its stubby plastic arms pushed itself upward and standing, took wobbly toddler steps, arms outstretched and jaws masticating unrelentingly.

Sarah laid on the ground clutching at her head, tears welling as she watched this demon doll teeter away from her.

"I hear you're hungry," Katelyn shouted, running back toward the Cabbage Patch Doll with full hands.

"Mama, feed me!" shrieked the doll, mouth opening wider than its gearing would ever allow, its tongue snaking, ready to strike.

Katelyn ran circles around its outstretched arms and tongue, throwing handfuls of capsules into the hole, filling its cavernous mouth. When her hands emptied, she turned and ran again.

Sarah stared in confusion, pushing herself up to her knees. She struggled to crawl toward the officer, who was only across the hallway. A clack clack clack sound from behind caught her attention and she spun around toward where the dolls were, only to find them staring at the source of the sound, as well.

Katelyn emerged from the center aisle of Toys, wearing a backpack water soaker connected to a brightly colored gun in her hands. It was their highest marked product in the store, full of pressure chambers and water reservoirs. She pumped the slide again, clacking more air into the canisters, then placed her hand on the handle on top of the barrel.

"Stay hydrated, Cabbage Bitch," she yelled deep from her chest.

She pulled the handle and unloaded a high-pressure stream of water directly into the Cabbage Patch's waiting mouth. It drank and guzzled and drank some more from her steady stream.

The doll gaped its impossible jaws to drink further, but the seams of its design started to spread in front of Sarah's eyes. The doll expanded to its threadbare limits. The toy distended, its clothing splitting piece by piece as its body bloated to the final limit of its plastic shell.

With a sickening pop, the Cabbage Patch Doll split along its seam lines and through the gaps of plastic stitching began spilling out small sponge dinosaurs like innards of roadkill.

"Looks like wetter is better." Katelyn smirked.

Sarah gaped at her understudy, struggling against shock to stand again. Her congratulations were cut short as she toppled and grabbed at the clothes rack next to her. It fell on top of her, pinning her to the ground. The weight of the over-wide pant legs trapped her in place. Mariah came over the speaker system again and Sarah started crying. No wage was worth this ending.

She was not yet free.

Elmo's red hand appeared over a sequined shirt, dragging its bisected top half one pull forward, then another, hand over felt hand. "Your turn to tickle," Elmo croaked in a fractured electronic threat and broke into giggles again.

Katelyn stood, struggling to take in her surroundings. She forced herself to draw her attention to the red menace bearing down on her leader, the toy giggling and moving ever so forcefully for Sarah.

The clap of the officer's gun pulled Katelyn out of her daze as she watched him fire again and again at Elmo, bullets undaunting the toy's march toward Sarah, fist by fuzzy fist, giggling with each bullet strike.

"That tickles," it mocked.

Katelyn unholstered the toy bow from her shoulder. "You're doing it all wrong," she shouted at the officer. She pulled back the string on her bow. "It's NERF, or nothing."

The arrow flew through the air in a chaotic spiral, striking dead true to Elmo's head, but didn't bounce as expected. Into the plastic and felt it entered, causing Elmo's head to distend and then explode in a shower of sinewy fluff and plastic shards. The toy fell limply to the ground. A demonic "oh no," escaped from its electronic voice box and then nothing.

The three sat there in silence, breathing deeply and looking around.

From Appliances came muffled shouts. Steve came running at full sprint. He helped lift the officer and carry him toward the plugged-in appliances.

Blood dripped heavily from his masticated leg.

Opening a chest freezer, they attempted to lift the officer in to chill him and slow the bleeding that spread across the floor. It was all for naught as his life drained from him.

"Steve, this night has been hell," Sarah said.

"I am so sorry for that," he replied, pausing to get the attention of both Sarah and Katelyn. "But let me tell you how proud I am."

Sarah's emotions ran wild with the pain of what she dealt with and her supervisor congratulating her all at once, but she turned to him for a moment. "You're proud of me? Of us?"

"Absolutely," Steve said, and he smirked, pausing for a moment to consider his next words. "And let me tell you: next seasonal staff, all I want for Christmas is Y—"

"As if!" drowned out the end of his sentence.

Mathew Wend loves working with books as a librarian, but writing has always been his dream. You can find his work in rejection piles of your favorite publishers. He has an amazing dog on Instagram at @arrowdoggo and an amazing wife at @baileyjeanadventures. If you want to follow him for whatever reason, he's on twitter @matwend and on Insta as @matograms. He's boring, he swears.

"Caution: Choking Hazard" is illustrated by Jenny Kiefer.

RETURN TO GRAY SPRINGS: BLOCKBUSTER BLUES

P.L. MCMILLAN

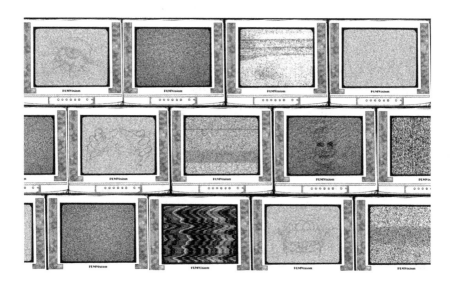

*"The world drowns in small chat,
Nobody really cares
Only in the beats between silences
Can our hearts truly share"*

Soundwave, "Beats Between Silences"

Blockbuster on Bramble Street: Gray Springs, CA
August 3, 1998
7 p.m.

"Beats Between Silences" by Soundwave comes through the speakers. I sigh and slump against the offensively yellow counter, by my elbow is a stack of twenty VHS movie returns that need to be put back in their homes on the wire racks that dominate the interior of Gray Springs's one and only Blockbuster.

The windows drown in sheets of rain. Thunder booms overhead. Lightning casts brief flickers through the glass. It makes me feel trapped. Trapped in the store, trapped in this town, trapped in my life. The abrupt ringing of the store phone is a welcome interruption to my miserable thoughts.

"Blockbuster, Colin speaking," I intone. "How may I help you?"

"Colin, have you noticed anything tonight?" It's my best friend, Patrick O'Halloran.

"The Blockbuster isn't haunted, Patrick," I reply, flipping through the movies, cataloging them in my head.

The Silence of the Lambs: thriller.

FernGully: kids.

Tremors: thriller.

Child's Play 2: horror.

"Lori said she heard strange noises under the floor when she closed two days ago," Patrick says.

"Lori smokes enough weed to cause world peace, Patrick," I reply. "And can't keep her alphabet straight. I'm sure she hears all sorts of things."

"Dude—" he starts.

"Can we not do this tonight?" I cut him off.

There is a pause on the line. In the static, I hear what sounds like the echoes of the rain on the line, hollow as though coming from a long way away.

"Is it your mom?" he asks softly.

Patrick's known me since we were tiny. We've been through thick and thin. Even a black ritual or two, back in high school. He is the brother I always needed.

"Yeah, she's back." I ignore the lump in my throat. "Back from rehab and already...well you know."

"Yeah, I know." Patrick pauses. "Do you want me to come by?"

"Nah." I shake my head, then feel dumb when I remember he can't see me. "We're closing in an hour anyway."

The door opens and its bell chimes throughout the store.

"Gotta go, Patrick," I say and hang up.

A young woman walks towards the counter. She looks familiar—but who doesn't in a small town like Gray Springs.

"Hey! I rented this yesterday and the tape is broken."

I recognize her and my heart races, my face burns. Amani Jones. More beautiful than when I last saw her, when she left Gray Springs after high school. Left me. It's been three years.

She looks at me, looks past the shitty Blockbuster polo shirt, looks past the long hair I have now.

"Colin?" she says, still holding out a copy of *Poetic Justice*.

A moment of complete awkwardness hangs between us. We kept in contact for a few months, mainly awkward phone calls. I couldn't stand how happy she seemed in L.A., so I stopped calling. Eventually, so did she.

She is dressed in simple jeans, a white t-shirt, a leather jacket studded with silver diamonds. Her dark hair is styled in tightly braided rows back over her head, with gold beads. She looks cool. She looks Anti-Gray Springs. And here I am, in a cheap navy polo and khakis.

"It's so good to see you," she says. She must be lying.

"I didn't know you were in town," I say and regret how weak I sound, how pathetic.

She looks down at the movie she's holding, as if it will save her.

"I had some time," she says. "I thought I'd come back and visit my parents."

Of course, I think. Why would she ever visit me?

"Uh huh." I move on, what else can I do? "And what's the

problem?"

I take the VHS from her. I imagine her watching it with her parents, with popcorn, soda. I imagine her laughing. A normal home. Standard.

"We tried playing it," she says. "It showed these weird, messed up images. A cat drowning, a child screaming, a woman crying."

I look down at the movie. Standard paper cover, generic VHS with label.

"Watch it!" Amani looks at me with that smile of hers that has always driven me crazy. "You'll see."

"Alright, I can refund you and—" The chime goes off again.

I look over and there's Patrick. I have no idea if I hate him or love him for interrupting. His hair is bright blue, he's dressed in black jeans studded with safety pins and spikes and an army green shirt with the words: NOBODY ASKED.

"Colin, I –" he's saying, and here comes the awkwardness I knew would happen.

Patrick stares at Amani. Amani stares back.

"It's been a while, Patrick," Amani says.

Patrick looks at me, back to her. He's holding the new Sony Nightshot camcorder he bought. So different from what he used on Homecoming night. And yet things do change. She left. After all the things that were said between us. She left.

"Yeah," Patrick says and comes straight behind the counter, next to me.

I feel both embarrassed and justified.

"Uh," Amani says. "I'm happy with a refund but trust me, you don't want to rent it out again. The movie is completely messed up."

I look down at the VHS. These things go weird all the time. Magnets, mold, use. Anything can warp those old tapes.

"What's wrong with it?" Patrick asks, and he brings his camera up.

"It's seriously freaky, you should watch it," Amani says. "I honestly wasn't sure if I was going to mention the weird stuff when I returned it. But seeing you…"

I know what she's talking about, of course. I told her everything after Homecoming. I told her about Scott Stark, my uncle, my Mom. I trusted her. Then she left. Left to chase her future, her career with a full scholarship to UC Berkeley and college basketball. Her future, which didn't have room for me.

"Fine," I say, because in the end, I still don't know how to tell her no.

8 p.m.

I switch the outside lights off, I lock the front door. Patrick and Amani wait for me in the back. My heart skips a beat. I wonder who she's dating now, what kind of cool life she has. And here I am, working at a Blockbuster. How pathetic.

"So you're saying something happened to the tape?" Patrick says as I approach.

"Yeah, it's beyond bizarre," she replies. "Seriously. *Twilight Zone* levels of weird."

I take them through the employees only door, where the store has a large storage room with old promotional material, damaged goods, a computer for management, and a TV and VCR for checking tapes.

I want her to leave but I also don't. I want her to be with me. I want to know what she's been doing. I want to know her.

A rich boyfriend, maybe another college student, or a movie director. That's who I picture her with, while I'm here, stuck in Gray Springs.

I take them past the shelves collecting dust, to the desk with the small TV and the VCR. I am overly conscious of Amani's body heat as she stands behind me, too close for comfort. Too close to remain ... distant.

Patrick brings his camcorder up and it hums in the silence of the back room. I can hear Amani breathing.

The tape whirs. Static erupts on the TV's screen.

"Let's just see what we see," I say.

That's when everything gets out of control.

On the TV, the static morphs to a black screen. Then a white dot. A woman's face weeping. A figure behind her, enormous, incomprehensible. A sound like buzzing bees. A smell of burning plastic. A child. Blood. The sound of breathing speeding up. Stopping. My heart races. I want to puke. I can't. I'm not me. There is something else in the backroom. A sense of presence. The smell of other. Taste on tongue. Death. Picture changes. A man screaming, A building burning. Uncle Will. I see him. Screaming. Trying to run. Trying to stop them. It escalates. It's too much. Vision spots. Bitterness on my tongue. Nostrils burn with dry air.

Fingers reach out. Fumble. Seek.

Then I find the button. I turn it off. But is it too late?

The present is a weight that sinks in, brightening my view. I find myself, I find my center. I'm in between Patrick and Amani. The video has stopped.

"Holy shit," Patrick says and lets the camcorder drop.

"See?" Amani adds.

This isn't the first complaint I've gotten about romance movies. I'd never bothered to watch the returned tapes. It's never worth my time, especially at minimum wage. I just issued refunds. But now something itches at the back of my mind.

"This is crazy," Patrick breathes.

"My mom wasn't impressed, that's for sure," Amani adds. "I figured some sicko messed with the tape."

"Let me just check the computer." I lead the way back to the store, to the counter, and start navigating the clunky DOS system.

"Mrs. Barnett rented it before you." I tap through the screens. "I doubt a kindergarten teacher is up to something like what we saw."

Amani laughs, and my cheeks heat up. I jump through a couple more menus. The warmth from my cheeks disappears as a chill settles over me.

"Oh," I say.

"What is it, Colin?" Amani leans over the counter to try and peek at the screen, she's close enough that I can smell her lavender body spray.

"All of the refunds in the past month have been romance movies." I page down and down. "Actually the past six months. Since we opened."

"Wait!" Patrick pulls his camera up and points it at me. "Say that again, I wasn't recording."

I roll my eyes and head to the back corner where the romance movies are. A light flickers over the displayed cardboard VHS sleeves.

"Let's grab a couple and check," I say and pull a few movies off the white wire racks.

Amani grabs a couple. Patrick keeps on filming. And narrating.

"We've taken more movies off the shelves," he says, "We are bringing them to the back to test them. Who knows what we might find."

"Can you quit it, Patrick?" I say, fully knowing he is going to ignore me.

In the back office, I put in the first tape and hit play.

Static, a black screen, wails of pain, a woman weeping, a massive growing smile.

"It's the same as my tape," Amani says. I feel her breath on the back of my neck, and I shiver.

"Try the next one," Patrick says, holding it out.

But we all know the result before we see it. All the tapes are the same.

Static, black screen, sounds of dying, a woman crying, a giant's mouth, chains, whispers, the smile grows and grows.

9 p.m.

"Can you smell it?" Amani says. "It smells like... mildew."

We stand in front of the romance section, under the flickering light.

"I can smell it," I say.

It reeks of salt, damp, cold. The air around the romance section is thick with the stench of it all. Overhead the light flickers an indecipherable morse code.

"It's been raining all week, it's probably seeped through the roof," Amani says.

"What about the crazy shit on the tapes then?" Patrick pans over to her face, then to mine. I shrug.

I don't want it to be anything weird, but Gray Springs is no stranger to the unnatural. Drowned in fog and mist and drenched in endless rain, Gray Springs has been home to bizarre sightings in the woods, to shadowy creatures in the reservoir, disappearances, a cult, and of course, an undead Homecoming incident.

I lean close to the display shelves and press a hand against the bright yellow wall, not knowing what to expect. All I feel is a cold wall. But that close, I spot something near the corner.

Hinges.

"Mr. Fellstone is gonna fire you when he sees this," Patrick mutters, stepping back to get the whole door in shot.

All the romance movies are in scattered piles on the thin blue carpet, the wire shelves thrown off to the side, a couple of screwdrivers next to them.

The wall is a mess, the paint's damaged and drywall lays in chunks on the floor, but we managed to open the door so cleverly disguised in Blockbuster yellow and blue, revealing a set of concrete stairs descending into the darkness. The walls closest to the door are scorched with old smoke damage and I can smell a hint of burnt wood.

"Did you know there was a basement?" Amani asks, leaning in and peering down.

"No, I mean it was completely covered up," I reply.

The air coming from the lower level is thick. The smell lingers on the back of my throat, coats my tongue and nostrils.

"This is so messed up," Patrick says. "I love it."

Amani just stares, hands clenched in front of her chest like she's praying. "What do you think is down there?"

I step up to the threshold and reach out, flipping a switch. A light flickers on, at the base of the stairs, revealing nothing but a concrete floor and unpainted walls. And in the distance, the far, far distance, I hear something cry out. A coyote maybe. Something mournful, hungry, alone.

"This must be where the Children of the Gray met," I say.

"I think you're right!" Patrick replies. "Who knows what horrors still remain in their old haunting ground."

"Children of the Gray?" Amani asks.

Amani wasn't a Gray Springs local, she'd moved here sometime in sixth grade so she wasn't steeped in Gray Springs lore like Patrick and me. The three of us stand at the mouth of the doorway that leads who knows where.

"The Children of the Gray was a religious group here in the eighties," I start.

"Ha. You mean a cult, Colin." Patrick pans to me, then Amani. "They never figured out how many were in the cult. Most of them were high society—the richest of Gray Springs: doctors, business owners, probably even the mayor at the time. Who knows. But they held power. All men of course, regular boys club."

"No one knows anything for sure —" I start.

But once Patrick got going, he couldn't be stopped.

"People went missing and everyone said that the cult was sacrificing them." Patrick points his camera back on the doorway. "Then they all died in a fire. Most of the building was destroyed, my mom says it was during one of their rituals. At least she said they all died. But if no one knew who was really all in the cult, probably some of them survived."

"This is ridiculous," I say, turning my back on them both, on the open door.

"When was that?" Amani asks.

"1988," Patrick says. "Ten years ago."

"And this all happened in a Blockbuster?" she laughs.

Patrick looks at me and rolls his eyes. "No, Amani. This used to be the Family VHS Center until ten years ago. It burned down, remember?"

"And how am I supposed to know that?" Amani replies. "Not everyone is as obsessed with this stupid little town as you, Patrick."

"We get it, you hate it here." He zooms in on her face. "No wonder you left so fast for your fancy life in L.A."

"Patrick, come on." I push the camera down and offer Amani a weak smile. "The building was rebuilt and this Blockbuster was put here only like six months ago. It's all new."

"And since the opening, people have seen signs of a haunting," Patrick moans in a theatrical voice. Overhead, the light blink, blink, blinks. "Maybe the dead cultists have come back!"

"To what? Rent *Sphere*?" I say and Amani laughs, making my heart skip.

Thunder rumbles over the building and I can't help myself, I shiver.

"Let's go down then," Patrick says, panning to me, then to Amani. "As long as you're not scared, Colin dear."

"Dude, I just finished work," I sigh. "I want to go home."

"After what you did to the wall, you're gonna get fired," he says. "And then they'll cover this up again, and I'll lose my chance."

"After what *I* did—"

"Okay, let's chill." Amani laughs, hands raised.

She plants her left hand on her hip and raises the other one like she's holding a microphone. "I'm Amani Jones with the Gray Springs Investigatory Team. Join us as we dive deep into the secrets of the Children of the Gray."

"Hell ya," Patrick says. "That's the Amani I love! But do we have our muscle to protect us from the baddies?"

I stare at them, at their smiles. After Homecoming in 1995, the three of us became an inseparable trio, exploring the many abandoned buildings, mist-wreathed woods, and abandoned reservoir as part of a series Patrick dubbed "The Gray Springs Investigatory Team

Adventures". I think, for a brief time, we actually thought about sending Patrick's raw footage to some company in L.A., that we could spawn careers, become famous. In the end, only Amani left, to go to college on a sports scholarship, leaving me behind.

Patrick zooms in on me and I realize I can go down in whatever creepy basement is at the bottom of those stairs and get to hang out with Amani, or I can leave and ...what? Be boring old Colin, working at a stupid Blockbuster—or not, 'cause Patrick is probably right in the fact I'll be out of a job as soon as Mr. Fellstone comes in tomorrow and sees this mess.

So I flex my arms as my answer and Patrick lets out a whoop. A moment later, after grabbing the singular flashlight from the office, Amani, Patrick, and I descend.

The singular light at the base of the stairs buzzes, its yellow light coating the bare concrete walls and floor. I am in front, Amani behind me, and Patrick last, filming everything. As I reach the bottom, I find myself staring down a hall with three closed doors, two close to me, and one at the very end.

"Can you describe what you're seeing, Colin?" Patrick prompts.

"A hallway," I say.

"Come on, Colin." Amani plants a foot on my ass and gives me a push further down the hall. "You can do better than that."

I laugh. It's so easy to slip back into the old rhythm, into the illusion that everything was as it was when we were still in high school. When I still had Amani in my life, when I still thought I had a future outside of Gray Springs. So I turn to the camera with a smile.

"I'm Colin Hayes, reporter for the Gray Springs Investigatory Team," I say in my best TV voice. "And I am here in the secret cult tunnels beneath Gray Springs' one and only Blockbuster. What will we find down here? The burned remains of the Children of the Gray? Ectoplasm? Mutant rats? Stay tuned!"

Amani shrieks with laughter, clapping her hands, and Patrick gives me a thumbs up.

"Do I still got it, or what?" I say.

"Bravo!" Amani says between gasps. "Bravo!"

Intoxicated on the ego boost her laughter gives me, I go to the first door. "And now, dear viewers, what lies behind door number one?"

Patrick pushes past Amani to get a good shot as the door swings open.

I gasp loudly, throwing myself away.

"What?" Amani shrieks. "What is it?"

I turn to her and point. "Brooms."

The door leads to a cramped storage room crowded with steel shelving units, stacked with boxes, plastic bottles of cleaning fluid, and bundles of wire. A half dozen mops and brooms stand against the wall in the corner, next to a rusted old A/C unit.

"Exciting stuff," Patrick says, switching the light on.

A bare bulb buzzes to life, revealing more shelves, more boxes, more cleaning supplies. The air reeks of bleach and lemons.

"My turn next!" Amani skips past to the second door.

"Amani Jones here," she says to the camera, hand on the doorknob. "Ready to reveal the horrors behind door number two!"

The door opens on complete darkness and a stench of mildew wafts out. The light from the hall doesn't reach far enough in to show anything.

"Light switch?" I ask.

Amani fumbles, refusing to step into the room, instead choosing to wrap her arm around the doorframe, pawing at the wall.

"And a werewolf grabs your hand in three, two..." Patrick starts.

"Oh shut up," Amani laughs and light blooms in the room.

"Whoa." Patrick steps past her.

Inside are several bookshelves packed with VHS cassettes, a folding chair, and a desk with a dusty TV and VCR on it. The tapes are a mix of blank cassettes and old movies from the 80s. Amani goes to the table and Patrick walks slowly through the room, filming everything. I pick through the movies closest to me. At first I recognize some of the titles, automatically cataloging them: *The Princess Bride* - romance, *Sixteen Candles* - comedy, *The Goonies* - kids, but it gets progressively weirder.

I pull out a cassette with a cardboard cover featuring a hand-drawn illustration of a bunch of children in a burning building. The title—in hot pink bubble letters —reads *The Screams of the Innocent*. I pull out the next with a cover done in faded marker, a naked woman is tied to an upside down cross, a knife through her chest. The title reads *In Hart's Trust We Cri*. The next one has no childish art, just the title *Raintime Rituals*.

"Have you seen these, Patrick?" I say, pointing.

"Oh man, home movies?" He zooms in, taking each VHS off the shelf and focusing on its cover.

"Do you think the cult made these?" I ask.

"It looks like it." He puts *Raintime Rituals* back and takes out another one, *The Creature of the Gray Lagoon*. "This must have been part of their old stock. I guess it survived the fire because it was down here."

The sound of white noise erupts and I nearly shit my pants. Amani is in front of the TV, her face flickering with the staticky light.

"There's a tape in here," she says and, like every bad horror movie out there, she hits play.

Static morphs to grainy black and white movement, figures swaying and the sound of a keening voice, plaintive and pained. It's interrupted by cruel laughter and the footage cuts out.

"Okay, weird," Patrick says.

"Try this one." I pull *The Creature of the Gray Lagoon* cassette out of its sleeve and hand it to Amani.

The VHS clunks in place and the VCR whirs to life, jumping right in.

"Someone wasn't kind, didn't rewind," I say as the film opens mid-pan, over a moonlit reservoir.

Also in black and white, the light on the still waters are stark, cartoon-like. The only sound is the distant wind through unseen branches and the breathing of the camera person.

"Is that Gray Reservoir?" Amani asks.

The view zooms in. There is a line of people, hand-in-hand, along the reservoir's shore, dressed in gray robes. Lanterns glow like tiny ghosts at their feet.

The waters ripple, multiple things beneath the placid surface rise. My breath catches in my throat and I can't recall what it was like to breathe.

The ripples grow into waves and the sky above the reservoir is laced with lightning. Muted thunder, overshadowed by the camera person's rapid breathing. The black water domes. Something is coming.

The camera zooms in. The people on the shore drop to their knees and fall forward, prostrating themselves at the water's edge.

"What the hell," says the unknown camera person.

Footsteps from the side, the camera spins, a figure in a gray robe has their hand raised. The camera drops with a thunk to the pebbly shore. Only a sliver of the reservoir's water can be seen from the new angle, waves splash, growing larger and larger. Drowning out the crash of waves is the sound of dragging.

Finally, to my relief, the footage cuts out. I realize I've been holding my breath and I let it out with a hiss, my lungs burning.

"Was that...was that real?" Patrick lets his camcorder drop.

Amani looks back at us, eyes wide. "Did we just watch a snuff film? I am pretty sure that was a knife in that guy's hand!"

"The mystery grows," I say with a forced smile and hold out another tape. "Come on, Patrick."

Tape after tape, there is grainy footage, fragmented scenes, sometimes just audio and no visuals. We joke at first. Then lapse to silence.

We move from the homemade movies to the titles we recognize and immediately notice something off.

"Wait, wait!" I lunge past Amani and jab the pause button. "What was that?"

"What was what?" Patrick asks.

I rewind it, hit the pause button over and over again, moving the film forward by seconds. The images tick forward in miniscule motions. Cartoon dinosaurs looking at a leaf, their mouths jarring open to dialogue we can't hear. I keep hitting pause until...

"There!" Amani points at the frozen screen.

The dinosaurs are gone. The screen is black with three words in white: SEEK THE STATIC.

"Subliminal messaging!" I say. "This is crazy!"

"Those nutty cultists were trying to brainwash Gray Springs!" Patrick laughs, panning to Amani and me. "Explains us, huh Colin?"

"Do you think all the normal movies down here have these messages?" Amani asks, ejecting the tape.

So we watch another, pausing in the middle, and slowly parsing through the scenes, finding more messages hidden in the recognizable films.

JOIN THE GRAY nestled in with a coyote and his fowl nemesis.

OBEY THE CHILDREN hidden in the scenes of a groundskeeper and a groundhog.

THE STATIC DEMANDS SUBSERVIENCE in weekend detention with five misfits.

Amani shuts off the last movie and turns slowly on the stool to face Patrick's camera. Holding up her left hand curled in a 'c' shape, in a deadpan voice and no expression, she says, "Guess these cultists put the C in VCR."

She looks from the camera to me, then to Patrick, the corners of her mouth quivering in a way I know so well as her trying not to smile.

"Wow Amani," Patrick responds. "That was bad. Like I might just need to erase all my footage bad."

"Oh whatever, our audience will love it." She stands, kicking the stool out of the way and jams her hands into her jeans pockets. "Anyway, mystery solved. The Children of the Gray believed you could actually brainwash people with movies. Do you all wanna go to Pizza Corner and catch up?"

More than anything, I want to get out of this weird smelling basement and spend the night with Amani like we used to. But I already know Patrick's answer.

"No way." He turns to leave the movie room. "We have one more door!"

Amani and I catch each other's gazes and roll our eyes at the same time with a laugh. But we follow him anyway, as we always have when we played at investigators in high school. When we all thought we'd be getting famous together.

The last door is at the very end of this hall and Patrick waits by it. "Come on, Colin. Let's do the big reveal."

And as I put my hand on the cold, moist door handle, I wish more than anything I'd tried to convince Patrick to go for pizza instead. Especially when we find another set of stairs.

"I'm not going down there." Amani's arms are crossed. "Seeing those creepy videos was enough excitement for one night, thank you."

"We have to go," Patrick says. "Who knows what's down there!"

"Exactly!" Amani snaps. "We don't know what's down there!"

Then they both look at me and I'm caught in the middle. The best friend and the old flame. But Amani left us, left me. There is only one way my loyalties can go.

"I say we go down." I wonder if this is something I'll regret. "You don't have to come with us, Amani. If you're scared."

I wonder if this is like old times or if there is some real bitterness behind my words. Before I can stop her, she grabs the flashlight from me and heads down the stairs.

"Amani, wait up!" I hurry after her, watching as the buttery illumination from the flashlight reveals snapshots of old wooden stairs and concrete walls covered in wires.

The air grows thick, cold, and smells of dead, wet plants, moldering in darkness. I make the mistake of putting a hand against a wall to steady myself and find the concrete slimy with moss. With a shiver, I wipe my hand on my pants, but the feeling of unclean remains.

At the bottom of the stairs, Amani casts the light along each wall and spots a panel of light switches. She flips all of them and a dozen bare bulbs spark to life along the ceiling.

"Happy?" she snaps.

"Amani, I—"

"This is awesome!" Patrick pushes past us. "I bet we're the first ones down here since the fire!"

The hall is narrow, black mold speckles the walls, moss grows along the ceiling, and soggy cobwebs hang from the wiring that garlands from one light to the next.

"I'm just surprised this place didn't go up too," Amani says, pointing at a steady drip of water tapping the top of a bare bulb. "This is an OSHA nightmare."

"Do you hear that?" I ask, staring down the hall, my eyes straining.

"Not funny, Colin!" Amani snaps.

"No, seriously, listen."

In the distance, down the hall, behind one of the dozen doors, is the soft sound of static.

"Is that...a TV?" Patrick whispers. "Do you think someone is down here?"

Patrick heads down the hall towards the sound of static. I am drawn along too, mainly because I can't let him go alone. He is my best friend, after all.

The hall ends in a T junction and we follow the static to the left, where a partially open door sheds flickering light into the hall. Amani is right next to me, holding the flashlight up like a weapon.

"This is such a bad idea!" she hisses.

I can't help myself. "Just ditch us then, you're used to that aren't you?"

She flinches away from me like I've slapped her. Like a coward, I jog a bit to leave her behind, to stand next to Patrick. He pushes the door fully open with his foot, still filming.

Inside is a downward sloping hall, lined with TVs on every side, from floor to ceiling. Patrick steps onto the landing, filming the TVs. I follow, searching for a light switch, but there is none. The only light comes from the dozens and dozens of TVs emanating nothing but static. It feels like the screens are closing in, eating the space between us and them, tightening a white noise noose around us.

"Okay," I say, my voice barely a whisper. "Patrick, I think it's time we head back."

"Why?" He pans back to me.

"Someone had to turn these TVs on," I hiss and reach for his arm. I'll drag him out of this freaky basement if I have to.

The next few moments happen on fast-forward. Behind me, back in the lit hall, Amani screams—a short cry of fear and rage. I turn. Someone tall, in a gray robe, face covered with a blank, white canvas mask, has the front of her shirt bunched in his fists.

Amani reaches up, still gripping the flashlight, and whacks it against the side of his head.

He roars, shoves, she comes flying through the open door into me.

We fall.

And the man slams the door shut, the lock turning with a clear, metallic *shik* like the blade of a guillotine.

"Amani! Are you okay!" I am selfishly pleased that I get to hold her again, feel her warmth, smell her flowery shampoo.

"Hey!" Patrick shouts, kicking the door, and still filming, always filming. "Hey! Let us out!"

"I'm fine!" she snaps and gets up, leaving me on the ground.

"It's locked." Patrick finally lets his camera drop.

Amani and Patrick turn and look at me as I stand. Their faces are eerily illuminated by the TVs, the shadows dancing over their cheeks, their chins, and in their eyes like living creatures. Like the white noise is possessing them. Possessing me.

"Uh, and I am Colin Hayes of the Gray Springs Investigatory Team, here with a special deep dive into hell!" I gesture to the tunnel as though welcoming them to my house and bow.

A beat of silence then Patrick barks out a harsh laugh. Amani giggles.

"You're so lame, Colin," she says. "I love it."

"Hey now, hey!" I reply in mock indignation.

"Well, since we're diving in." Patrick kneels. "Let me switch out my battery."

The three of us assume the team huddle, kneeling in a circle as Patrick swaps batteries in his camcorder, puts in a fresh tape.

"My heart is still racing," Amani says, pressing a hand to her chest. "Who the hell was that guy?"

"Could he be a surviving cult member?" I try to keep the growing panic out of my voice.

"Maybe." Patrick replies as he methodically manages his camera. "Who else would know this place was down here?"

Camera work done, he puts it on the floor and holds out his hands. We did this before every "mission". We take each other's hands, completing the circle. It all started after we went into the rain culvert by Patrick's house and got scared by a rat the size of a house cat. Patrick had just read *IT* by Stephen King and decided we needed to start channeling our friendship for protection, sans the weird sewer orgy bullshit.

It was silly. But so were our little ghost hunting or Bigfoot chasing adventures. And right now, locked in this bizarre tunnel, it helps. I feel a little better, knowing that I am down here with them, my friends.

"Three, two, one," we chant. "Suck it, ghosts!"

Then we let go, though I really don't want to, and stand again.

"At least we know there has to be another way in and out," I say.

"How so?" Patrick cradles his camcorder in his hands.

"That guy didn't get in through Blockbuster like we did." I look down the tunnel, filled with dancing shadows. "There has to be another way, so maybe if we are lucky, it's down there."

Armed with Amani's flashlight and Patrick's camcorder, we head down the tunnel.

The constant buzz of white noise makes me paranoid, there's no way we'd ever hear someone coming up behind us until it was too late. I keep glancing over my shoulder but see only flickering light and an empty hall.

"So, uh, how's L.A.?" I finally say to interrupt the flow of static.

Amani glances at me and shrugs. "Same old."

Patrick turns, filming us. "How's UC Berkeley? Heard you quit basketball."

"You quit basketball?" I guess this is what happens when you stop calling someone, you stop hearing about their life.

"Her mom told my dad when he was dropping off the milk." Patrick continued.

"I thought you loved basketball?" I say. "And didn't you get a scholarship—"

"Sheesh, guys!" Amani exclaimed, her voice echoing over the static. "You are worse than my Mom's church group for gossip, shit."

She softens her tone with a half smile, but I don't think she's completely joking either.

"Yeah, I didn't end up having time for it," she continues. "I got an offer to model. You have to go to a lot of auditions and photo shoots."

"You're a model?" Patrick pans from her face down to her toes and back up. "Yeah, I guess maybe for Sears or something?"

"Oh shut up, you overgrown Smurf!" Amani laughs and takes a swipe at his camcorder.

The air is thick with the taste of pennies and stagnant water, my skin feels damp from the humidity, it's hard to breathe, like I'm drowning on dry land. I can't stop imagining Amani in L.A., in a city not swathed in near year-long fog and drenching rains, I imagine her in the sun, in magazines, in someone else's arms.

"Must be nice to be able to just leave." And I wish more than anything I could take those bitter words back.

Amani stops, turns and looks at me. "Why don't you just come out with it."

I look at the floor, the TVs, Patrick, everywhere but her. "What do you mean?"

"The reason you stopped calling me back, the reason you stopped answering my calls, Colin. Just spit it out already."

I can't look at her. I'm angry and bitter and a stupid part of me blames her for us being down here. After all, she's the one who brought the tape in.

"You left me, us, Gray Springs," I say. "After everything we've been through. You just left like we were nothing."

"Is now really the—" Patrick starts, dropping his camcorder.

"Now you listen here, Colin Hayes." Amani steps right up to me, left index finger stabbing me in my chest. "You chose to stay here. You don't even like it here. You told me that, straight from your goddamn lips."

"I—" I start but her finger jabs me again.

"No, Colin. No." Her eyes glitter like diamonds in the white noise light. Glitter with tears. "You knew I planned on going to UC Berkeley. You decided to stay here. Stayed for a mother who half the time doesn't even realize you're not her dead brother. You chose to stagnate yourself here. You didn't even try to apply to UC Berkeley, did you?"

"Guys—" Patrick again, always butting in.

"Not now, Patrick!" Amani whirls on him, and that's when we see the TVs.

All the screens show the same image: Amani and I in this very tunnel, fighting. Patrick raises his camcorder up, presses record.

The TVs change. One shows me punching Amani and she drops. Another shows Amani hammering my face in with the butt of the flashlight. Another: we start kissing passionately. Another: we melt into the TV screens behind us, disappearing as Patrick screams silently.

"What is this?" Amani whispers.

The TVs throb in unison, fade to black, dousing us in darkness. At the end of the tunnel, a light appears and approaches. The only sounds are our rapid breathing and the steady drip of water from the ceiling.

The light nears and now I can see the TVs are displaying a person walking towards us, his body fragmenting across the screens. A man in a Gray Springs's police uniform, holding a gun up and at the ready, his face tense. I recognize him though years have separated us. A shudder rocks my body, my scalp tingles.

"No," I breathe.

Uncle Will walks past us, intent on wherever it is he's going. He leads the way down the tunnel and disappears from view. My body is numb as the TVs blare back to static and white noise. Patrick knows better than to pan to my face. He lets the camera drop again and looks at me.

"Was that?" he says and I nod.

"Let's go." I lead the way down the tunnel, following the path my dead uncle had taken just moments before.

The tunnel bottoms out in a huge cavern, its rough stone walls covered completely in buzzing TVs—broken in two places where small slits in the stone lead elsewhere—and a low ceiling studded with moldy looking stalactites dripping with moss. The majority of the cavern floor is taken up by a dark pool of still water, reeking of sediment and rot. Its water eats the light of the dozens of TVs and reflects nothing back. Besides the pond and TVs, the cavern is empty.

"I honestly didn't think we could get any freakier than a hall of TVs," Patrick says over the blaring white noise. "But here you go."

"This smells like the gross water from the reservoir," Amani replies.

She switches on the flashlight she's holding and shines its light over the surface of the subterranean pool.

"I'm no cave pond expert, kiddos," Patrick says. "But shouldn't we be seeing some reflections?"

I watch the TVs. Will he appear here too? And what was that? How did he appear down here on those TVs? Old footage? A death echo? But Uncle Will is gone.

"This place is giving me the weirdest vibes," Amani says. "Look, all the hair on my arms is sticking up!"

"It could just be all the static from the TVs?" Patrick zooms in on Amani's arm.

As if in response, the TVs cut to complete silence. Across one wall, they display this very same cave, but instead of us they show a circle of people in gray robes around the pool of dark water. Their arms are raised above their heads, they might be chanting, or singing, but the TVs have no sound.

Behind them, through the same tunnel that we just came

through, appears Uncle Will. He stops upon seeing the group of people around the water, the shock clear on his face.

"What is he doing here?" I say, watching my dead uncle as he takes another step into the cave.

"He must have been investigating the cult." Patrick keeps his camcorder aimed at the TVs, capturing every moment. "Did your mom ever say anything about it?"

"No, she was wrecked after he died." So was I. "I think she burned everything of his. The only thing I was able to save were his cassettes."

Uncle Will had been the rock of the family after Dad left one day and just never came back. Mom started drinking, but he'd at least kept her in check. He shielded me from it, took me camping during her benders, introduced me to Soundwave, came to my school events even. And then one day he was gone and Mom just let herself escape into her bottles of vodka.

Behind the video-ized phantom of Uncle Will, I spot another robed figure and it all happens fast. Uncle Will must have heard something because he whirls, fires, and the TVs flash white. Blinded, I shield my eyes with my arm, but it's too late. It takes a while before the spots disappear and the TVs are back to static. It leaves the three of us in limbo as we stare at each other, our faces mottled by the flickering light.

I feel like I did back when I was a kid. When Mom told me Uncle Will had died. Lost into my own screaming thoughts, a maelstrom of grief and pain and hate and sorrow. Then Amani takes my hand. Hers is warm, mine cold and clammy. Her warmth anchors me.

"Let's get out of this shithole," Patrick says.

Amani leads the way to the left-most tunnel, skirting the silent pool. She squeezes my hand again.

"You never brought him up much, your uncle Will I mean," she says and even hearing his name again causes a wave of nausea to roll in my belly.

"He died when I was nine," I reply. "My mom said it was a heart attack. It was a closed casket though and she just got rid of everything, you know? I guess I just tried to remember him how I last saw him."

Uncle Will across from me in the fishing boat, glowing with early morning light, as we both hold fishing poles on Lake Chabot. He laughs at some lame joke I make, there's a cooler of soda and sandwiches between us. I can forget everything, mom drunk at home, the bully at school.

Amani shines her flashlight into the tunnel, all we can see are craggy walls, moss, and dripping water.

"Uh, guys?" Patrick sounds scared.

I turn. The cave pool's surface is broken with erratic bubbles. Ripples cause its edge to caress the stone floor as the bubbles increase in frequency.

"Oh my god." Amani's voice is a breath in my ear.

The water boils, bubbles, then bursts as something shoots upward. Amani's light catches the figure, exposing them.

But it's not a monster.

It's a cop and, for an insane moment, I know it's Uncle Will. I push past Patrick as Uncle Will gasps for air, struggling in the water.

"Colin, stop!" Amani calls, but I jump into the ice cold water.

The smell of grit and minerals hits the back of my throat hard and I gag as I wade deeper into the pool. The bottom is slick with slime and I almost tip over several times. Eventually, the bottom pulls away and I have to swim. Reaching for the struggling man, I grab his arm and pull him to shore.

It's then I see it's not my uncle. Of course not. Still, it's a familiar face.

"Lance?" I say, looking down at the face of my one and only high school bully.

I haven't seen him since graduation, though he stopped bullying me after that fateful Homecoming night. I hadn't even known he'd started working as a cop. He's somehow gotten even taller and leaner, but his hair is now cropped close to his head and his chin is covered in a bit of stubble.

Now he's looking up at me, in the exact same uniform that my uncle once wore, his face pale and eyes wild.

"Where did you even come from?" I look at the small pool as its waters settle.

"Lance Foster?" Amani approaches, shining her light at him.

Patrick zooms in. "The great bully appears."

"Not the time, Patrick," I say and kneel next to him. "Dude, are you okay?"

Lance rolls to his side and vomits up a bellyful of gray water, coughing so hard I am surprised there weren't bits of his lungs mixed in. I watch the pool while Lance catches his breath. The sight of the quiet water makes me feel uneasy. Like it's one great big eye watching me as I watch it.

"D–dead," Lance forces out through his coughs. "All dead."

"Who, Lance? How did you get here?" I ask.

He shakes his head and takes a couple more deep breaths.

"We got called out to the reservoir," Lance finally says. "There'd been reports of bonfires, suspicious people gathering."

I exchange a look with Patrick and Amani over Lance's prone body.

"Did those suspicious people happen to be wearing gray robes?" Patrick asks.

Lance pushes himself up to a seated position and nods.

"Oh god, Lance." Amani kneels on his other side. "You're bleeding."

The back of Lance's head, neck, and the upper back of his uniform is dyed scarlet. A brutal looking wound sweeps from behind his left ear to the base of his skull, but I'm relieved that it's not deep enough that any bone is showing.

"It looks like something took a chunk of skin right off you," Patrick says and holds out the blue handkerchief he's had around one wrist.

Amani thanks him, takes it, and presses it against Lance's head.

"Five of us were sent to break it up," Lance continues, seemingly unaware of his wound. "But something in the water..."

He looks at the pool and trails off. I shiver and follow his gaze, but there's nothing there and the waters are quiet.

"Hey, Lance, hey." I snap my fingers in front of his face. "How did you get here from the reservoir? What happened?"

"Something pulled me under. It was fast," Lance says, almost dreamily. "I kept kicking and kicking. I even tried to shoot it. I must have nicked it because I got free. But I was in an underwater tunnel. I swam desperately, trying to find the surface again. I found pockets of air here and there, that's the only way I survived. Then I ended up here."

"Holy shit, dude," Patrick says. "That's one hell of a tale."

I think back to the tapes we watched. I think back to the footage of *The Creature of the Gray Lagoon*. Could it have been referring to the reservoir? To what was *in* the reservoir?

"The things in the water took them." Lance's voice cracks. "Jameson, Steve, Kim, and... and Natalie. All gone."

"You're okay, Lance," Amani says, taking his hand in hers. "We're going to get you to a hospital."

I look away so she can't see my annoyed expression at her being tender with the same guy who called me Gayes all through high school, and my gaze lands on the pool.

Which is no longer quiet, bubbles popping on the surface.

Something is coming.

"Guys," I hiss and wrap my arm under Lance's arm, lifting him to his feet.

"Oh." Patrick pans to the pool.

"Not the time, Patrick!" Amani grabs his arm and yanks.

Behind us the pool waves and churns, the TVs go white and silent, as the four of us flee to the tunnel. The tunnel cuts to the left, hiding us from view instantly, so I slow and let Lance stand on his own. I press a finger to my lips and everyone nods. I have to see. We all want to see. So Amani, Patrick, and I cling to the edge of the rock outcropping that hides us and watch the pool. Lance leans against the wall, clutching the handkerchief to his head, and doesn't join us.

The water explodes in waves that splatter across the stone floor as three gray figures crawl to shore.

At first I think they are robed people, swimming up after to recapture Lance. But as I watch the figures, whose backs are to us, I immediately notice how *off* their movements are. Draped in rubbery gray cloth, they slurp over the stones like slugs. All three are hunched over, overly long arms clutched in front of them like priests wringing their hands in despair. Their capes drag way behind them, ends still beneath the water's surface. Even from where we hide, I can hear their breathing—bubbly, wet sounds, like someone with a terrible chest cold.

One reaches to the other on its right and I can see it only has two long fingers and a thumb, each with six knobbly knuckles. It presses these three digits against its closest companion and they pause, the first one leaning its head in close, as if whispering secrets.

Amani presses against me, her lips to my ear. "What the hell are those things?"

Her voice is the barest whisper but the three things whip around to face our direction.

And that's when I fully realize that those things are most definitely not human.

What I thought was clothing at first, I can now see are folds of gray, rubbery flesh freckled with black splotches. Their bodies trail off, ending in long tails that lead back into the water. They remind me of those ugly blobfish that occasionally get pulled up from the bottom of the sea—except these things don't have faces—no eyes, nose, or facial structure at all. They only have giant, human-like mouths filled with crooked yellow teeth and surrounded by thick black lips.

Their double-jointed arms sprout above the mouth, where a person's shoulders would have been, and all three wring, wring, wring their hands as if worried they might have left their creepy-ass ovens on. The three monsters don't move. They are incredibly still besides the wringing of their hands.

"Those things killed them!" Lance shoves past me, gun raised.

The crash of two gunshots slice through my ears like white hot knives. I'm pretty sure I cry out but I don't hear anything but a heaven-shattering ringing. Lance is right in front of me, legs spread wide, pulling the trigger but nothing happens—out of ammo.

Still, the monster in the middle of the trio has fallen, yellow goo jetting out of a bullet hole just above its right arm. Its front buck teeth are shattered, enamel littering the ground like ostrich eggshells. I have to give it to Lance, he's a pretty good shot.

The other two monsters point in our direction, mouths gaping—maybe if I wasn't deafened, I would hear them screaming. The injured monster's tail goes taut and its limp body is dragged back into the water.

Maybe it isn't a tail after all. Maybe those long fleshy appendages are something else.

Either way, I'm not waiting to find out. The other two monsters speed towards us, their gelatinous, soggy bodies gyrating across the stone. Standing, I grab Lance's arm, spinning him, pulling him along as Patrick, Amani, and I flee down the tunnel.

10 p.m.

"Great, a dead end," Patrick says, slowly spinning in a circle.

My eardrums throb painfully in time with the racing tempo of my heart, and I press fingers to each ear, checking if they are bleeding.

Piled in a narrow dead end is a mound of debris: scraps of tire rubber, crushed beer cans, moldy newspaper dating back ten years, wet garbage bags among other things.

Lance sinks to the floor, pressing the heels of his hands to his eyes with a groan. Amani stands at the edge of the garbage pile, gripping her elbows, shaking. And I know Patrick well enough to see how pale he is, how scared.

I look over my shoulder at the tunnel for the millionth time but those monsters aren't there. Whatever those tails of theirs are, they must keep the creatures on a short leash. Not that it matters much. We need to go back through that main cave if we ever want to escape, if there even is an escape.

I look up at the dripping ceiling and suck in a deep breath of humid air. I can't explain the calm I feel, or maybe it's numbness. As a kid, I used to cry about everything. Especially right after Dad left. I remember Uncle Will taking me out in his squad car, while Mom was passed out on the living room floor. He'd taken me to Gallows Overlook, a cliff that hung over the reservoir just above Crystal Cove, and we chilled to Soundwave, watching the stars.

"Life sucks, huh, kid?" he'd finally said, breaking the silence.

Immediately tears threatened. "It's not fair, Uncle Will."

"No, it never is," he had replied. "I'm not gonna sit here and lie to you, tell you life will always get better, cause sometimes it doesn't. Sometimes it's a whole lot of suffering, a whole lot of hurt. In those moments of darkness, it's up to you to define yourself. Do you fold under the weight, kid, or do you make it fold before you?"

Now, in this cold dead end with only Amani's light to break the darkness, I realize I am facing that moment. Uncle Will had been here before me and who knows what he saw. What would he have done?

I kneel. "Gray Springs Investigatory Team huddle."

Amani barks out a sharp laugh, shakes her head, but joins. Patrick follows after. Lance stares at us.

"Gray Springs *what*?" he says, looking tired as all hell.

"The official Gray Springs Investigatory Team, kid." I hear Uncle Will in me then and let my false confidence carry me forward. "You're now an honorary member, welcome to the team."

"Don't worry, we don't do blood pacts or anything." Patrick turns his camera off, preserving the battery. "We might throw some buttermilk at you, though."

"Let's break down what we know," I start. "We know the Children of the Gray operated out of what is now Blockbuster."

"Yeah, it was an independent video store," Patrick adds. "Apparently they were tampering with movies to add subliminal messaging."

"Yup," I say. "The original store burns down and the Blockbuster is built on top, six months ago. Immediately romance movies start getting returned for being damaged."

"And the romance movies are right in front of the door to the secret cult basement." Amani wraps her arms around her long legs, resting her chin on her knees. "And there was some sketchy dude down here who locked us in."

"The cult is obviously still operating." I glance at Lance. "The cops were called out to the reservoir where a bunch of people in robes were doing some kind of ritual similar to what we saw in *The Creature of the Gray Lagoon*."

"Summoning something." Patrick glances down the tunnel. "Or waking it up."

"And somehow my uncle was involved," I say.

"Somehow?" Lance finally speaks. "You mean you don't know?"

"What?" My whole body rolls with hot and cold and for a moment, the world tilts.

"Your uncle was the key investigator into the Children of the Gray," Lance says. "He was in the video store the night of the fire. I mean, you really didn't know? He died from the injuries he got then...it wasn't pretty."

"I —my mom said he had a heart attack."

Lance looks away, looks at Patrick, at Amani, everywhere but me.

"It was a closed casket funeral, wasn't it?" Patrick says. "I always thought it was weird for someone who died from a heart attack."

I don't say anything, I *can't* say anything.

"Look, sorry I brought it up," Lance mutters.

I shake my head. "It's fine. Can—what happened to him exactly?"

My ex-bully shifts awkwardly on the stone floor. "Uh, listen dude. I don't know—"

"Spit it out, Lance," Amani snaps. "Now's not the time to hold back anything that could help us get out."

I shoot her a grateful look and then remember how immature I was earlier. When the fact she went to L.A. seemed the worst thing that had happened to me—the ultimate betrayal. Now it's hard not to feel mortified.

Lance sighs, rubs his face with his hands. "Colin, do you remember Natalie Dune?"

I nod. "Uncle Will's partner on the force."

"She's my partner now, mentor really," Lance says. "She's still obsessed with the fire and the cult. Everyone in the precinct calls her Nutty Nat."

"Wow," Patrick sneers. "That's a Lance-level nickname."

Lance at least has the self awareness to flinch and blush a bit.

"About a month ago, she showed me the file she keeps on it," he says. "We spent hours in our squad car, she told me everything."

"Was there a reason she showed you all that?" Amani asks. "You'd been working together for how long? And only a month ago she shows you everything?"

"That's when people started to disappear again," Lance says. "She was convinced it had something to do with the cult, even though they hadn't been seen since that night Colin's uncle died."

A faint high-pitched chittering—much like a dolphin's squawk—causes us all to freeze. The call is answered by another. Then the sound fades. The four of us look at one another, our faces underlit by the flashlight on the ground between us.

Lance continues, his voice even lower. "Natalie told me that she and Will had been investigating the Children of the Gray for months before the fire. There were a ton of disappearances while the group was active. But the night of the fire? Nat's daughter was taken."

He pauses and we all listen. Nothing.

"She and Will tried to get a warrant to search the Family VHS Center but they were denied," Lance continues.

"They busted in anyway," I say and Lance looks at me with a surprised expression. "We saw him, Uncle Will, on the weird TVs here. He finds the cave pool and gets attacked while Natalie was getting her daughter out."

"Yeah." Lance nods. "They interrupted some kind of ritual. Will was attacked but Nat saved him. She said something came out of the pool and started snatching cultists. It must have been *those* things."

"How did they get away though?" Patrick jumps in. "Was there another exit?"

Lance shakes his head. "They went back up to the video store and grabbed the gas canister Nat always has in the back of her car. They lit the fire that destroyed the store."

"And Uncle Will?" I can picture him so clearly even now, in my memories. His smile, his humour, his generosity. "Did he die from burns or smoke or...?"

"Nothing like that. Listen, Colin." Lance looks up at me, and I swear to God I see actual pity in his eyes. "She showed me the pictures and it wasn't pretty."

"Just tell me, Lance," I say. "You owe me that after all the shit you put me through in school. You owe me the truth."

Out of the corner of my eye, I see Patrick pick up his camcorder. For being my best friend and all, he can completely lack tact. Amani reaches out and pushes the camera back down to the floor, shaking her head.

"It wasn't the fire," Lance whispers. "Nat said that when she got down to the pool cave, the cultists painted some symbols on his chest. When those monsters started coming, they went after Will first. They did something to him. Nat got him out of there but it was too late. His skin started to go gray. After a few hours, he started to look like those things in there. He was in a lot of pain, Colin. He begged Nat to— well, I think you can figure out what happened."

"Oh my god." I stare down at my hands and they fracture as my vision blurs with tears. "Uncle Will."

"Nat said that the cultists wanted to go with those things." Lance speeds up, as if wanting to get it all out. "She thought that maybe they wanted to go with the monsters, maybe they wanted to become one too. Just like what they did to your uncle."

More silence. I suck in a shuddery breath and wipe the back of my arm across my eyes. I try to imagine the man who had been my uncle, who had fed me when mom forgot, who paid the heating bill when she ran off with some guy for a summer and didn't pay any bills, leaving me without hot water. I try to imagine him writhing and screaming in a hospital bed as he changed into something monstrous. I wonder if he thought of me as he died. I wonder if he knew that Mom would spend all the money he left us on rehabs and fad recovery clinics, trying to get "better" but then diving into a bottle as soon as she got out.

"Oh, Colin." Amani sits next to me and wraps her arms around me, resting her head on my shoulder.

Did Uncle Will have any regrets in those last moments? He would have had no idea when he woke up that morning, got ready, got dressed, that it would be his last. And what if this was my day, my last day? Would I have regrets?

I reach up, grab Amani's hands. My tears are gone and I feel the strange calm I had before. Maybe I'm just nuts but I know in my gut that my uncle died thinking of me, thinking that I'd be fine on my own because he had taught me how to face those dark moments.

"Listen, Amani," I say. "You were right. I should have gone with you."

"Colin, you don't—" she starts but I shake my head.

"I was afraid to leave," I say. "I took it out on you because you weren't. I'm sorry, Amani."

She smiles, squeezing my hands. "I'll forgive you if you take me out for some pizza after all this shit."

"Deal." I return her smile.

"I'm all for this romantic growth, guys," Patrick says. "But I really do think we need to figure a way out. Plus my camera is off."

"I think it's obvious there's only one way out," I say, standing.

"What? Where?" Patrick asks, turning his camcorder on and panning up to me.

"We go out the same way Lance came in," I say. "We go through the pool."

11p.m.

The two monsters are still in the cave, leashed by their tails or tethers or whatever it is that trails back into the water.

I glance over my shoulder. Amani, Lance, and Patrick are right behind me, and I press my finger to my lips. Back at the dead end, we made our plan and one thing we thought was that the creature reacted to sound. They obviously don't have eyes to see, and they managed to hear Amani's whisper from across the cave, so this would be the Gray Springs Investigatory Team's stealthiest mission yet.

Armed with a broken beer bottle I took from the trash pile, I take a step into the cave, my heart racing.

The TVs blare out a national alert screen, its tell-tale tones screaming into the cave. The creatures don't react, they only go still, their hands wringing in front of their oversized mouths. Mesmerized, I watched the screens.

NATIONAL ALERT
GRAY SPRINGS IS ADVISED TO FOLLOW THE CHILDREN.
CITIZEN WARNING IN EFFECT
DO NOT ATTEMPT TO HURT THE CHILDREN. STAND DOWN.

"What the hell?" I can't help but mutter.

The creatures turn towards me, slowly. The message blinks on the screens over and over again, wailing. Then, blaring out one last siren, the TVs flicker to a new program. Uncle Will.

The footage is shaky. He is struggling on a hospital bed, two nurses trying to get him to hold still. His body bloats out, stretching his clothes, tearing them, as his skin goes gray. He screams and screams, begging someone to make it stop.

Then he goes limp, the nurses step away, and Uncle Will looks at the camera. It feels like he's looking right at me. He smiles.

"Follow them, kid," he says to me as gray water begins to rise all around his hospital bed. "I'm waiting for you. I've been down here this whole time, but you haven't come to visit once."

My brain drowns in static as I watch Uncle Will sink into the gray water, his eyes close, his eyelids seal and fade away as his body expands into rubbery folds. Ears buzzing, I take a step forward, staring at the screens, watching Uncle Will transform into a monster.

That's why the casket was closed. Uncle Will was never in there. He's been waiting for me this whole time.

I take another step, and I hear someone yelling my name, but the static is too loud. The static is everything.

I fall to the side as Amani barrels past me, holding the hubcap she'd pulled from the trash pile and, as she squares off, I swear I hear her scream, "Eat this! Moon Tiara Action!" as she flings the hubcap like a frisbee. It smashes into one of the TVs in the top row and it comes crashing down. Wires attach the TVs to one another and these stretch, whine, and pull down each set one by one, in a spray of sparks and hissing electricity.

I fall back into my own mind, the static fades with the end of the TVs' siren call, and I can feel my feet on the floor, my hand gripping the broken beer bottle, the throbbing of my head. The gray monsters stop wringing their hands and clutch at the sides of their flabby heads in agony, baring their massive tombstone teeth.

This is our moment. I reach out my hand and Amani grabs it, we run. This time I am expecting the shock of the cold water, the gag-inducing smell of minerals, the slippery slimed bottom, and I don't hesitate until I hit the hole in the middle with Lance and Patrick right behind us.

Sucking in a deep breath, I grip Amani's hand tight and plunge into the water. The next part of my plan was the most dangerous, the part I based on gut instinct and nothing else. Back in the dead-end, Lance had said he wasn't sure he'd be able to lead us back to the reservoir and I knew that, even if he could, we wouldn't be able to out-swim the monsters in the cave.

In the water, I force my eyes open and I spot one of the gray tails right away. I have to let go of Amani's hand so I can grab the tail. It's as rubbery as it looks, but with an iron core of pulsing muscle. Amani grabs it as well and, next to us, Lance and Patrick swim to the other.

Now for the gamble.

I catch Patrick's eye and he gives me the devil horns with his free hand, before grabbing hold of the tail in front of him. We're both holding beer bottles and as one, we stab the jagged ends into the thick fleshy tails. Nothing. My lungs burn. I stab again and again, twisting the bottle on the last one, drawing thick yellow goo. The tail goes rigid and I only have a second to let go of the bottle, grabbing the tail with my other hand as it yanks.

The tails whip us down the tunnel. Down a left turn, my body slams against the rocks, then up right. I can't keep my eyes open against the water pressure. All I can hope is that I was right that these things would have come from the bottom of the Gray Springs reservoir.

I slam against another rock wall, then another, and I feel something in my left arm crack. I scream out the last of my air, taste sediment on my tongue. My left hand goes weak, falls away from the tail, and now my fate rests on the right. It's not even my good hand if you know what I mean.

I force my eyes open. I see bubbles, I see spots, I see darkness, and I lose hope, until I'm whipped into the air, straight up into the night sky. The tail arcs, Amani below me, and the creature below her, just breaching the surface. I hit the top of the arc, the tail jerks back down, reeling back into the water, and that's when I lose my grip. I fly through the air, seeing the clouds above, the reservoir below, the clouds, the water, the clouds, the water, and I know I'll hit a cliff or the shore and I'll die.

Instead I hit water, plunging deep.

Beneath me is a fissure in the reservoir bed, glowing with a sickly yellow pearlescence and from it trail the dozens of what I thought were tails, but now seem more like umbilical cords. At the end of each is a monster, floating in the water, wringing their ugly little hands. But not all the monsters are the same. Some are still half...human.

The cultists. The ones Lance must have seen on the shore before he got grabbed. They are all naked with the flesh cords stuck to their backs, in various stages of bloat and mutation. And one other, a face I recognize though it's older now.

Natalie Dune, Uncle Will's old partner. Unlike the cultists, who seem to have embraced their transformation, she claws at her ballooning throat and cheeks, at the growing folds of skin. I know I can't help her and I'm glad she doesn't notice me.

All the cords lead back to the trench and that's when I see it.

If the gray monsters are the Children, then this must be their mother.

A massive face, as wide as the reservoir is, presses against the confines of the fissure, its massive mouth open, but instead of a tongue, there is the twisted braid of the Children's cords. Its gray skin has the same Rorschach pattern of black splotches as its Children and based on what I can see, I know it has to be massive. Its lips are grossly sensual and plump and unlike its Children, the leviathan has eyes. And in those eyes I can see a horrible intelligence and cunning. Its lips curl up in a coy smile.

As one, the Children twist towards me.

Definitely my cue to leave. So—thanking Mom for enrolling me in swimming lessons all through grade school, more time for her to drink alone—I swim like my life depends on it.

Which, of course, it does.

I hit the surface, suck in air, and kick. On the shore I spot Patrick, Amani, Lance, and someone else. Someone in a gray robe.

"You don't know who you're messing with, asshole!" Amani's voice carries over the reservoir.

Behind me, something splashes to the surface, then another, and another. I don't look back. Cutting through the water, I wish time would freeze, I wish I was faster, stronger, but I only have one arm.

"And through the static comes knowledge," the cultist shouts. "And the Children of the Gray shall inherit the Earth! She will guide us and we—"

Amani crouches, stands, whips her arm back, and fires. The rock knocks the cultist's head back, cutting them off, and causing them to stumble. Behind me, I can't tell if the things are closer but my muscles are burning, all I want is a break.

Then my knee hits gravel, I'm at the shore. Scrambling, I stumble to my feet, thrashing through the water. I don't know what kind of reach those Children have and I really don't want to find out.

The cultist straightens and Lance charges, swinging.

"Holy shit, this is amazing," Patrick says, pulling his camcorder from the garbage bag he wrapped it in.

I risk a glance back and see the Children pulled into the air by their cords. They hover above the reservoir, swaying as the cords rear back like a snake ready to strike.

"This is for Nat!" Lance shouts, slamming his right fist across the cultist's face, knocking the mask from their face.

It's Mr. Fellstone, the owner of the one and only Gray Springs's Blockbuster, and he pulls a gun from beneath his robes, points it at Lance. This dark moment unfolds in stuttered seconds. Lance stumbles back, hands raised.

He tries to reason with Mr. Fellstone. Behind us, the Children chirp and snicker.

I scream at everyone to duck. Amani drops to her knees, Patrick follows suit, still filming.

Mr. Fellstone laughs and I lunge, my left arm still limp, as he pulls the trigger. I shove Lance with my right shoulder, pushing him out of the way.

A sky splitting bang. A blinding flash of light. A burning pain that dives deep into my left shoulder.

Hitting the ground, everything is spinning, and all my strength is gone. The Children swoop through the air, but the only one standing is Mr. Fellstone, who opens his arms to them.

They oblige.

Or, I guess, the thing controlling them obliges, and two Children snatch him up, pulling him back into the water.

Pain washes over me, I taste copper on my tongue. My vision fills with static and it pulls me down into a deep darkness.

Highway 101 - Eastbound
Gray Springs, CA
August 15, 1998
10 a.m.

Amani slaps my hand away from the radio in her canary yellow Jeep. "Driver is DJ, guests keep their hands to themselves."

"Careful!" I pretend to flinch. "I've only got one left!'

My left arm resembles a mummy's—all gauze and bandages. But it'll heal. At least that's what the doctors at Gray Springs Memorial Hospital told me. Squeezed in the backseat with some of the luggage is Patrick, snoozing.

We left Gray Springs behind over an hour ago. I convinced Mom to try rehab again and we said goodbye to Lance over breakfast at The Nook. I'm surprised he stayed after everything we saw. After what we know is still down there, under those gray waters.

When I had passed out that night, the three had laid on the shore as silent as they could until the sun rose and those things gave up, sinking back into the depths. Amani and Patrick dragged me to the hospital, Lance went back to the Blockbuster and—in the footsteps of Uncle Will and his partner Natalie—burned it down.

"Someone who knows about the cult and about those things needs to stay and keep watch," he said. "We don't know if there's more cultists out there, waiting for things to quiet down so they can wake that thing up again. If there are, I'll be here to stop them. Until then, I'll be working my way up to run for mayor."

"Mayor? Why?" I ask.

"So he can get that shithole of a reservoir filled in, duh," Patrick says and shares a little smile with our ex-bully.

We left him standing on the sidewalk, waving, on our way to L.A. Patrick is convinced we can cobble together what footage he managed to get into a decent B horror movie. Break into the scene in Hollywood.

There're some gaps we'll need to fill in—like why the romance movies were corrupted. My guess is the mother monster's influence leaked through that secret door, just like she managed to influence the TVs all throughout that underground base. Some kind of telepathy.

Who knows if anyone will pick it up. I might end up working at a different Blockbuster, honestly. But that doesn't matter.

And a part of me knows that I may have left Gray Springs behind, but a little bit of Gray Springs is coming with me. I know because I hear it in the radio static when we hit pockets of dead air. I hear Uncle Will begging me to come back, I hear Mr. Fellstone screaming, I hear a woman crying. Then the music returns and everything is normal. Except for a cold ache in my left arm and a wayward shiver.

But that doesn't matter either.

What really matters is I faced that dark moment. We all did. And we made it bow before us. Of course, there'll be more dark moments ahead, but—as Amani reaches over and rests her right hand on my knee, giving it a little squeeze—I know I can handle it.

P.L. McMillan is a writer whose works have been known to cause rifts in time and space itself... Well, not quite. But writing often makes her feel that powerful. With a passion for cosmic horror and sci-fi horror, P.L. McMillan sees every shadow as an entryway to a deeper look into the black heart of the world, meant to be discovered and explored. Infatuated with the works of Shirley Jackson, H.P. Lovecraft, and Ridley Scott, her dream is to create stories of adventure, of chills, of heartbreak, and thrills. P.L. McMillan lives in Colorado, with her large selection of teas, her husband, and her two chinchillas (Sherlock and Spuds) – all under the supervision of their black cat overlords, Poe and Zerg. Find her on her website: https://www.plmcmillan.com/ Or on Twitter @authorplm.

"Return to Gray Springs: Blockbuster Blues" is illustrated by P.L. McMillan.

ALIVE AND LIVING (PILOT)

CARSON WINTER

FADE IN:
    Swirling colors introduce us to the world of our main character, BRIAN PARKER (14). He smiles at the camera, a baseball bat resting on his shoulder. A look of terror comes over his face and he runs out of frame.

. . .

HIS OLDER BROTHER, MATT PARKER (17), holds a whoopie cushion. His face is twisted in fraternal rage. Mid-screen, he stops. He looks at the audience and flashes shiny white teeth.

HE TOO PASSES beyond the swirling background, then PRESTON PARKER and MEREDITH PARKER enter. The man wears a button up, he grins haplessly. The woman wears a dress and is holding a feather duster. They sigh with their entire bodies.

THROUGH ALL OF THIS, the credits roll—a dozen names none of us have ever heard, and never will again.

CUT TO:

INT. BRIAN'S ROOM. EVENING

BRIAN IS SITTING on his bed in the upstairs of his parents' two story house. His friend, ETHAN (14), sits at the small desk across from the bed.

BRIAN
   You really think he's not gonna notice?

ETHAN
   Let me tell you something, Bri. Parents are smart, but we're smarter.

. . .

BRIAN
You think?

ETHAN
Occasionally.

PAUSE FOR LAUGHTER.

BRIAN
So, how do you want to do it? I don't want to get in trouble.

ETHAN
You're not going to get in trouble. Besides, I have a plan.

BRIAN
It's not going to end like the Grand Cherry Bomb Fiasco of 1994, is it?

ETHAN
More like the Toilet Paper Revolution of '93.

BRIAN
You got caught for that too!

ETHAN
(Whimsically)

But I never broke.

LAUGHTER.

BRIAN
I just don't know, man... Do you really think we can do it?

ETHAN
A guy like you can do anything.

CUT TO:

INT. PARKER FAMILY LIVING ROOM. EVENING

PRESTON AND MEREDITH PARKER are sitting on the couch, downstairs, enjoying a glass of wine as they watch TV. It's a quiet night-in for the heads of the household.

MEREDITH
Is Brian up in his room?

PRESTON
He better be.

MEREDITH
This could be our chance... Say, when's the last time we got to be a little...romantic?

. . .

PRESTON
> When was Ross Perot last in the news?

LAUGHTER.

PRESTON EXTENDS his arm around his wife's shoulder. They lean in for a kiss.

MEREDITH
> Maybe we can make some news of our own...

PRESTON
> It's 5 o'clock some—

THE FRONT DOOR opens and their eldest son, Matt, walks in.

MATT
> (Oblivious to his parents' intimacy)
> I can't believe Vicky dumped me!

MEREDITH AND PRESTON look at each other and throw their heads back.

MEREDITH AND PRESTON
> (In unison)

Oh no, Matt. Girl trouble?

LAUGHTER.

MATT
How did you know?

MEREDITH
What happened with Vicky, honey?

MATT LEAPS over the couch and settles in between his parents, further ruining the mood.

MATT
Just the usual. I'm not cool enough, apparently.

PRESTON
Son, there's more to life than being *cool*.

MATT
(Sarcastic)
Yeah, right!

LAUGHTER.

MEREDITH

Why aren't you cool enough for this girl?

MATT

She says it's because I'm not on the football team. She wants to date a quarterback.

PRESTON

You don't have to be a quarterback to be cool, son. I'll have you know that I was pretty cool back in the day myself. And I was no quarterback.

MATT

Is that true, Mom?

MEREDITH

It's true, Matt. Your father was no quarterback.

Laughter.

Matt looks around the living room.

MATT

Where's Bri-guy?

PRESTON

Upstairs. Probably telling his delinquent friend what a horrible father I am.

. . .

MEREDITH
Oh, stop it. He'll be fine. It was just a tiff.

MATT
What happened?

PRESTON
I told him that he couldn't go to Minneapolis with his buddies and he got mad. He's acting like I'm a dictator just because I won't let him go off to the big city with a car full of criminals and no adult supervision!

MATT
Those teenagers, huh?

MEREDITH
Yeah, those teenagers.

They both stare at Matt.

MATT
You want me to talk to him, don't you?

They keep staring. Matt hangs his head down.

. . .

MATT
　　Fine. You got me. Older brother, to the rescue.

PRESTON
　　Thanks, son.

MATT GOES UPSTAIRS.

MEREDITH LEANS in close to Preston.

MEREDITH
　　Now, where were we?

　　　　　　　　　　　　　　　　　　　　　　　CUT TO:

INT. BRIAN'S ROOM. EVENING

BRIAN AND ETHAN are throwing a softball back and forth. When Matt walks in, they stop.

BRIAN
　　Weren't you supposed to be on a date?

MATT
　　Let's not talk about it.

　　　　　　　　　　. . .

ETHAN
    Dumped? Again?

MATT
    (To Brian)
    Your buddy here is just full of questions, isn't he?

BRIAN
    He's the inquisitive type.

MATT
    He's the inquisitor type.

THE TWO BOYS share a conspiratorial glance.

ETHAN
    You have *no* idea.

MATT
    (Sitting down on his own bed)
    So, Dad says you're bummed about him not letting you go into the big city?

BRIAN
    Are you here to tell me that I need to forgive him? To remind me that he loves me, that he knows best, that he knows exactly what I'm going through and...

. . .

MATT
> No, I don't care about any of that.

BRIAN
> Then why did you come up here?
> Matt lies back on the bed.

MATT
> Uh, I live here.

BRIAN
> Ignore him.

ETHAN
> Easier said than done.

Riotous laughter.

BRIAN
> When should we do it though?

ETHAN
> Tonight, of course. When else?

BRIAN
> Will it work?

. . .

ETHAN
  Of course it'll work.

BRIAN
  How do we know it'll work?

ETHAN
  You've been over to my trailer a bunch, right?

BRIAN
  Yeah. So what?

ETHAN
  When's the last time you've seen my parents?

BRIAN THINKS TO HIMSELF, his eyes go wide.

BRIAN
  Oh my god.

ETHAN
  They prayed. But he had nothing to do with it.

MATT OPENS HIS EYES. He sits up on the bed, exasperated at the two boys.

. . .

MATT
I'm sensing a scheme here.

BRIAN
Schemers? Us?

ETHAN
We're not schemers.

MATT
No? Then what's this little pow-wow about here? Something you wanna tell me?

BRIAN
It's not a scheme. It's just... Ethan has a plan to deal with my Minneapolis troubles.

MATT
Oh? And what is that?

ETHAN
You ever made a problem disappear?

MATT
Minneapolis is pretty big, Copperfield.

. . .

IN THE BLACKENED seats of the audience, someone SCREAMS, HOWLS. Their body hurts from what they're seeing.

BRIAN
   No, Matt. He doesn't mean the city. He means Mom and Dad.

MATT LOOKS at his brother and his friend. He cocks his head.

MATT
   Your friend's lost it, huh?

ETHAN
   I haven't lost *anything*. It works. I did everything right and my parents are gone.

MATT
   They must have gone out for smokes.

ETHAN
   Trust me, they already tried that.

MATT
   So, you're going to just make them disappear? How are you going to do that?

BRIAN
   (to Ethan)

Tell the man!

ETHAN
(digging into his backpack)
This is called the Demodorum.

HE PULLS OUT AN OLD BOOK, comically thick, bound in old worn leather with straps and buckles that close the cover.

ETHAN
It's an old book.

BRIAN
No kidding.

ETHAN
They don't make 'em like this anymore!

MATT
I wonder why.

BRIAN
Keep an open mind. This is going to be cool.

ETHAN OPENS THE BOOK, one buckle at a time. The wind HOWLS outside, the windows FLY OPEN, lightning CRASHES, and a DEEP, GURGLING ROAR sounds all around the three young men in the suburban home. The pages flutter and Ethan's eyes roll back into his head.

CLOSE UP ON ETHAN.

ETHAN
(In an unearthly tone made of icy consonants and bottomless vowels)
Ka'thar! Qi psol'uta! Barati narku!
THUNDER ROARS again, LIGHTNING FLASHES.
Brian's mouth opens in shock.
Ethan shakes his head. He's coming out of it. He closes the book.

ETHAN
Dude, sorry. I didn't mean to...

MATT
What do you mean...?

THEY BOTH STARE in horror at Matt, who's body is fading away in front of them. First they see his skin turn translucent. Then Matt looks down in utter terror to see his rippling insides wither away to nothing. When he tries to scream, he realizes he no longer has vocal cords. He VANISHES into thin air.

THE TWO BOYS look at each other, their expressions commingling in awe and horror.

. . .

ETHAN
　Told you it'd work.

　　　　　　　　　　FADE OUT TO COMMERCIAL.

INT. BRIAN'S ROOM. EVENING

THE BOYS ARE RIGHT where we left them, they're staring at each other in awe at their new powers. The hint of horror is gone. They're now clearly excited, their mouths agape.

BRIAN
　We did it.

ETHAN
　Sure, if we're not grading on accuracy.

FOUL LAUGHTER FROM A DEGENERATE CONGREGATION.

BRIAN
　He's really gone.

ETHAN
　Cut from the cloth of reality, just like that.

BRIAN
　(beat)

Cool.

MEREDITH
(Off screen)
Dinner's ready!

BRIAN
Quick, start reading again.

ETHAN
She's not even in the room.

BRIAN
So?

ETHAN
C'mon, man. If we're going to make your parents disappear, we can at least look them in the eyes.

M<small>EREDITH ENTERS</small>.

MEREDITH
Are you staying for dinner, Ethan?

ETHAN
Yes, ma'am. If it's not too much trouble, that is.

. . .

MEREDITH
No trouble at all... Where's Matt?

BRIAN
Date.

ETHAN
Bathroom.

BRIAN
He's on a date... in the bathroom. He's getting ready for the date.

MEREDITH
I thought he just got dumped?

BRIAN STANDS UP, affecting sympathy. He pushes her toward the door.

BRIAN
Please, Mom. I thought you'd be more sensitive to this sort of thing. He's going through a lot right now. I think Matt deserves a chance to get back out there without our cruel jokes.

MEREDITH
But—

BRIAN

>   (Pushing her through the door)
>   No buts, Mom!

HE CLOSES the door behind her.

ETHAN
>   (Yelling to the closed door)
>   We'll be down in a second!

BRIAN
>   Phew, that was close!

ETHAN
>   Cool, calm, and collected... I think you've made it to the big leagues.

BRIAN
>   Really?

ETHAN
>   Nope. But give it another hour.
>   Brian takes a deep breath and smiles. His friend <u>hugs the Demodorum tight to his chest.</u>

FADE TO:

INT. DINING ROOM. RIGHT AFTER

Brian and Ethan are helping themselves to massive amounts of mashed potatoes. There's a great heaping pile of food on the table. Preston is slicing a slab of ham slathered in ketchup. Meredith is sipping chardonnay. They eye the boys suspiciously.

PRESTON
　You know, boys, when we said we had plenty, it didn't mean you had to have plenty.

MEREDITH
　Is this a puberty thing?

Brian and Ethan share a glance.

BRIAN
　Yep, Mom. Nailed it as usual. We're going through a lot of puberty.

ETHAN
　That's right, Mrs. Parker. My bones ache as we speak. And—
　(He raises a hand to his face)
　Ope! I think I just sprouted a mustache.

PRESTON
　(Squinting)
　I think that's gravy.

. . .

LAUGHTER, cruel laughter.

ETHAN WIPES HIS MOUTH QUICKLY.

ETHAN
  Clean shaved and soft as a baby's bottom!

MEREDITH LOOKS TO PRESTON.

MEREDITH
  Is there something wrong, boys?

BRIAN
  Wrong, Mom? What's wrong? What could possibly be wrong—why do you think something is—

ETHAN SLAPS his hand across Brian's mouth.

ETHAN
  Brian is having stomach issues.

BRIAN
  Stomach issues?

. . .

ETHAN
    Yeah, diarrhea. *Verbal* diarrhea.

PRESTON
    Something's up. Where did you say Matt was again?

BRIAN
    Matt? Who's Matt?

ETHAN COVERS Brian's mouth again.

ETHAN
    Matt's on a date.

PRESTON
    (Nodding)
    Right. A date.

BRIAN
    Matt's just out there... dating away. Food's great, by the way.

MEREDITH
    (Suspicious)
    Thank you.

BRIAN

Hey, Mom. I was wondering if we could start a new tradition tonight?

MEREDITH
Depends what you had in mind.

BRIAN
Well, Ethan here has this book.

THUNDER.

BRIAN
(Continued)
Maybe we could let him read from it. Like dinner and a movie, but a story.

PRESTON
Oh?

MEREDITH
A book? I didn't know Ethan read!

ETHAN
Oh, I'm a big reader.

ETHAN PULLS the <u>Demodorum</u> from under the table.

. . .

ETHAN
And this bad boy is my new favorite.

PRESTON
Looks older than dirt.

BRIAN
You know, Dad, that's surprisingly accurate.

COLD LAUGHTER FILTERS in from the soundstage, because THEY REALLY DON'T KNOW.

ETHAN OPENS THE BOOK. The THUNDER ROARS outside. Preston and Meredith turn their heads to see RAIN PELTING their windows. WIND HOWLS.

ETHAN
C'thyn har'kh c'ollata...Ka'thar! Qi psol'uta! Barati narku!

THE BOYS LOOK at each other and smile wickedly.

MEREDITH
I don't feel so good.

PRESTON RUBS HIS CHEST.

. . .

PRESTON
   Me neither. I feel... strange. Like... I'm—

BRIAN
   Dying, Dad?

ETHAN
   Erased?

PRESTON
   (Standing up)
   Yes, actually.

Meredith turns to her husband, her eyes watering.

MEREDITH
   What's happening? Boys, what did you do?

Brian gets up from his seat to stand apart from the table. The wind SCREAMS outside. Preston and Meredith claw at their own bodies as they begin to waste away.

BRIAN
   Sorry, Mom. You're just collateral damage.
   (To his father)
   He was the one I wanted.

. . .

ETHAN
Yep, guess that'll teach 'em.

BRIAN
(High fiving Ethan)
Minneapolis, here we come!

MEREDITH
But—but—we love you.

MEREDITH BEGINS to bleed from her eyes. She's holding on to the table for support.

PRESTON
I just wanted you to be safe. That's all I wanted. I just wanted you to be safe. Please, please, please. Stop it. I don't feel so good. I'm dying, son. Do you understand what's happening?
(He looks at his hand, dissolving into wispy black liquid)
This is forever. I don't want to die. I don't want to be dead forever.

ETHAN
Yeah, my parents didn't want to either. But they haven't complained since.

WICKED, wicked laughter.

PRESTON AND MEREDITH weep openly as their bodies dissolve. They reach out to each other, but they can no longer touch. On contact, their bodies dissolve further. When they touch each other, it's like sand hitting sand. They scream as they realize they will be no more. These are their last moments and they can't even touch each other. They look upon themselves and their son in pain and horror. And then, they are nothing. Gone. Forever.

BRIAN
   (beat)
   Well, that's that.

ETHAN
   Yep. What's done is done.

BRIAN
   What do we do now?

ETHAN
   Whatever we want.

THE HOUSE IS SILENT. They look at the spot where Brian's parents used to stand and seem to consider what the rest of their teen years will look like. The silence is deafening. The STORM has stopped.

ETHAN
   To Minneapolis?

BRIAN
   (smiling)

I call shotgun!

WE FREEZE frame on the boys in their glee.

THE AUDIENCE RUSTLES in their seats, they get up to leave and tell their loved ones about the pilot they saw that one afternoon. They misremember jokes and retell them at dinner. They lie about the actors. "This starred so-and-so" or "It was the kid from that thing." But they don't remember, not really. Decades later, they recall sitting in a dark room, wondering which parts were real and which parts they invented. They wonder how the parents dissolved live on the soundstage. And then, they shake their heads and think, *No, no, no. That's not what happened at all.* And sometimes, when they're especially brave, they'll wonder what *did* happen that day. Why it lingers like a bad dream. Why the pilot never made it to air. But they do know one thing: that for 22 minutes, they were entertained.

AND THAT'S SOMETHING.

THE CREDITS ROLL. We realize we don't know anyone here. We don't know who these people are. We've never seen this show before. And yet it is here, right before us. It is alive and well and living. It exists. It exists. It exists.

CARSON WINTER IS AN AUTHOR, punker, and raw nerve. He's a minimalist weirdo, a conversational absurdist, and a vehemently bleak-minded artist making his home in the Pacific Northwest. You're looking for his words? You don't want those. But if you're going to insist, poke around the cold alleys of Vastarien, Apex, and The No Sleep Podcast. You want something longer? Okay, well, he also has a novella called Reunion Special. If that's not enough and you want more Carson Winter roiling in your stomach and mind, find him on Twitter @CarsonWinter3 or at carsonwinter.com. But please, be careful.

"Alive and Living (Pilot)" is illustrated by P.L. McMillan.

THE END OF THE HORROR STORY

PATRICK BARB

T hey say the snow's a distraction. It's the cold that kills you in the end.

--UNTITLED SLASHER FRANCHISE SEQUEL, 1ST DRAFT, BEN SHAW,1994

BEN SHAW MEDITATED on the final line from his first draft of the summer camp slasher franchise sequel he'd soon helm. With filming set for the most unlikely of locales—the frozen wastelands of Siberia, Ben had plenty of time to run those old lines over and over in his head.

First came the 30+ hour flight from LAX to the Russian airport in Irkutsk. Then, Ben crammed himself and his bags into a car that appeared leftover from the height of the USSR rather than from its more recent downfall. In a thinly-padded backseat, he sat beside his bulky, taciturn local liaison, a man named Grigori who'd also brought his pet mink. Finally, Ben suffered through a too quiet and far too awkward ride from the airport to the village outskirts tucked away in the heart of Siberia. The driver, whose name Ben never got, kept the privacy divider up the whole way there, though occasionally the throbbing bassline of some Russian dance-pop song filtered through to the back.

The cheery, bouncy pop didn't match Ben's mood in the slightest.

At least, I'm not in Germany having to listen to the Baywatch guy, Ben thought.

Over and over, he returned to his screenplay's words. Doing so also stirred up memories of Murray Goodwin, the movie's producer, and what he'd said during their first script notes call.

It wasn't pleasant.

"Mean" Murray G.—sower of an ever-growing number of embittered *former* personal assistants into the Hollywood ecosystem—pulled no punches. *"Look, pal, no one cares about the cold or the snow or what-the-fuck-ever. You wanna write that flowery shit, go work for my brother. You're not a writer anymore, kid. You're a director. You're Quentin, Jon Demme, one of the Scotts, you're that sex lies and videotape pervert. Second, forget that heebedy-jeebedy nonsense about the franchise being cursed cuz some folks had some bad luck in the past. This is a movie about a murdering mask-wearing psycho and this time he's loose during a snow-*

storm because we're...because I'M getting serious moolah for y'all to film in fucking Siberia. Nothing more than that."

The words *"Fucking Siberia"* rang in Ben's ears as the hired car pulled up to a concrete block of a building situated in the middle of nowhere. In one week, the entire cast and crew would stay in the Gulag-esque accommodations for the planned three-week shoot. But until then, it would be Ben, Emma his cinematographer, and Jennifer his leading lady, doing prelim work for the picture, with Grigori around to ensure they didn't freeze to death or get eaten by wolves or whatever other dangers might prey upon the clueless Americans.

As the driver put the car in *Park*, Ben wondered how the others were settling in. Their flight had arrived earlier in the day, so they'd been alone in the complex for many hours while Grigori and the driver fetched Ben. Ben's arrival came at nightfall, which meant he'd have to spend less time in the strange, unsettling building before work commenced the next day. But even then...*he was arriving at night—in the middle of nowhere.* He wasn't sure if he should envy the other Americans or vice-versa. It didn't seem like anyone came out as the winner.

Grigori launched himself from the back of the car, his long limbs exploding into the blistering chill outside. The big man left his mink curled into a fuzzy ball on the seat beside Ben. The creature gnawed on upholstery. Then, it unfurled and inched closer and closer to the American. Ben glanced down and noticed his nervously drumming fingers in the direct bite path of the tiny, beady-eyed mammal.

Suddenly, the door on his side of the car opened. Ben yelped, setting off a chain reaction, with Grigori's mink darting across the frightened American's lap, dragging its tiny claws across Ben's jeans on the way over before it finally leaped from the car and into the waiting arms of its giant owner. The Russian reciprocated with tender kisses on the creature's head, not paying attention to the small white claws pulling at the flesh on his hand. He muttered to the mink. "Seychas tixo. Ne budite ved'mi."

There were no lights in what passed for the parking lot outside the complex. From the darkness extending from Ben's side of the car and out to the surrounding woods, a loud cracking sound echoed. Ben figured it a branch on one of the spindly black trees he'd noted on their approach down the winding snow-packed road had become overladen with snow and broken free, before plummeting to the ground.

Still in the car, Ben's cheeks reddened, partly from the skin-searing high-whistling winds outside and also from the sting of embarrassment at being frightened by a tiny rodent. With a shudder, he unhooked his seat belt and slid out of the car. Grigori, his black-eyed mink resting on top of his head, didn't offer a hand to help Ben from the vehicle. "I thought you were big-time Hollywood horror director, Mr. Shaw. You're not scared of little Mishka, are you?"

"No, of course not."

Out of the car, feet on the ground, Ben surveyed the empty lot in front of the building where he was meant to stay for the duration of the shoot. A dusting of white that might normally seem like powdered sugar, appeared more like anthrax against the concrete gray. A faint bluish light emanated from the entrance and windows. The car's high beams shined bright against the building. The driver, with a chauffeur's cap sitting high on their head, remained in the front. Shadow-draped and silent.

His unease growing, Ben turned from the car. He was dumbstruck by the realization he had no memory of the driver's face. If pressed, he'd recall an androgynous figure in a drab gray uniform that looked as though it was once favored by some not-so-long forgotten secret police before being repurposed to fit whoever was ferrying one of *Variety's* "Hot Young Screenwriters of 1994" around through the Siberian countryside. But beyond that? Almost nothing.

Whoever the driver was, they had a pointed chin and cheekbones that could've been chiseled from an ice block.

Usually, Ben was great with faces. He'd read a life story in a stranger's glance. Watching movies on mute at the video store while he wrote his first spec scripts had helped him develop that skill. He blamed jet lag for his utter failure in this instance.

That and Grigori and this driver are just really fuckin' weird.

As though Ben thinking about him had summoned the Russian liaison, Grigori's hand, bare and mannequin smooth, fell on the director's shoulder. "It's good you're not scared. We have plenty more scary things here in Siberia than my Mishka."

Ben resisted the urge to scream at Grigori's cold, clammy touch. One embarrassing moment was enough. Instead, he bit his lip. A tiny dribble of blood trickled out but froze into a crystalline scab almost immediately. Ben hoped the Russian wouldn't notice.

Grigori held Ben's suitcases, including the scuffed silver briefcase containing the most essential piece of equipment for the pre-production work ahead—the neophyte director's very own home handheld video camera. Being trusted to helm what Mean Murray promised would be the franchise's re-emergence as a force to be reckoned with in the 90s, Ben pulled out all the stops in planning the shoot and pre-production. He was damned sure going to make using his *lucky* handheld part of those pulled-out stops.

"Shall we?" Grigori asked. His voice emerged like a plow dragged across frost-laden snow determined to break through and make itself heard.

Even though Ben filled his scripts with clever asides about the attractive Victoria's Secret supermodels he'd sleep with, Lamborghinis he'd drive, and other pie-in-the-sky dreams he planned on fulfilling once he made his mega-million-dollar spec sale and became the next Shane Black or Joe Eszterhas, Ben was lost for words again.

Indeed, he worried he'd lost all of his in-person banter and bluffing skills at the initial pitch meeting. "I'll write it, Murray. But only if you let me direct." (Never mind how Ben had rushed to the bathroom and sprayed about a half-gallon of fear piss into the nearest porcelain urinal once the meeting wrapped.)

Come to think of it, Murray signed off on the deal pretty quickly. Like he didn't give a damn one way or the other...

Standing outside the strange, severe, blue-lit building in an otherwise desolate part of Siberia, accompanied by his giant Russian liaison, Mishka the mink, and a driver of mysterious origin, that combination should've been weird enough. Yet, as the snow fell in heavy sheets around him and his escort, Ben couldn't shake loose the feeling that something else was wrong. He looked to his right, back to the car. Then, he looked to the left. Dark trees grew together in tight formations, marking the boundary between the barely-paved veneer of "civilization" and the skeletal woodlands beyond.

He rubbed the back of his head, making sure all his hair was under his knit wool cap. Then, he tried his damnedest to shake away the feeling of dread.

"Anybody live around here?" he asked.

When Grigori shook his head, his black hair swished left and right against the fur-lined collar of his coat. From her perch atop Grigori's head, Mishka twirled, offering her retort in squeaks, chirps, and bared chicklet-sized fangs.

"No person lives out here," Grigori answered as they passed through an enclosed atrium-like passageway from the outside and moved toward an inner set of doors. "Not any longer. Is now for Hollywood movie types like yourself. Rich capitalists coming to spread your Western culture all over us."

Ben couldn't tell if the big man was serious or joking. Or falling somewhere in between. *There's the dry wit of the Russians, I suppose.*

Lost in thought, not watching where he was going, Ben slammed into the back of Grigori who'd stopped mid-stride.

"Owww...*oh*."

Grigori turned, bending slightly so his face was even with that of the screenwriter/first-time director. The Russian's breath smelled of black-market liquor with hints of discontinued aftershave. Traces of wet fur made their presence known as well. Ben conceded that the fur smell probably came from Mishka.

Trying not to breathe too deeply, Ben forced a smile, playing the part of the too-cool, unphased auteur to the best of his ability.

He pointed back the way they'd come. "You're tellin' me with all those woods around us, there's *no one* living out there?"

Grigori straightened. In doing so, he appeared to grow a few more inches from what Ben remembered.

"In those woods? Only *vedma*."

"Vedma. You said something like that before. By the car. What's it mean?"

Acting as though he'd said too much, Grigori turned on his heels and marched forward, deeper down the flickering fluorescent-lit hallway extending past what looked like the abandoned check-in area of a YMCA. There was no concierge desk, no night clerk waiting with bellhops in the wings to take bags.

Ben shuffled along trying to keep up with his guide. He heard the whirr and grind of the old generators powering the structure through the walls or in the walls or wherever the hell the noise was coming from. He pictured Charlie Chaplin in *Modern Times*, getting caught in the clockwork gears. Except in his vision, the Tramp's guts spilled as metal teeth tore across his stomach and pierced his scalp. The sounds of mechanical consumption real and imaginary almost ate up Grigori's answer.

"*Vedma* is witch. In many forest here, there are…things we believe in long ago. Things more *scary* than your American monster-movie films."

Grigori counted the doors lining the hallway, muttering the numbers in Russian. Finally, he stopped.

He placed a massive hand against one drab, maroon-painted door among the other drab, maroon-painted doors, grabbed a handle, and pushed the door open. Then, after dropping Ben's bags inside the entryway, he flicked a light switch and illuminated the American's accommodations with the now-familiar pale blue light.

Ben entered the room, as Grigori faded back into the hallway. "Do you all still believe in witches?"

Grigori's face became a mask, all straight lines and bland features, a hollow visage ready to be filled. "Do you all still believe in a God?"

An awkward beat passed between the two. Then, Grigori sighed and continued.

"In USSR, we were raised not to believe in fairy stories. We were raised to believe in science. In the rational. In doing what is best for country. For Party. For Communism."

"Uh-huh." Ben glanced around the room. A bed and a dresser

were on one side and, on the other, a makeshift plywood false wall was erected in the far corner with a door that Ben assumed led to a toilet and sink. Observing the whole setup made for a quick tour.

"Of course, now there is no more cause. No more Soviet Union. So, perhaps we were wrong about other things as well…"

Ben forced himself to make eye contact with Grigori and nodded, seeking the most efficient way out of the conversation.

The big man got the hint and pulled the door toward him, shutting Ben away in the tiny room. Before the door closed all the way, Grigori made eye contact and added, "I will go and check perimeter. You start filming tomorrow, da?"

Ben shook his head.

"Oh no, no. *Actual* filming starts next week when the rest of the crew and actors get here. We've got a team coming from Romania. Murray promises they're the best. My camera that's just for pre-production work. That's what me and Jennifer and Emma are working on. I wanna check out the area and get a sense of the best places to film. Don't suppose you have any summer camp cabins out in the woods? I mean we can always use a cabin from the studio backlot and dress it differently…"

"Cabins? No. But…"

"Yeah?"

Grigori gave him nothing more.

"Okay, nighty-night."

The sound of the door clicking shut was as matter-of-fact as the Russian's abrupt farewell.

Once he was certain the door had completely closed, Ben pressed his ear to its thick surface, hoping to pick out Grigori's footfalls moving along the cracked linoleum hallway. The grind and crunch of hidden machinery filled his ears instead. It was like living inside a giant, hearing the ogre's teeth rubbing hard, one against the other in restless slumber.

Wrapping himself in overtired thoughts about giants and witches, Ben slept in a fog of fairy-tale nightmares.

[RECOVERED CAMCORDER FOOTAGE, SEPTEMBER 1995]

BEN SHAW: Is this thing...okay...

Camera's recording.

Do I...fuck...got a double chin at this angle...

[Noise, movement off-camera]

How's that? Better. Okay, yeah. This does look better.

Great, let's see...

Hi, everybody. This is Benjamin...Ben...shit.

[slight skip in recording]

Hi everybody, it's Ben. I'm the director of the movie. I also wrote its screenplay. With this latest installment of the [CENSORED] franchise, we're moving things out of the typical summer camp mill...mill-ew?...

[skip in recording]

With this installment of the [CENSORED] franchise, we're moving away from a summertime setting and instead going for a winter-set slasher. And, wouldn't you know, our producers found the perfect spot here in the Russian republic, up in Siberia. You should see it—and I guess you will soon—it's creepy as hell.

Now, to answer the questions you no doubt have: yes, it's as cold as it looks in those old spy movies; and yes, the icy, desolate terrain does look exactly like a Midwestern summer camp.

[laughter, coughing]

There's no phone in the room. No shower. The adapter works at least. So I'm charging the camera as much as possible. It's a Sony Video8 Handycam Camcorder, professional-grade, for you gearheads out there watching on your...

Whatever.

We'll edit these parts later.

AFTER HE FINISHED RECORDING HIMSELF, Ben peered out the narrow window set into the back wall of his room. The rooms on Ben's side of the hallway faced the back of the property. Given the prevalence of snow and darkened, leafless trees outside, Ben knew he wouldn't have to worry about him and Emma being able to identify creepy enough spots for Jennifer to run through.

Ben left his room and returned to the hallway of unremarkable maroon doors. He hadn't showered, but he'd managed to change his clothes and brush his teeth, before swiping a damp hand through his hair to put any bedhead he might've accumulated to rest. Every cough or scuff of shoes against the dusty hallway sent rippling echoes behind and before him.

Jennifer and Emma were waiting at the front of the building. Despite traveling without her usual Hollywood glam-girl entourage, Jennifer Leeson remained every inch the horror movie scream queen. Ben didn't know how Murray'd talked the starlet into flying out early for this skeleton crew assignment. But he was grateful to have her. *After all, a stand-in just wouldn't have been the same.*

As far as Ben was concerned, there was one Jennifer Leeson and this movie provided an opportunity for them to remind the world of that fact. Her pitch-black hair was straightened to her shoulders. Brown lip liner outlined magenta-hued lips. Her parka was unzipped to the navel revealing a black-ribbon choker around her neck and a burnt-sienna sweater whose fabric wasn't that thick given what poked quite visibly through from the other side. Her long legs were covered in gray stockings. Her ensemble met in the middle with the merest hint of a black skirt. Given the cold and the wild nature of their surroundings, Ben didn't consider it the most practical of outfit choices.

Still, he'd followed her career since her days dancing in hair metal music videos and he admired how she could still pull off a look that appeared both dangerous and stupid all at once. Of course, the way she rolled her eyes at him on his approach made Ben suspect Jennifer thought he wanted to sleep with her.

Which was true. It just wasn't *all* he wanted.

In contrast to the star's voluptuous and scantily-clad snow-bunny look, his cinematographer Emma Vinson wore a wool cap of her own, covering simple, short blonde curls. A scarf was pulled low enough so her lips were visible. The rest of her outfit consisted of practical GoreTex snow gear, embracing her in its puffy heat-retaining fabric.

Despite the fact she was his DP, Ben had only spoken to Emma once—on the phone, but he liked what he heard from her *and* about her.

"Murray tells me I'm to indulge your requests, keep you on track, and keep you away from Jennifer," she'd said.

She'd delivered the line in a deadpan Ben considered the best he'd ever encountered. At least until he'd met Grigori.

Truth was, Emma didn't exactly need to issue a warning about trying to hook up with their movie's Final Girl. Ben had heard the rumors about who his starlet dated…or used to date. He didn't feel qualified to toss his proverbial hat into the ring given the blowback that might follow.

Hugs and cheek kisses were exchanged when Ben made it to the front. To avoid smudging whatever make-up Jennifer might've applied, Ben made sure to kiss the air beside her cheeks. "You look amazing," he said, talking fast, hoping not to make a thing out of complimenting his star's appearance.

"I know." Jennifer smirked, no stranger to men making fools of themselves before her.

"Are we still catching a ride into…town?" Emma asked.

She held a wrinkled print-out of the rough itinerary Ben faxed to both ladies the week prior. Emma had worked in the business for at least half a decade longer than Ben. Her NYU student film "The Bagman's Gambit" was a cult hit on the underground tape trading circuit during Ben's time in undergrad. Since going to Hollywood, she'd gained a reputation as the best of the best among the new generation of cinematographers. The films she worked on always looked gorgeous. And yet, she'd never broken through to the big leagues, never worked with the big-name directors. And she'd never had a chance in the director's chair again. Ben felt hopelessly outclassed in her presence and he tried his damnedest to make sure it didn't show.

"I dunno," he answered. "Last night, Grigori said these weird things about the—"

"—woods." Emma interrupted, finishing his sentence. Her eyes sparkled with enthusiasm. "Yeah, yeah, strange guy but have you looked out there? It looks perfect. I can picture the dolly cam shot for the chase sequence. Or we could even do it handheld, long as I can watch where I'm going."

Ben smiled, having a pro like Emma agree with him made for sure-fire empowerment.

While the film nerds gushed, Jennifer extracted a lighter and pack of Marlboros from her jacket pocket. Soon, smoke curled around her head and the hand with which she held her cigarette, adding another layer of glamor to her appearance. The sizzle of the cherry at the end of the cigarette caught Ben's attention, then Emma's.

"Where is he?" Jennifer asked.

"Who? Oh, Grigori, he was supposed to be here with the car, and…" Ben trailed off, again struck by a strange sense that something was off with the scenery as it revealed itself to the trio, extending past the last set of doors. He couldn't put his finger on what exactly made for this unease, other than a certain flatness and constructed angularity to the corners of the building and the trees beyond. *Like something out of Caligari…*

As the leader, Ben didn't want to upset his starlet or his DP. So he kept those comments to himself.

"There's the car." Emma pointed to the makeshift parking lot.

Sure enough, the hired car from the day before remained in the spot where it'd dropped off Ben. He wondered if the car waited there all night long, idling.

He took a deep breath, then passed his camcorder to Emma with a nod. "Alright, showtime," he said.

Before she proceeded with filming, Emma paused to inspect the equipment provided. She checked the camcorder, like a doctor evaluating a bloody and screaming newborn, trying to find flaws noticeable on the outside but also understanding that any internal flaws wouldn't show until later, once it was put to use.

"Turn it on," Ben directed.

Emma flipped open the viewscreen and her thumb pressed the power button. "New tape?" she asked.

"Mostly."

"How do you want to do this?"

"I dunno. Just...keep filming. On me, on Jennifer, anyone we talk to. It can be for the LaserDisc features."

Training the camera on Jennifer, Emma flashed a thumbs-up to the side of the equipment. "Congratulations, dude," she said to Ben. "You just gave your first directions."

Ben couldn't hide the goofy smile breaking out on his face like acne, even if he'd tried. When he exhaled, he willed the calm to take him, blaming his earlier unease on first-time jitters.

Once they were headed toward the car, Emma started filming.

[RECOVERED CAMCORDER FOOTAGE, SEPTEMBER 1995]

[Boots stomp across cracked concrete, and asphalt]

JENNIFER: *Are we gonna talk to the old woman? What? Why are you all looking at me like that?*

BEN: *I'm not, I'm not trying to look at you in any way.*

JENNIFER: *Em will back me up. Won't you? Remember the old house. Like some cottage from a fairy tale or...*

EMMA (behind the camera): *You didn't say anything when we got in... and I was talking to Grigori.*

BEN: *Are you sure you're not thinking of the cottage from the original [CENSORED]? Did you watch the tapes I had messengered over? The bootleg print from the first screening? I know it's scary and all, plus you throw this place's weirdness into the mix and—*

JENNIFER: Whatever. It was right over there, through the trees. It was...

[Ben's fist knocks against the driver's window of the hired car]

BEN: Okay, okay. Maybe Grigori knows what you saw or our driver might. What's there... hey! Oh, were you sleeping? Sorry, we just... is Grigori here?

JENNIFER: Ask him about the house. Ask him.

BEN: Sorry, I'm Ben. You picked me up last night. With Grigori, um, I didn't get his last name.

EMMA (behind the camera): Pervak. Grigori Pervak.

BEN: Yes, him. With the mink, Mishka.

JENNIFER: That *name* you remember?

[Emma, laughing from behind the camera]

BEN: Listen, um....

EMMA (behind the camera, whisper): I don't know their name...

BEN: Okay, look, could you just tell us where—

[Ignition turns, tires spinning]

BEN: Hey! Hey! What the fuck, dude? You almost...shit!

[Car backs up, spins. Engine roars as it speeds down the road.]

JENNIFER: Oh. My. God.

EMMA (from behind the camera): You okay? Ben?

BEN: Yeah, I...damn. The dude drove like a crash-test dummy.

JENNIFER: I'm going back inside to find a phone. Then, I'm calling Murray. Then, I'm getting the hell out of here.

BEN: Jen, Jennifer! C'mon, wait! [...] Shit, she's not waiting.

EMMA (from behind the camera): Do you want me to keep...?

BEN: Ehhhh. No, I don't wanna waste the battery.

As Emma powered down the camera, Jennifer slowed as well, stopping a foot or two from the front of the building. Walking across the lot to intercept her, Ben watched the starlet's eyes drift away from the double-doored entrance and over to the forest. He called out. "Jen, you okay there?"

No answer. Walking closer, he tried again.

"What's going on? Do you see something? Someone out there? Is it Grigori?"

Emma followed close behind. The silent observer with the camcorder. A tiny, but growing part of Ben felt judged. Here he was, not even Day 1 of filming, and things were falling apart. He wondered if Emma was in touch with Murray, feeding him information somehow. He'd heard stories of Murray's spies. The way he'd use inside sources on film sets to take control of a picture and cut it up to shit.

At the tree line, dried-up husks of plant life existing in a permanent yellow and brown state of near-death were encased in ice but still moved like fingers sprouting from the earth, bending back and forth despite the lack of the slightest breeze.

"Jennifer? Are you okay? If you want, we can go back inside, maybe they have a CB or something and we can find someone in charge to help us and explain what the hell's going on here," Emma said.

Not wanting to let his DP have the last word or suggest *he* wasn't the one in charge, Ben felt obligated to chime in. "Yeah, we'll call Murray, somebody, and we'll get help to…"

"Shhhhhhhhh!"

Jennifer did a half-turn, so she faced her companions. Her cheeks were flushed and she held a finger to her lips. With her free hand, she signaled for them to crouch. She did the same and her gaze moved to the ground.

After duck-waddling to their star's side, Ben and Emma followed Jennifer's extended finger, as she pointed toward the frozen brush.

Black eyes sparkled from slick brown fur glistening with morning dew.

"Is that—"

"—Mishka," Emma said, answering Ben's query before he'd finished it.

Grigori's mink stood on hind legs at the tree line, staring back at the building—that anomalous, crumbling site of industrialized Russia. Ben wasn't sure *how* he knew the mink was the same shifty-eyed creature who'd scratched his hand the night before.

But he was certain of it.

Before anyone else spoke, Ben took the lead. "Hey buddy," he said, speaking in the sing-song voice he used when meeting a stranger's dog. "Whatcha doing there?"

The mink dropped to its forepaws, then tested the cracked asphalt before it.

Ben stepped forward.

Mishka withdrew, slinking back behind the trees.

Ben stopped.

"Okay, okay, easy, pal."

"Is that the same one?" Jennifer asked.

"I think so," Emma whispered in response.

Ben took another step forward, his heel scraped a chunk of debris, sending it spinning toward the trees.

Mishka turned tail, taking off like a bullet, tiny claws crunching the underbrush. Ben slapped his thighs in disappointment. "God-dammit!"

Facing his companions again, Ben noticed Emma had the camcorder open, preparing to film.

Then, Jennifer waved them all down again. "It's back!"

Sure enough, the mink's black eyes appeared, gazing from the trees. When the trio moved forward again, the mink remained still. Not moving forward or backward.

"It wants us to follow," Jennifer whispered.

"Really?" Ben and Emma both asked at the same time.

Their star nodded. "I've done a lot of kids' movies, worked with animals. Their trainers tell me I'm *really* in tune with their natural spirits."

Ben coughed, stifling a laugh. Ahead, Mishka bristled and looked set to flee. But she stood fast. The trio moved closer. The wheels turned in the young director's head. He gestured for Emma, aiming to get his cinematographer's attention.

"Start filming," he whispered.

She raised an eyebrow, not a question but the implication of one all the same.

"C'mon," Ben continued, "this is too weird not to get down. We won't go too far. Once we connect with Grigori, he can tell us what the hell's going on with that asshole driver of his and—"

Before he finished, Jennifer had crossed the tree line and entered the forest. Her cries for the mink drowned out Ben's words. "C'mere, Mishka baby. Come here."

Ben gave Emma a shrug and followed his star. Emma sighed. Then, she powered the camera back on.

[RECOVERED CAMCORDER FOOTAGE, SEPTEMBER 1995]
[Damaged footage, low-quality picture and sound for this segment.]
JENNIFER: ...such little legs. Didn't expect it to move so fast.
BEN: Yeah. [...] How we doing back there, Emma?
EMMA (behind the camera): Thumbs up here, boss-man. [...] What?
BEN: Could you not?
EMMA (behind the camera): But that's what you are, right? When I wanted to turn back a good...I dunno five, ten minutes ago, you told me you were the boss, yeah?
BEN: I didn't...I didn't mean...Jennifer, hold up. [...] I didn't mean it like that.
EMMA (behind the camera): Of course not.
[heavy breathing, frozen woodlands crunching underfoot]
BEN: You know Murray wants to cut the flaming chainsaw chase from the climax.
JENNIFER: There's a flaming chainsaw chase?
BEN: Oh yeah. I mean, not now. But it was in my original draft. I wanna put it back in. It's like...Exterior Forest Path - Night, the remaining survivors huddle together in the cold, snowy conditions. Tina (that's you,

Jennifer): My stomach's growling, I'm so hungry. Then, Katie says, 'I don't think that's your stomach...'

POW! The killer jumps from behind a tree wielding two chainsaws. Blades spinning, flames flickering across the teeth. Like Dennis Hopper in Chainsaw 2. But more fiery.

EMMA: Whoa. Hardcore.

BEN: Thanks. Thanks a lot.

[...]

BEN: I bet you could shoot it so it looked cool as hell.

EMMA: Yeah. I probably could.

BEN: What do you think, Jen? Jen? (Goddamn she walks fast.) Jennifer, can you please wait for us. I...

JENNIFER: Everything keeps disappearing in these woods. First that house, then this rat-thing...ferret...Next my career...

BEN: Hey. C'mon, we're gonna open huge. I swear there's still life in [CENSORED]. And Murray agrees with me.

EMMA: That's what he told you?

BEN: Huh?

EMMA: Murray told you they were planning a wide release?

"Yeah, he..."

When Ben turned around, he discovered Emma had already turned the camera off.

"What are you doing?" he asked. "Why'd you stop filming?"

Even Jennifer stopped her pursuit of the elusive mink and returned to join the others. "What's going on? Are we gonna keep looking for the big Russian guy and his pet?"

Ben held up his hand, cutting his starlet off. "We are. It's just...we need it on *film*. If it's on film that makes it real." The last part was addressed very pointedly at Emma.

But she shook her head. Ben recognized pity in his cinematographer's eyes. His stomach did flip-flops in response. Suddenly, he felt the thirst and hunger he'd ignored since he was picked up at the airport come crashing down on him. After the realization that he hadn't eaten anything in over half a day, the resurging fear came next, attacking him at his most vulnerable.

"You told Jennifer you sent her the tape of the first film's premiere. So I assume you watched it too, right? Were you a fan?" Emma asked.

"Of course. I mean, I was always more of a French New Wave, Hong Kong cinema kinda guy, but I'd heard the rumors. Knew plenty of gorehounds who flipped their shit for it. I remember they had that big piece in Fangoria..."

"Did you *watch* the movie?"

"I mean, I've watched plenty of slashers, Em. I know all the tropes and motifs. I've—"

Emma cut him off. "Have you seen the movie? The first one?"

Ben nodded. "Yeah, I saw it."

"Then, you saw the old woman in the woods?"

Ben nodded again. Everyone remembered the inexplicable appearance of the old woman in the woods in the middle of the goofy summer-camp slasher film. Not a drop of blood was spilled onscreen, but every ounce of it drained from audiences' faces after the infamous "old woman" scene finished. Then, the movie made another strange jump-cut, returning to typical summer camp massacre fare.

"So, you know about the curse? About the filmmakers' claiming they hadn't written, shot, or edited that particular sequence with the old woman and her cottage?"

"Yeah. I know all about it."

"Everyone who worked on the movie—the director, the editor, the main stars—they're all dead. I think only the writer's left. Though he's mostly doing script polishes now. Hasn't got *his* name on any other films. Just...the one."

Ben tried on a slight smile as he responded. "Phew. Good to see the writer made it."

Emma shook her head again, pity drifting toward frustration and disgust. "You don't get it, do you? The studio could look the other way over the past decade. As long as there were asses in the seats, they overlooked the misfortunes, the accidents, the ODs, and...you get the idea. But now...all the sequels, killers with the cornball catchphrases, cliché piled on cliché, nobody wants it anymore. Not quite life and death anymore. Not literally at least."

Ben's retort died before it left his lips. Realization dawned, falling on him like an avalanche. Pebbles to start, then sheets of snow burying him until his whole face felt like it was on fire.

"We're not getting the theatrical release, are we?"

Emma shook her head one more time. Ben looked at Jennifer. The starlet bit her lip. Then, she joined the silent chorus of no.

"Murray cut a deal with Blockbuster. And Cinemax. He told me the horror movie was dead, but he still wanted to squeeze the last dime out he could. Told me he just had to find someone dumb and desperate enough to fall on the sword, someone to blame for killing the franchise once and for all..."

Emma cut her answer short when Ben started wiping tears from his cheeks.

"Aww, kid, I didn't mean...it's just..."

Sniffling, trying his best to spurn his DP's attempted pity, Ben asked, "Jennifer, do you see Grigori's mink out there?"

Jennifer scanned the surrounding woods. Then, she nodded, filled with enthusiasm and pleased to be the center of attention again.

"Lead the way," Ben ordered.

Jennifer pushed aside branches and did as she was told. Ben looked back over his shoulder at Emma. "Action."

That time the command felt more like a burden than a pleasure.

[RECOVERED CAMCORDER FOOTAGE, SEPTEMBER 1995]

[...]

JENNIFER: Hey, you guys?

BEN: We're coming, we're coming.

JENNIFER: I think he's up here!

BEN: Oh, shit. Really? [...] C'mon let's go!

EMMA [behind the camera, heavy breathing]: Heh, heh, he. Okay, I'm coming.

JENNIFER: Hey there, Mr. Uh, Mister...

BEN: Grigori. Phew. Sorry, I, fuck, haven't run like that in...goddamn. [...] Grigori?

JENNIFER: First of all, Mr. Grigori Whatever, what the actual hell is going on? First, your driver ditches us in the middle of nowhere. Then, your little Fievel runs off, leading us on a wild goose chase through these scary fairy tale woods. And not the Disney kind either. Now you're standing there, leering at me, like you're Jeffrey Goddamn Dahmer. What the hell, man?

GRIGORI (?): Vedma...

EMMA (behind the camera): What's that? What'd he say?

BEN: Ah, God. He said...

GRIGORI (?): Vedma.

JENNIFER: Jenn-i-fer. That. Is. me.

GRIGORI (?): Ved'ma khochet, chtoby vy uvideli yeye dom.

EMMA (behind the camera): Hey, Jen, babe, why don't you come back here, okay?

BEN: Uh yeah. Come..c'mon. [...] Grigori, you just, you stay there. We're gonna...

EMMA (behind the camera, whispering): His voice, the sound's not coming from the right direction. I mean...it is, but it's also...not. Like it's all around us.

GRIGORI (?): [laughter]

BEN: Where are you going? Emma...

EMMA: I need to get around, something's not right here. He's not moving...

JENNIFER: His face isn't moving you guys. He's not...

EMMA: Jennifer Leeson, you get back with Ben right the fuck now!

JENNIFER: I wanna see. I wanna see it, too. I...

EMMA: No, don't...

[Jennifer screaming, Emma screaming]

[high-pitched animal screaming, whining, paws on the ground]

BEN: *Oh fuck. Oh, God. Oh fuck. Oh, God.*
[wet sound, like smacking lips, off camera]
JENNIFER: *Get them off! Get them off! Get them off!*
EMMA: *Jen, calm, fuck...Ben, these minks, rats, all these animals, fuck... how were they all inside his skin [...] Ben!*
JENNIFER: *No, no, no, no!*
BEN: *Jennifer! Wait! Come back!*
EMMA: *Jennifer!*
BEN: *She just...she ran off.*
EMMA: *Fucker.*
[squishing sound below]
EMMA: *Was she headed back the way we came? To that concrete prison or whatever the hell?*
BEN: *I guess. I mean, I think. I'm so turned around.*
EMMA: *Then that's where we're going. Follow me.*

HEADING BACK THROUGH THE FOREST, trying to find their direct-to-video starlet and a way out of whatever madness they'd stumbled upon, Ben considered how absurd it might be to offer an apology to Emma in their shared moment of distress. *Hell, it's the exact sort of thing the secondary protagonist does at the top of the third act, before making the noble sacrifice to kick off the climactic final confrontation...*

"How could she have gotten so far ahead?" Emma asked, interrupting Ben's musing.

"I dunno," he said, "She's quick. Quicker than I would've thought. Tough too. Ya know considering all this..."

He waved his hands wide, unable to articulate and hoping to capture the immense strangeness of the moment they'd been swept up in.

Emma held some drooping branches, allowing Ben to duck underneath them. "She is tough."

Ben waited for Emma, holding the branches from the other side.

They went side-by-side as often as they could unless some obstruction blocked their path. "You know what happened to her? Before all this?" Emma asked.

Ben shook his head. "I try to stay out of gossip."

Emma chuckled, her laughter colder than the air around them. "She turned down Lester. And he's not a man you say no to if you want a career out in Hollywood."

Ben stopped. "Lester? Like Lester Goodwin? Mr. Academy Awards? Mr. Prestige Pictures? Mister...our producer's *brother*?"

Emma nodded. "One and the same. But he's had her locked up with a contract and other legal wranglings, basically traded her to Murray to make this schlock—no offense—and stall whatever momentum her career might've had. Like she was some prized racehorse he'd shot in the leg. Just because he could."

"I had no idea."

"You never do," Emma whispered. Ben understood her *you* didn't refer to him alone. But it still hurt like hell all the same.

"This film's our purgatory," Emma said. "We're all dead. Now we're waiting to find out what happens next.

"So, what'd you do to end up here?"

Emma shrugged. "Me? I just like scary movies."

With more foliage blocking their path, Ben took the initiative to lift the branches allowing Emma to pass through. The ice encasing the bark leaked through the lining of his gloves, sending chills up his arm. With a slight chatter in his teeth, he told her, "I really do love your work."

"Thanks."

Emma passed through to the other side. She turned, ready to hold the branches from her side so her director could follow. Through the crisscross pattern of blackened branches, he caught glimpses, pieces of her face.

Then, the ice cracked under her feet. And Emma fell away.

Blackbirds took to wing, exploding from the trees the same as the tiny mammals had burst from Grigori or the Grigori skin-suit or whatever the hell it was they'd left behind when Jennifer fled. The birds' raucous cries nearly drowned out the quick grunt and subsequent keening wail from Emma on the other side of the tangle.

Panicking, Ben dropped onto all fours. Feeling at the ground, testing its firmness inch by inch, he sought a safe path forward. Spiked branches kissed by the cold scraped his coat and gloves, exposing his skin to the elements. He pressed on, listening to the gasps and sobs up ahead. When he finally made it to the other side, crunching and crashing through the tight-knit brush, Ben's fingers were curled and aching from the cold.

He rose to his feet, grasping the same branches that had passively attacked him moments before for support. Once he found firm footing again, he inched closer to where Emma had fallen.

The toe of his boot scraped the ragged edge of the hole she'd dropped into. Ben crouched, waddling back a bit so he wouldn't accidentally tip over and join her in the pit. Peering down into the hole, which looked to have been dug by someone's hands, Ben gasped.

Below, he saw the shattered layer of ice, the broken branches used as camouflage. And then Emma. Huge stalagmite-type icicles rose from the bottom of the pit, like teeth. And Emma was the morsel caught between them. The semi-translucent, blue-tinted spikes were soaked red at their tips, pressing up through Emma's neck, her limbs, her belly. Her lips moved, coughing up blood, then choking it down when it splattered back into her mouth.

"Emma..."

Her eyes locked on Ben. Wild, savage with pain. The proverbial fox in the bear trap, ready to gnaw off its paw for a slim chance at freedom and survival. Ben lay with his stomach flat against the ground and kicked the toes of his shoes into the permafrost for leverage. He crept forward propped up on his elbows until he dangled over the hole with his arms stretched toward Emma. Bypassing the surrounding spikes, his hands wrapped around one of her wrists.

He yanked, but nothing changed. It was like holding onto Silly Putty. She was a broken shapeless mass of flesh to the touch. "Come on..." Ben gritted his teeth and tried again. Emma's blood spray sprinkled his face. He inhaled the blackened serum up his nose. Ben tried again and again.

Until he noticed the spray of red and black slowing, and he let go of her arm. Down in the pit, Emma's eyes rolled back white. A pink tongue, quickly turning blue in the cold, lolled from between her lips. Blood bubbles popped, then froze. Then...

...nothing.

She's dead.

With life drained from her, Emma's corpse provided an up-close view of mortality. "I'm so sorry," Ben whispered.

Then, his eyes fell on the tiny red glowing light balanced atop one of the spikes that'd missed Emma. The camera was opened once again and switched on in the fall. Ben imagined the viewfinder displaying his broken, confused, and terrified face as it stared down into the death trap.

What hands could craft these? he wondered.

Up ahead, the sound of boots crunching snow caught Ben's attention. He dragged himself back from the hole and turned toward the noise. When he stood, his hands weren't empty. He'd grabbed the camera.

[RECOVERED CAMCORDER FOOTAGE, DATE UNKNOWN*]

[*While the events depicted appear to be in sequence with earlier footage from September 1995, the dates listed on the screen at this part of the recording are indecipherable glyphs.]

JENNIFER (off-camera): *I found it! I found the old woman's house!*

BEN (behind the camera): *Jennifer! Emma is, she's...Wait for me! Please!*

[running, heavy breathing, tree limbs breaking]

BEN (behind the camera): *Jennifer...I'm...*

[Thirty seconds of black]

BEN (behind the camera): *Oh my God. It's real. Like she said. The* cottage from the first movie. All that snow, it's...so beautiful. Gotta get closer and...

[low voices, women talking]

BEN (behind the camera): Jennifer! Psst! Jen! It's the old woman. Who the hell is she? What'd Grigori say...

GRIGORI (whisper): Ved'ma...

[car horn's blast, repeated over and over again]

BEN (behind the camera): Jesus! Who the fuc...oh shit, it's the car. It's the car! Hey, hey, hey! Stop! Stop!

[running, breathing]

DRIVER: Come! Come!

BEN (behind the camera): Oh my God! Look, I don't care why you took off...I mean, shit, I get it now. This is all...

"...TOO MUCH."

Sprawled across the backseat, looking through the open privacy divider, Ben was face-to-face with the same driver who'd left them behind that morning. Everything spilled out of him all at once, as though he'd slipped into the confessional and not the back of some geometrically strange Soviet vehicle. "There's an old woman back there. In the woods. She has..."

The driver, their features dark and obscure under the brim of their chauffeur's cap, shook their head. "Nyet, there is no woman."

Ben sat up straight, pressing buttons on his camera. "Dammit, there is. Grigori or whatever he was...he told me about the ved'ma, the witch in the woods. I think it was her. Look! Look at the view screen here and you'll see."

The driver took the camera, their finger slid across the fast-forward button, and then a long black nail flicked record.

Ben watched as the driver rolled down the window and threw the camera to the ground.

The driver turned back to the passenger. They took off their hat, and long white hair, white as snow, shook loose. The face beneath was plain, a blank, another mask. The driver's long fingers and longer nails scurried up the sides of their face, stopping below the scalp.

Then, they pulled. The smooth, unremarkable skin gave way, revealing something gray and wrinkled. Teeth sharp and glimmering like icicle spikes.

[RECOVERED FOOTAGE, SOURCE UNKNOWN, DATE UNKNOWN]
[The click and whirr of a camcorder, rolling against broken asphalt]
[an engine roaring]
[metal breaking, giant chicken legs emerging scraping the frozen ground]
[...]
[the soft, near noiseless pitter-patter of snowflakes against the lens.]
[cracking, breaking frozen glass]

POST-CREDIT NARRATION: *Following the disappearance of the film's star, director, and cinematographer, producer Murray Goodwin scrambled, sending over a former ad agency executive turned music video director to work with the remaining crew and actors to finish what many considered the last, dying gasp of the [CENSORED] franchise.*

The movie premiered to little fanfare—and many questions from the family and friends of the missing—in Blockbuster bargain bins and a late-night stint on Cinemax.

Years later, near the close of the decade, after the runaway success of the indie film, found-footage pioneer The Blair Witch Project, Goodwin released a re-cut version of the franchise sequel, incorporating the footage recovered from Ben Shaw's camcorder with no explanation for its inclusion. Many believed it was an attempt at re-creating that unsettling experience of the original film's "old woman in the woods" sequence. No answers were given regarding how Goodwin came to possess the footage.

Following an investigation of his brother for potential sex crimes that appeared likely to result in arrest and prosecution, Murray and Lester Goodwin both fled the country. Their whereabouts remain unknown to this day.

PATRICK BARB IS an author of weird, dark, and horrifying tales, currently living (and trying not to freeze to death) in Saint Paul, Minnesota. He is the author of the novellas Gargantuana's Ghost (Grey Matter Press), Turn (Alien Buddha Press), and The Nut House (serialized in Cosmic Horror Monthly), along with the sci-fi/horror novelette Helicopter Parenting in the Age of Drone Warfare (Spooky House Press). His debut dark fiction short-story collection Pre-Approved for Haunting is out Halloween 2023 from Keylight Books/Turner Publishing. For more information, visit patrick-barb.com.

"The End of the Horror Story" is illustrated by Jenny Kiefer.

THE FINAL AWAY GAME

J.W. DONLEY

The twenty seconds of anti-skip protection was in a losing battle with the bus's shocks and the rough state highway somewhere between Kingfisher and Enid. But I didn't notice. I don't think I could've told you what Adam and I were listening to. I was too busy wondering if Candice Fledecki had smiled at me, Gerard Beecher, a few miles back.

It was a long trip to the last away game of the season; the Tuttle Tigers hadn't won yet this year, so no playoffs. I, and most everyone else in the band, looked forward to the transition from marching to concert band. But, if she'd smiled, I'd happily spend an infinity of late Friday nights sharing a bus seat with Candice.

"G-man! You're not even trying to balance the Discman. Just ask her out," said Adam, my best friend. He'd hoped to get his own Discman for his birthday, but didn't. So, I shared my extra jack with him. I flipped burgers to pay for it, along with my growing horror library. His parents wouldn't let him get a job since he was always on the verge of failing a class or two. *Gotta study, study, study*, he told me with a smile. I'm pretty sure he was just avoiding the dreaded J-O-B for as long as possible.

"Since you aren't even listening, I'm gonna jam out to something more my speed. Let's see. *Vulgar Display of Power* or *101 Proof*?"

"Fine. You hold it though. I'm gonna read." Adam's music gave me a headache. I was more into, what Adam called, *brainy* shit, like Radiohead and The Pixies—I had to toss the booklet for *Surfer Rosa* though; my mom would've flipped if she saw the topless woman on the front.

Some Lovecraft would take my mind off Candice. I was on my third pass through a best-of collection and about to start on *The Music of Erich Zann* again. I dreamed of becoming a composer and one day writing the music the old man played night after night, keeping the demons at bay.

The bus rolled to a stop over crunching gravel.

"Pit stop!" Mr. Straker yelled from the front of the bus. "Pee if you gotta."

Candice was in the gas station before I was outside—*Like I would've said anything if I'd had the chance.*

A long line had already formed outside the Honeybucket off to the side of the parking lot. Standing must've rushed everything into my bladder because I was about to burst. A clump of scrub brush behind the porta would have to work.

After relieving myself on some dry dirt, I started back through the overgrown weeds. My toe caught on a stone, and I stumbled, nearly slamming my face into a patch of cacti. Sand and rocks embedded in my scraped palms. My first instinct was to poke my head up and check that no one saw me fall. I didn't need to give more fuel to the snare jocks. It was already enough putting up with the usual 'nerd' and 'gay' stuff. Anyone not currently dating a girl must surely be gay —thus is the logic of the drum slappers. It's not a rule that snare players must be shitheads, but that was the case at my school.

I started lifting myself off the ground, convinced no one witnessed my spill. I froze with my elbows straightened. A strange stone rested on the dry-cracked dirt between my hands. There were stones all around, but this was different. It had a hue that seemed to morph as I stared. Metallic greens, cerulean blues, obsidian blacks. And in its center; a symbol. Looking directly at it made it invisible, but it appeared in my periphery. Sorta like trying to see the dimmer stars amongst the brightest that make up the framing of the constellations. It resembled a ball of snakes or tentacles appearing to writhe, even though it was only a picture on a rock. Then, from one instant to the next, the stone was gone, leaving only an impression in the dirt. But the strange morphing symbol was burned into my vision.

"You okay?" Candice asked from the edge of the lot. "I saw you fall. Are you hurt?"

I'd rather one of the snare jocks had witnessed my fall.

"Yeah. Uh. Just tripped."

Before I could say anything to stop her, she was at my side and helping me stand. I couldn't speak. The feel of her hand on my arm drove away the unease of the weird after-image burned into my sight, which had already faded to nearly nothing.

Her eyes were a beautiful deep blue, unchanging and arresting. I had to force myself to look away. I couldn't ruin this once-in-a-lifetime chance.

"Thanks," I said.

"What were you reading back on the bus? The cover looked awesome, with all those skulls." Her smile was everything. I could float to the moon there and then.

"Just some Lovecraft. He wrote a bunch of horror stories in the twenties and thirties. Cosmic monsters, evil books, cults. All that creepy stuff."

"Sounds cool. Maybe I can read some with you on the way home? I have a little flashlight we can use."

"Definitely!"

"Looks like someone's in love!" yelled Justin, the lanky lead snare, leaning out a bus window. "Isn't your boyfriend Adam gonna be jealous? I didn't know you swung both ways!" In the next window was Bradley—a bass drummer, who wore his usual white cowboy hat—laughing at everything Justin said.

Heat rose up my neck and face but Candice and I both rolled our eyes.

She smiled and blushed and said, "Nice. We should get back to the bus though. See you later tonight."

With that, she turned and trotted across the lot. Her oversized army jacket bounced with each step, causing the giant anarchy symbol scrawled on the back to flutter.

THE GAME WENT AS EXPECTED. The Tigers lost, and we played our pep tunes from the stands and our *West Side Story* medley half-time show. I flubbed a few notes on my trumpet solo in 'Maria'—it was hard to focus when all I could think about was hanging out with Candice on the ride back. Adam didn't even tease me during the game. I think he was rooting for me, or he was worried he'd lose Discman privileges for the ride back.

After loading our instruments and equipment back onto the trailer, we hopped on the buses and changed out of the heavy uniforms. It always felt odd changing in front of everyone, especially the girls, but we were all practiced at it and wore shorts and t-shirts underneath.

Everyone had a special stench after an evening of marching and music, but that was a fact-of-life. We lived with the smell of sweaty teens for the ride back. When it was warmer, most vented their windows to siphon off the bad air. That night it was too cold.

I looked back to Adam a few seats behind. He already had his headphones on and gave me a sly smile. Toward the back half of the bus many were settling in for some rest, some with cowboy hats pulled down over their faces—some of them did work on farms, but most would never come closer to a cow than a Big Mac.

After a quick re-application of Speed Stick, I was ready for the ride back with Candice.

With the bus rolling out of Enid stadium, Candice and I shared her little flashlight to read *The Music of Erich Zann*. I kept looking up to check her face, eager to gauge her reaction to the story. Each time, she caught me and smiled before motioning to return my attention to the book.

We hadn't reached the next town before we finished the story.

"That was so cool," said Candice. "I wish the stuff they make us read in class was that good."

"I know, right? And that was one of his more tame stories. Wait until you read *At the Mountains of Madness*. So fu— I mean, freaking awesome."

It felt strange, finally talking with the girl I'd been crushing on since the start of last year. My nerves were settled, even. It felt like chatting with Adam, but better. He didn't like reading, even the Lovecraftian stuff. He was more focused on thrash metal and learning to rock out on his beater guitar. If he *were* to get a job, it would be to buy an amplifier.

"Is the *Mountains* one in here too?" asked Candice.

Before I could answer, the afterimage of the symbol with its mass of writhing snakes flashed in my vision, and a blast of sound bombarded my skull like a herd of out-of-tune trombones.

"Shit," I said, putting a palm over my right eye. "Did you hear that?"

"Hear what? Are you okay?" Candice sounded genuinely worried. Maybe she thought more of me than I knew.

"I don't know. That was so loud. And I can't see anything other than this bright symbol."

"What was loud? I didn't hear anything. And what symbol?"

"Ah shit! Hold on!" the bus driver yelled, then slammed on the brakes. The bus erupted in a slurry of screams and items slamming to the floor as the tires locked and the bus skidded along the highway. Even Mr. Straker joined in on the screaming.

I peered over the seats as Candice and I braced ourselves. Slightly ahead, in the middle of the highway, was a bonfire. We came to a stop only a few yards from the licking flames. It was a huge pile of burning, mutilated cattle. Horns and hooves stabbing from the light in haphazard patterns. How many cattle would it take to make a bonfire so big, to block an entire highway? It smelled like one of my dad's backyard cookouts.

"Okay kids," said Mr. Straker, now standing at the front of the bus aisle. "Settle down. I'll go out with the driver to see what's going on. I want you all to stay in your seats and stay calm."

The bus door swung open, ushering the only two adults out into the night. Mr. Straker pushed the doors shut behind him. The heat of the bonfire made the glass of the pull-down windows hot to the touch.

The pain and symbol both faded from my head.

"Why would someone do this?" asked Candice. "All those cows."

I had no answer, but I met her worried gaze. The flames danced shadows across her face. She grabbed my hand and squeezed. I hadn't realized my need for the same comfort and squeezed back as we peered out the windows waiting for the bus driver and Mr. Straker to return.

No one on the bus spoke, there was nothing to say. Nothing to be done.

Eventually Evan Stevens, first chair clarinet and treasurer on the student council and only student in school to have a cell phone, spoke up. "I already checked for a signal. I don't think there are towers out here yet. Should we check on them?" A lot of the school jocks called him Mr. Banana Phone because his Nokia was one of those flip phones from *The Matrix*.

"Oh! Absolutely not!" yelled Bobby Pirelli, our lone sousaphone player, sitting in the back of the bus amongst the percussionists. He wasn't friends with them or anything, he just liked sitting in the back of the bus, and Bobby was a stout boy that could throw a serious punch if antagonized. "He's probably dead or something."

"Well, we should do something," said Evan.

A flurry of arguments erupted, many backing Evan but with no plan.

Candice pulled back into the corner of her seat like a snail hiding deep in its shell. She pulled her knees to her chest and nearly disappeared into her oversized army jacket. I was scared shitless myself, but someone had to stand for reason. Why was no one else speaking up?

"Quiet!" I yelled. I was surprised at both myself and the quiet in response.

Evan, who had worked partway toward the back of the bus, turned his attention from arguing with Bobby.

I spoke before he could, addressing the whole bus, "We don't know what's out there. It could be anything. I mean, Mr. Straker and the driver aren't back yet, we should wait for them. At least here, we are together and safe."

"Gerard's as smart as they come. I'm with him," said Bobby, breaking the silence.

"This is bullshit. I'm not listening to some fairy and his fatso butt buddy. I'm with Evan," said Justin. The way he flinched, he probably felt Bobby's dagger eyes stabbing him in the back of his head. "Evan. You lead, and we'll follow."

Evan, the goody-two-shoes student council member, scanned the other faces, looking for further support.

"Let's get out there and see what's going on," said Evan, voice more sure than before. "Feel free to follow me, or continue to hide in the bus like Gerard and his goth *girlfriend*."

I felt the blood flush my face. I wanted to punch him, but it wasn't the time.

Bobby stood in the back as if to block those who would take the rear exit. I jumped to block Evan, but he easily pushed me aside to get to the folded doors.

Evan pushed open the double door and the heated night air flowed in, carrying that savory smell of charred steak. Something seemed off about it though. A smell of rot rode the top and stuck to the inside of my nose. An acrid overtone.

"Wait! There's Mr. Straker!" A freshman flautist with a bowl cut and braces shouted.

Evan stopped pushing with the doors only half open. "It's him. I can see him."

"Hold that door closed. Something's not right," I said.

And it was him, but he wasn't walking. His head didn't bob with each step. Instead, he glided into the firelight.

Eyes wide, staring at our approaching director, Evan grabbed the lever used to control the door and held it in place.

Everyone stopped their arguments and crowded that side of the bus to get their own look at Mr. Straker.

I joined Evan at the door lever. Mr. Straker stared through the glass with an empty expression, his eyes watery and the bags under them, puffy and red. He then pounded the glass with a closed fist and studied it from bottom to top as if he'd never seen a school bus before.

"Mr. Straker," said Evan. "Are you okay?"

He stopped prodding the door and looked directly at Evan.

I saw a tear run over Evan's cheek.

"Please. Mr. Straker. Please tell me everything's okay. My phone's not working. I can't call my parents. Please."

Again, a sharp pain shot through my head as the symbol burned into my vision like the after-burn of staring into a spotlight. Mr.

Straker started to dig at the rubber seal between the folding doors, attempting to pry them open.

"Stop! Please stop!" screamed Evan, frantically holding the lever fast to keep Mr. Straker from getting in.

Adam rushed to help control the handle as I shook the fresh pain from my head, clearing my vision.

The bus erupted in more confused fear.

Screams, prayers, sobbing.

"What the hell is that?" yelled Bobby from the back. "There's something coming out the back of his head!"

Mr. Straker got a hand in and nearly grabbed Evan's shirt. I hit him with the spine of the Lovecraft book to get him to back off.

A meaty umbilical tube, throbbing with light, punctured the back of Mr. Straker's head. Each pulse pushed along the appendage from the sightless dark beyond the fire's light. It was like his bursts of energy used at tearing and pulling the bus doors grew with each pulse into the back of his head. What was once Mr. Straker began to scream and grunt with his effort. His eyes glowed with the same pulsating rhythm.

"Fuck this!" yelled Justin over the din of screams. "I'm out!"

Before I could yell to stop, he had his bus window down, and he was crawling through the smallish opening.

Then he was gone.

Ripped away through the window like a wet rag doll through a tiny hole. Blood painted a three-seat radius around the open window and ran down the glass both in and outside the bus. His surrounding percussionists were still in shocked silence as they realized they were covered in their bandmate's blood.

"Holy fuck! Holy fucking fuck!" screeched Bradley, shaking bits of his friend from his cowboy hat.

"Close that window! Now!" yelled Bobby. No one near the open window budged, so Bobby abandoned his post at the back. Pushing the panicking teenagers out of the way, he reached the window and pushed it up, the latches clicking at each stop until it snapped shut at the top. "No one else touches the Goddamned windows! Got that?"

I was relieved to hear another voice of reason.

Out the driver's side window, the bus driver held the bloodied body of the snare player. Another meaty appendage pulsing with light fed into the back of the driver's head. He tore an arm away from his victim and held it high up, the blood dripping into his mouth. The light began to pulse in reverse as he gulped down the blood. With each swallow a ball of light flowed along the umbilical and deep into the darkness behind the bonfire of cattle.

Candice was curled into a ball on the floor in front of our seat, wrapped in her jacket. Only her eyes shone through the opening at the top, but it was enough to see the absolute shutdown. She stared forward at nothing and did not move. Her breath was fast.

"Keep holding that door!" I yelled to Evan and Adam as I hopped into the driver's seat. I cranked the engine and threw it into gear.

I made a sloppy three-point turn and felt a sickening crunch as the bus rolled over something. Human, animal—I didn't care. I wanted to get us out of there.

"Wow, I didn't know you drove stick," said Adam.

"I'm getting us out of here," I said both to myself and to Candice.

I pointed the bus tires in the other direction and slammed the gas to the floor. The diesel engine jumped and sputtered at the sudden push, but engaged, and the bus rolled onward. It was wonderful to see the bonfire fade over the hill in the rearview mirror. What was once Mr. Straker watched as his students left him behind.

Everything was pitch black beyond the illumination of the bus's headlights except for a sickening glow ahead.

"Is that another..." said Adam beside me.

I eased up on the gas, but not enough to trigger worry from those who had yet to notice the second bonfire. "Get Bobby. You and him, talk to the others and gather up anything that could be used to defend ourselves."

Others noticed the slowdown and fresh prayers and tears swelled.

There was movement around the fire. Other people and large animals, each with their own luminescent umbilical cord reaching over the flames and into the darkness beyond.

Ahead and to the right I noticed a gravel drive leading into a field. I remembered the turnoff from the drive out to the game in daylight. There would be a red barn out in the middle of that corn field.

I slowed the bus to turn onto the rough path meant for farm trucks and grabbed the intercom mic. A back wheel dipped into a drainage ditch—I'd forgotten I was driving a bus and had cut the turn too short, eliciting a handful of curses and shouts from the rear.

"Okay, I have a plan," I said as we all jounced side to side in our seats. "Please work with Bobby and Adam to gather up anything we can use as a weapon. Pencils, lyres, whatever. I know this sounds crazy, but all this is crazy." I held up the copy of Lovecraft's collection I'd tossed on the dash. "In all the scary stories, the monsters only come out at night. There's a barn up ahead. Whatever is out there expects us to be in here. I say we abandon the bus and hide in that barn until morning. We go from there when the sun comes up. I know it's not much to go on, but it's all we have."

I looked over to Evan, who stood in the entry well. He nodded in agreement.

"Any objections?"

There were none.

The headlights flooded the front of the barn, and I stopped the bus.

I was impressed with the resourcefulness of the band. Many wielded inside out three-ringed-binders with the rings bent open as defensive claws. Little Peter Beauchamp didn't look upset about having to dump his meticulously sorted and sleeved POG collection and was ready to go into battle with the metal hook of a lyre in one hand and the open binder rings in the other. Adam held the Swiss Army knife he liked to hide in his denim jacket pocket. Even Candice was out of her shell and brandishing a pair of sharpened pencils. Bobby only had his fists, but he seemed as fierce as any of the others.

Adam handed me the Discman. It had a few spots of blood spatter across the digital display. I popped out the Pantera disk and snapped it in half, creating a shiny cutting weapon for each hand. I felt a little bad breaking my friend's disk, but I would buy him Pantera's complete discography if we survived.

"Okay, when I open the door, get out of the bus and run into the barn as fast as possible. We'll regroup once we're inside."

I began to open the door when once again the symbol burned into my vision. I flung the door open and screamed, "Everyone, go! They're here!"

Before more than a few students were out the door, something slammed into the side of the bus and almost turned it on its side. My vision returned and outside was a massive lump of gelatinous flesh made up of the same meaty glow as the umbilicals. The symbol in my head flashed an outline of the creature. It had tendrils writhing from its central mass, each ending with the slack body of some animal or human, each glowing with an emanating power, each like a lure dangling in front of deep-sea angler fish. But instead of a small point of light these were glowing, reanimated corpses used as appendages to feed the central maw.

It attacked the bus, mouth wide and ready to swallow anything in its path.

I grabbed Adam. "Get Candice and everyone else into that damn barn! Now!"

Most of the back of the bus was empty when the creature bit off everything beyond the center seats. Bobby barely dodged the bladed teeth that tore away metal and faux leather seating. He didn't flinch. Instead, he pulled the few remaining students behind him and stood his ground, feet planted, and fists raised. Mr. Straker, glowing and on the end of a meaty appendage, came forward. Bobby collapsed the corpse's face with a solid punch and it backed away. Next, a creature like a mountain lion, another victim of this horrible monster, attacked on another appendage. Bobby tried to swing his other fist into its face, but missed, and the cat-thing grabbed him with all of its claws.

"You motherfucker!" he yelled, before it pulled him out of the bus and tossed his body into the central creature's maw.

Only five surviving band members remained on the bus, scrambling to get free of the carnage as I stood transfixed.

Outside, many of the others ran in panic, attempting to avoid the searching bodies feeding the large beast. I screamed at them to get to the barn, but it made no difference.

Peter fought hard against what could've been a cow mutated like the monsters from John Carpenter's *The Thing*. He slashed it a few times with the binder rings before its body unfurled like a bloody Venus fly trap and snatched Peter from the ground.

Adam waved frantically from the barn door. As I scrambled over the rutted path, others around me were snatched up and ripped in half. There was nothing I could do for them, so I ran into the barn, tears streaming down my face.

Adam, Candice, Evan, and a handful of others were inside. Far fewer than half of the band had made it.

"Okay, everyone. Search for somewhere we can shelter." I had to keep these few of us alive.

Everyone spread out looking for anything amongst the rusted farm equipment and stacks of hay. There were a few empty animal pens, but they wouldn't provide real protection.

"Over here," yelled Evan from the back, behind a tractor.

We rushed over to find Evan climbing down into a tornado shelter dug into the barn floor. No one said anything; we simply followed him in.

We all settled in for an uncomfortable night on benches set against the walls of the shelter. There were a few canned goods, all the generic-yellow of the Always Save brand blandness, but no can-openers. Bradley collapsed into terrified sobs when he sat down across from Candice and I, still covered in Justin's blood.

The hours passed in the dark of the bunker. An occasional whispered conversation asking about family left behind and God's plan. Me? I avoided conversation. What god would set that creature loose on a busload of teenagers? God had no place there. He may've been watching over our families back home, but we were on our own.

"Are we going to be okay?" asked Candice, whispering in my ear. These were the first words she'd spoken since the onslaught on the bus.

I thought hard about making promises I could not keep. Her body slumped when I did not respond.

"Yes. We will be fine. I promise." And I meant it, I really did.

I still do.

I hugged her close and kissed her on the forehead. She fell asleep in my arms in the dark of the bunker while the beast searched the barn above us for meat.

Eventually I too fell asleep. My nightmares filled with the faces of every victim, that writhing symbol branded into their foreheads. Each screamed in despair as the beast tossed them into its great maw.

I'VE BEEN in therapy for months now. My parents sympathize with the trauma I've been through, but no one believes my truth. They all think it's some sort of coping mechanism for what really happened.

No one will listen.

In the bunker I woke with a stabbing headache behind my eyes. It was strange now for that symbol to be absent from my vision. Slivers of daylight bled around the edges of the shelter door. I could see everything in the bunker clearly. And the bunker was empty.

Only I remained.

I scrambled up and out of the bunker and into the barn.

Also, empty.

"Candice! Adam!" I ran out the barn door and into the morning light.

The remains of the bus were also gone. And none of the expected gore littered the yard around the barn or the edges of the corn field.

There was no evidence of any of the horrors we had gone through. And no witnesses...other than me.

Everyone was gone.

The police are convinced that Mr. Straker and the bus driver drove off, kidnapping the whole bus and that, somehow, I escaped. A nationwide search continues for the missing bus or any of the other band students.

Last week I ran away from the hospital.

I manage to steal enough food from gas stations to survive in the corn fields north of Kingfisher.

I spend my nights hiding in haylofts.

But my days?

Those I spend searching the ground in every field and parking lot between Kingfisher and Enid.

I try to remember the symbol. It must be the key—the pass between here and that other place where my friends wait.

Where Candice waits.

Where *it* waits.

I have to find the stone again.

In the last few days, I've started seeing faint reflections of the symbol when I first open my eyes in the mornings. I must be getting closer.

I will not give up.

I made a promise.

J.W., HWA and HOWL Society member, lives with his wife and son in the Pacific Northwest where the Cascade Mountains meet the Salish Sea. Growing up he enjoyed R. L. Stine's Goosebumps books. Later he discovered Mark Danielewski's House of Leaves and authors like Clive Barker and Laird Barron. In July 2021 J.W. published Cats of the Pacific Northwest, a horror chapbook available from your favorite booksellers. J.W.'s short stories have appeared in anthologies from both Dim Shores and HOWL Society Press. You can sign up for his newsletter at JWDonley.com and follow him on Twitter @JWDonley.

"The Final Away Game" is illustrated by Jenny Kiefer.

ABOUT A GIRL

J.V. GACHS

If Kurt Cobain were still alive, I wouldn't need an exorcism right now.

That's me in the corner over there. No, not the worried nun. The teenager with dark circles under her eyes, biting her nails as if they were her first meal in a month, looking as languid as girls in underwear ads.

Sister Inés grabs my hand to stop me from biting into my flesh *again*.

I respond by spitting in her face.

Yeah, I know, I know. It's shitty of me, *poor Sister Inés,* and all that. But, what can I say? I didn't choose to be here or to be possessed by a little girl in a communion dress.

If Kurt Cobain were still alive, Sister Inés wouldn't be covered with spit. Which is *probably* more disgusting than it should be. Brownish, bloody.

For you to understand—and excuse—my behavior, I have to rewind a bit. Not just a few days. But a whole month.

IF YOU'RE like me and have no belief whatsoever in the afterlife, God, or any supernatural phenomena, you will agree that Ouija boards *shouldn't* work. At all. But, as an aspiring horror film director, the chance to shoot a séance with my friends as the unaware main characters and turn it into a short, unscripted film full of practical special effects... How could I resist?

"Tomorrow is the first anniversary of Kurt's death," Anahí said with tears in her eyes as we left for lunch.

At that moment, the light bulb went off in my head.

"Why don't we try an Ouija board to contact him?"

"Verónica, *tía,* that's dangerous," replied Virginia, who has always been by far the most gullible of us all. She was the only one who kept going to catechesis after communion, and is still going to church every Sunday.

"We could ask him what really happened that day."

Anahí's delighted voice indicated to me the idea had already caught on and Virginia's protests were going to be of little use against the tsunami of passion I had just unleashed.

Our parents allowed us to spend Friday night together in my room, and we prepared everything according to the latest issue of *Más Allá*. While I was changing my tampon in the bathroom I had the stupidest idea—which is why I'm now the one tearing my skin to shreds from the itch of possession—to use my menstrual blood to trace over the letters we had already drawn on the Ouija board at lunch that day. It looked creepy as hell after I was done. Virginia was too scared to notice, but Anahí shrugged and rolled her eyes when she saw it. She was too invested in the séance working out that she didn't protest. Good. My short film was going to be the best thing to happen to horror in the 90s.

Anahí brought candles and Virginia brought her rosary. My Hi8 camera, tripod and all, was ready. Faking a haunting couldn't be that difficult, right? Spell some lyrics to make Anahí go nuts, and freak out Virginia by spitting corn syrup on her. Easy peasy.

WE MADE sure my younger siblings were fully asleep before we started our little experiment with the afterlife, so it had been dark for hours by the time we started. We sat on the floor, surrounded by vanilla-scented candles. Anahí wore her In Utero t-shirt and Virginia rolled her rosary in her hand, looking like she was about to pee herself. Between us lay the Ouija board, with a shot glass as our planchette in the center of the bloody letters.

I hit record and, at first, everything unfolded as you might expect. Putting our fingers on the shot glass, we looked into each other's eyes trying to hold our nervous laughter, and Anahí, as an expert on the spirit we were trying to summon, played Mistress of Ceremonies.

"Kurt, love of my life, I know your spirit is here because you are always on my mind. Now, I beg you to take this opportunity to contact us."

I decided it was best to wait for the second or third attempt to push the glass and carry on with my plan for a terrifying, realistic, and all-around fucking great short film.

"That's not going to get you anywhere," Virginia said. Surprisingly.

"What do you know?" the Mistress of Ceremonies whispered, breaking character completely.

"I go to church more than you do, so obviously there are things I know *a little bit more* about."

And so, she proceeded with a ceremony I'm not disclosing here. I bet you would love to know, wouldn't you, you little demon worshiper? Sorry to disappoint. Starting an outbreak of demonic possession is not in my plans (for now). SO! Flash forward ten minutes!

It's not like I *saw* her. Not exactly, at least. I just knew she was there, in front of me, standing, in her white communion dress. Crying. Suffering.

Hating.

Her presence was as clear to me as my feet, even if I couldn't see them tucked under my knees. The certainty of her existence was overwhelming. The fact her hatred seemed locked onto me... wasn't exactly pleasant, either.

Neither Virginia nor Anahí noticed the girl's presence. They had been left behind in a world where Ouija boards are teenage jokes, used to freak one another out, while I had just crossed a line no one should ever cross.

I stood very still. Mute. I didn't know what to do. How to get rid of the girl, how to send her back to the foul hole she had creeped out from.

"Well, nothing. Next year we'll try again," Anahí sighed. "My words were as good as yours it seemed, *Señorita Religiosa.*"

"Don't count on me, I've been scared enough tonight, all for nothing," Virginia replied, kissing the pink plastic beads on her rosary and making the sign of the cross.

"Come on, let's pack up," Anahí said. I did not turn to look at her. My whole body was frozen. Trapped in amber. "Stop being an asshole, come on," she scolded me.

But I remained motionless. Even blinking was out of the question.

Then, fed up with what she must have thought was my usual nonsense, Virginia pinched my arm so hard it was impossible not to scream and turn to look at her, rubbing the sore spot with my hand. Opening my mouth was all the girl needed to come inside me.

An inordinate force hit my chest like a wave, but unlike a wave, soaking me was not enough. It penetrated beyond my pajamas, beyond my skin, beyond my bones, muscles, and tendons. It filled me to overflowing.

I was a girl and I was hollow.

I was wearing a white First Communion dress.

The folds of the dress' tulle brushed my skin from the inside. Her vocal cords had been torn out from howling in pain, so much so now she couldn't even borrow mine to scream. All that came out of my mouth was an aching, airless, torn whistling sound. Her body inside mine felt wrong. Her skin was buckling, sagging. There was nothing left of her internal organs. I could feel that much as she moved inside of me. Contorting in impossible ways. Crawling under my skin. Peeking out of my eyes. Pulling my tendons as if I were nothing more than a puppet.

The next thing I remember, I was in a hospital bed, my wrists tied to the gurney, and my mother crying over me. Everything hurt. The pain was way worse than period cramps. Worse than breaking a bone. Worse even than your appendix exploding. Free hospital drugs helped, though.

My mother called it "The Episode," the capital letters implied by her tone whenever she brought it up. All the hospital tests came back normal, so she hoped it had been a one-time thing as the doctor said, and kept on with her usual brand of parenting: ignoring me.

I don't know what Anahí and Virginia saw that day. The Hi8 tape suffered a case of spontaneous combustion when I tried playing it on Sunday after the hospital. Whatever it was, it was enough for them to be scared shitless the next day.

When I sat down next to Virginia on Monday at school, she looked at me and held her rosary high. Her eyes couldn't have been wider.

"Who are you?" she asked, trembling.

"Madonna. Who do you think I am, stupid?"

"Ok..." she sighed and tucked the rosary into her jeans pocket.

"Are you okay?" Anahí sat on our table. "What did the doctors say? That was creepy as hell, what the fuck, Verónica? Better not have been one of your candid short horror movie schemes."

"How could she have... done what she did?" Virginia protested. "She's possessed. We opened the gates and something crossed them."

As it turned out, having a religious *loca* in our pack wasn't so bad after all.

"I *feel* her crawling under my skin," I muttered. "She's inside me. I want her out as fast as possible, so tell me, Sister Virginia, how do I evict the fucker?"

"First, we need to know her name. Who she is. She must want something..."

"How? We ask her? She is not particularly chatty...."

"Easy. You tell us all you *feel* about her."

"And then?"

"Then, we go to the library."

ANAHÍ CAME to our old-magazine-covered table as fast as she could without running—Mrs. García was very particular about speed in her library—and she threw an old issue of the magazine *Más Allá* open with the picture of a girl wearing a communion dress.

"Found her," she whispered, as excited as if she had just opened a pharaoh's tomb. "This is her, isn't it?"

I took the magazine in my hands to inspect her features carefully. The girl I saw in the candlelight the night of the séance had eyes puffy with tears, her skin swollen, and her expression one of pure horror. Her dress was brownish and bloodied, but in good enough condition to recognize the white underneath it. The pearly beads. The peter-pan collar. The girl in front of me on the glossy paper was smiling with rosy cheeks, hands in prayer, eyes cheerful.

But it was her. There was no doubt.

"What happened to her?" I asked.

"According to this article" Anahí said, "her mother was a healer, a water-reader in a small village. A woman from the neighborhood started working with her. But not only working. It says here they were lovers. Witnesses said they got into some weird stuff. Well, weirder than the usual prophecy thing.

"They had visions of Hell and decided the little girl was possessed by Satan. They started calling her *Perra de Satán*. So the mother and her lover tried to perform an exorcism on her... They were, like, super high on some herbs they picked in the backyard or something. Apparently, other women joined them, and what started as an orgy, got awful real quick."

"How awful?" Virginia asked.

"They pinned her to the floor," I mumbled, rubbing my aching wrists, "and emptied her..."

The memory of the events awoke the little girl inside me. Trying to stay still, ignoring the itch of the tulle behind my skin, was the hardest thing. But we were in the library, I couldn't start to act weird and turn "The Episode" into a whole series. We needed answers, a solution before the Hollow Girl showed herself again. I didn't want to end up institutionalized when all I needed was a good old exorcism.

"How did they..." started Virginia.

The broken fingers of the Hollow Girl grabbed my ribs, scratching them with her dirty nails, and she pushed herself upwards. The taste of blood gone bad filled my mouth. Her hands fondled my tongue and my teeth, searching for a way out. Nails scratched my gums. Pushed against my jaw. I pressed my hands to my mouth, gagging, as she managed to squeeze one blackened finger out of it.

Luckily, no one saw.

"It seems like her mother shoved her hand into her... you know... and started tearing out organs saying they were demons," Anahí clarified in dismay.

As Anahí's words echoed inside my skull, a sharp pain overcame the Hollow Girl, who retreated her hands from my mouth and curled up inside me. She started to cry her communion dress was heavier now, warm, wet, soaking my insides, making me dizzy and fragile.

"Verónica..."

"What?"

"You're bleeding," Virginia said pointing to my jeans, which were rapidly turning red from blood flowing from my crotch. The library spun around me. Or I spun around it. The floor wasn't steady, the lights were too bright, the silence too loud.

I passed out.

VIRGINIA AND ANAHÍ went on a mission to collect all information available about the exorcism of the girl in the communion dress while I was tucked in bed trying my hardest to keep Satan's bitch calm. Watermelon bubblegum was her favorite. I don't think she had ever tried it when she was alive. Morning cartoons seemed to work too for the first couple of days.

There were a fair amount of news articles for us to go through. Her exorcism was only five years ago, back when we were just kids watching Heidi and Marco cartoons.

"Maybe they were right," Virginia said, sitting on the corner of my bed while I read the file they had put together, blowing bubblegum bubbles against my will.

"About what?" I asked.

"She has possessed you, hasn't she? Maybe her mother and the other women were right. Maybe she had a deal with the devil going on. Maybe they were interrupted and the exorcism wasn't properly completed."

The Hollow Girl protested inside me. She pulled at my tendons and slapped Virginia.

"Sorry, sorry, sorry!" I jumped towards her to hug her. "She didn't like that."

"Well, there's only one way to figure it out," Anahí said. "We think we know why she's roaming over here."

"Why?" I asked, trying to hold my arms still with Virginia's help. My hands kept trying to scratch her face. Anahí showed me a picture of a hospital. only two towns over.

"Her mother is *here*."

THE FIRST STEP of our plan was to try to send the Hollow Girl back to hell ourselves.

The girls convinced their parents I was sick and needed some comforting. My mother wasn't pleased with the idea, but she had to work the graveyard shift and couldn't really say no. Or she could have, like I cared.

We didn't record this Ouija board session, but it was even more unpleasant than the first attempt. This time, the Hollow Girl took full control of my mind and body. She sent me back to her living room floor.

We were naked and shivering, sprawled over the tiles, the girl and I. The house smelled of blood, sex, and piss. It was dimly lit. Nude women danced around us, their faces contorted as if they had no control over their muscles. Chanting gibberish. Touching each other. Touching us.

We couldn't move. Maybe it was just fear, or maybe it was something else. Our limbs felt unnaturally heavy. Our mouths dry. I've never been so thirsty before.

We heard banging on the door. Shouting. Pleading to be allowed inside. To stop whatever was going on.

Hands clasped our ankles. Spread our legs open. Then there was pain.

Pain.

Pain.

And darkness.

OUR FIRST INSTINCT, after the failed attempt to get rid of the Hollow Girl, was to seek her mother's help. I wasn't convinced it would do much good, but Anahí and Virginia were certain that, at least, she would give us an idea of how to proceed.

We needed an adult to accompany us to the visit we lied ourselves into with the Hollow Girl's mother. Virginia suggested it would be wise to take a priest with us, so we could sort out the most pressing matter: whether she was possessed by a demon —making me possessed by a demon by proxy— or just a pissed-off ghost. The problem was the only priest we knew was the one at Virginia's church and...well, people talk, you know? I wanted an exorcism, not to be groped, so before we knocked on his door we had already repented. The three of us stood looking at each other in the hallway. The Hollow Girl began to scratch my uterus, making me fall to my knees. It was then that Sister Inés saw us and entered our story.

Sister Inés is the most *candid*, *sweet*, *beautiful* human being you could ever meet… And despite it, when she saw me doubled over in pain, she came running and offered to help. The Hollow Girl wasn't particularly happy with our plan and she was making it known.

I hadn't felt such hunger ever in my life, but she refused to allow my body to feed. Whenever I took a bite and swallowed, she squeezed my stomach so hard that food went back into my mouth.

I was exhausted and yet she wouldn't let me sleep. As soon as I closed my eyes, she would pinch my eyelids and force them open. Scratch my ears so I could only hear that nagging sound like termites eating away at my bones.

We were lucky my mother was at work almost twenty-four hours a day. Any other parent, more present, would have noticed their child was not doing all that well. Sister Inés saw it immediately.

"Girl, what is wrong with you?" she asked honestly.

We exchanged looks that said: *Well, better a nun than a handsy priest.*

Virginia filled her in while Anahí tried her best to keep me steady.

"Come with me, girls," Sister Inés begged to take my hand. Not to be dramatic or anything, but a warm sensation climbed up my hand and reached the Hollow Girl in my womb. It put her to sleep like a lullaby.

Was it… love? Inés' faith? Well, I'll need to think about it and get back to you when I've wrapped my mind around it.

Adults don't usually believe teenage girls, less so if they are babbling about Ouija boards, Kurt Cobain's spirit, and possessed girls in communion dresses. But Sister Inés was, after all, a nun. So, she had already proved to be somewhat into the unexplainable.

She knew about the Hollow Girl. It had been all over the news.

"Here, drink this," she said, offering me a glass of water inside her office.

It was like drinking lava. My insides burned. The Hollow Girl started her hissing, she contorted inside my chest. Her fingers pressed against my neck and chest, visible through my skin as if it were nothing more than a piece of cloth. I managed to climb up the wall trying to spit the last drop of burning water.

"Holy water," Sister Inés confessed while Anahí and Virginia hid behind her. "I'll help you, girls," I heard the nun say from the floor below me. I turned my neck toward their voices.

I didn't realize my head had spun backward until they screamed.

AND SO, here we are. Waiting for our turn to meet the Hollow Girl's mother. No one bats an eye at the nun and the teen, whether they don't give a shit or they see it often remains unclear.

"Sister Inés," a man says while she cleans my spit from her face.

She grabs my hand and we follow the man to a cold room where a woman is waiting. My heart sinks. The Hollow Girl's first reaction isn't hatred or vengeance. It is primal fear.

"She's harmless, but call me if you need anything," the man says before closing the door behind him.

"That little *Perra de Satán* escaped, didn't she?" the mother asks, leaning back on her chair.

"How do you know?" Sister Inés replies, still holding my hand tightly.

"We were interrupted before we could finish the ritual, I figured she would find a way to chase me down sooner or later."

"Do you truly believe your daughter was possessed?" As she asks this question, Sister Inés lets go of my hand. The warm watermelon bubblegum lullaby that put the Hollow Girl to sleep when Sor Inés' hand tethered me to steadiness leaves my body, unleashing the spirit's full potential to control my body and mind, again.

The Hollow Girl wriggles inside my belly like a fish squirming on a hook. She climbs up with her jagged nails, clawing at my stomach, clutching at my lungs. I propel myself forward bent over, my back very straight, as if made of wrought iron, vertebrae fused together.

Without heeding my will, and with a movement so fast neither Sister Inés nor the self-proclaimed exorcist has time to react, my hands grab the face of the Hollow Girl's mother.

I bring her lips close to mine and kiss her. My tongue tangles with hers. Her hollow daughter inside me, demonized and pissed off, crawls with the taste of rotten earth and sour blood across my tongue, entering hers, like a snail sliding from one leaf to another.

Chairs fall to the ground. Guards enter the room. They try to free the woman from my grasp. My nails tear her skin when they push me back, but our lips remain locked onto one another until the feet of the Hollow Girl and the last strand of her blood-soaked dress leave my unhinged jaw.

We both fall backward.

I feel nothing. There's no one inside me anymore. I look at my hands, nails bit to their beds, and flex my fingers. I'm in control of my own body again. Everything hurts, though. It's not a second-hand pain, but all mine. The damage the Hollow Girl did to my body is starting to show. But I am free.

Then I hear the howling. The loud crack of bones shattering.

Sister Inés helps me to my feet. I peek back and see, clearly, the Hollow Girl taking over her mother's body. Snapping bones and reaping organs, while a couple of orderlies try to hold the howling woman still.

She is finally getting her revenge. As we leave through the door, I escape Sister Inés' hands and turn back.

Hovering over the woman, the Hollow Girl looks back at me. Her mother lies motionless on the ground in a pool of blood. The communion dress is white again. Her cheeks are rosy. Her skin, clean.

She winks at me, smiling, and then dissolves into thin air like dust.

Right on.

J.V. Gachs is a Spanish classicist, and horror writer. Writing in English and Spanish her work has been featured in magazines such as Luna Station Quarterly or Mordedor, and anthologies like Scott J. Moses' What One Wouldn't Do and Cursed Morsels' Antifa Splatterpunk. Her first novel Epiphany will be published by Off Limits Press in 2023. Obsessed with sudden death and ghosts, she always writes with a cat (or two) in her lap. She can be found at jvgachs.com or on social media as @jvgachs.

"About A Girl" is illustrated by Jenny Kiefer.

THRESHOLD

DAMIEN B. RAPHAEL

2 6th of September, 1995. It's a date seared into Southampton's history, even though the events that day are hazy for most. Like a magic trick, the only lasting impression was something invisible: Laurence Holder's complete disappearance. The fallout of media frenzy was enough to poison his neighbourhood of Eastleigh, chatter in cafes and schoolyards reskinned and sculpted into urban

legends. Tales about the video game he was obsessed with—pirated on a floppy disk shared around amusement arcades, whispers overheard by spooked parents leading to an outright ban on visiting places like Quasar, Way Out West, and Big George's Fish Shop. Venues long since gone, or now, devoid of arcade games entirely.

26th of September, 1995 is a date woven into Wayne Connett's memory too.

He remembers it scrawled around the city at the time, simply the date painted in Dulux emulsion, sun-baked hope. An anniversary of Laurence's last known whereabouts. The vandalism caught on like a collective guilt, copycatted over bus stop windows. Etched with frenzied scratches. Wayne's attempts were nothing more than a fumbling with aerosol cans that dyed his fingers beetroot-red. A destructive means to ease his own personal guilt that he hadn't read the warning signs: Laurence's lack of basic hygiene, his sudden introspection. But like everything else, given time, the vandalism subsided in the flux of moving on, kept alive for a few more years in Wayne's GCSE textbooks, ground out in ballpoint, and once on a night of underage drinking, emblazoned across the seafront in liquid polish stolen from Woolworths.

Ever since, the anniversary for Wayne has been methodically internalised. Quietly encoded onto his soul. It was the reason for his vocation: his nurse training, his specialism in mental health. A career inspired by the assumptions of Laurence's suicide, any unanswered calls for help. A career that would end Wayne's unquenchable sense of guilt.

IT'S WITH WAYNE NOW, the guilt, parked up outside the meeting point.

Wayne's hands, chapped from an obsessive use of hospital sanitizer, clutch his steering wheel like it's an anchor to adulthood. The road is deserted, streetlights burning away the night in a ubiquitous, peachy glow. Wayne tries unsuccessfully to pinpoint the drum and bass music emanating from the brutalist flats towering over his VW Golf, a concrete mass bearing down with all the despair of untold below-the-poverty-line existences. Rechecking the autolock, he scrolls through his messages again to make sure he's at the right address. He is: Milton View, a notorious council estate that hasn't been ameliorated in the twenty-seven years he's been gone. A place he would never be seen dead in: and still wouldn't, if it wasn't for a text from Paul.

Wayne had been back in town helping his parents when he'd received it. No pleasantries, just an image: a picture of a floppy disk with Laurence's anniversary taped to it. And a meeting point and time, and a *see you there. Your old mate, Paul.*

Paul. One of the original kids of their video game crew from secondary school. He owed him that much, at least. A reunion. A sense of closure.

Wayne's anxiety spikes to the moon as a blurred face peeks through the misted passenger window, knuckles tapping on glass. A whisper-quiet *Jesus!* escapes Wayne's clenched teeth before he opens up, a whirring motor mechanism the only noise as they stare down one another. Not much more than three feet separates them, yet it was a gulf of decades. Because underneath the weathered face is the school kid that Wayne used to know, mummified beneath a nest of tired wrinkles.

"You made it then," says Paul. "Long time. Long, long time. Fancy a pint?"

Without much small talk—thanks in part to a heavy rain beginning to fall, and Wayne's preoccupation of having his car bonnet keyed—they make it to the nearest dive of a sports pub, the locals eyeballing Wayne's lack of football shirt or trackie bottoms. Paul gets a round in, and they nab a table in the corner, underneath a huge TV on a constant loop of Sky news and a faulty radiator intent on blasting out nuclear heat. It's the first time Wayne can get a proper look at his old friend and it's like his style hasn't evolved past the nineties. Paul's hair is combed forward, a tub of gel fixing it in place.

A 'step' runs around the back of his head: an antecedent to the fashionable fades that almost all men sport now, including Wayne. Also strange is how he fidgets with a gold necklace between generous sips of beer, knees bouncing amphetamine-quick.

Wayne was sure that Paul would just come out and talk about the picture he'd sent him, but the lack of conversation is unnervingly off-putting. Instead, Wayne chats about himself to fill the void. About his history from then until now, the nursing degree, the two-year rotation programme in hospitals and schools and psych wards, the daily grind from grade d to h, where the paperwork and abusive patients (shitters and kickers) and their perpetual relapses finally burnt him out. Deep down, he'd been strangely relieved when his mother told him she couldn't cope caring for his Dad anymore. Happy to leave the toxic workplace politics behind for the sake of his own mental health.

"How's life been treating you, then?" Wayne tries not to slur his words and wonders how he'd allowed himself to be talked into getting shitfaced on a damp Tuesday night in a corner of nowhere.

"I can't complain," says Paul.

"And the picture? What gives, sending me that old disc. Pretty sick joke."

He wanted to say it was an odd prop to cosplay, too. Oddly authentic, with scuffs and yellowed tape, and Laurence's anniversary typed out on an old-school Dyno label maker, the font all capitals and no nonsense. Supposedly, as Paul has insisted on a couple of random texts, it was the *actual* game that Laurence was playing at the time of his disappearance. An urban legend about as believable as the tale of those sixth form girls who used a Ouija board in Laurence's then-abandoned home, their wine glass planchette scratching out 2, 6, 9, 5 over and over until it snapped in two, a shattered stem impaling one of their wrists.

"Well?" asks Wayne.

Paul doesn't flinch, biting down on a piece of lemon before knocking back the tequila.

"You remember," says Paul, "all those days we spent hanging out at the arcades?"

"Absolutely."

"You. Me. Daz. Locksy. Laurence. How we skipped school and dominated all the regulars on Killer Instinct at Munchies Café? The force completions at Green Trees. Locksy being banned from Game Exchange, after beating their instore champion at Mortal Kombat II?"

"Yeah," says Wayne. "Course."

"You remember our allegiance?"

Wayne takes a sip of his cider, the memories flooding back. The night of vandalism along the seafront and pier. A swansong of ink drips and blood oaths.

"We swore," continues Paul, "that we'd never give up looking for Laurence."

Wayne nods and before he can respond, Paul pulls down his bottom lip. On the inner skin is a tattoo, its colour the same blue as arteries. 26/09/95. Paul's demeanor shifts as his glazed eyes become a touch more lucid. "Got something else to tell you, actually. Not sure what you'd make of it. They might cart me off to the madhouse. No offense."

Paul's confession lasts perhaps a minute. That, sometimes, when he zones out just before sleep, or after the first tokes of weed after work, or even in moments when he's entering different rooms in his high-rise flat, just sometimes, he catches glimpses of Laurence. Not a ghostly form, he assures Wayne, but physical. As if that detail made it okay. And with the apparition: an accompanying noise that's stretched like a signal too high to perceive. Like radio waves from the early universe. The admission creeps under Wayne's skin, snug as a splinter.

By the time they walk outside at quarter to midnight, after an evening spent boozing like they're students again, he staggers over to a set of industrial bins and throws up the evening's excess. Paul pats him on the back like it's a job well done. As if they are drinking Hooch behind the local Co-op. Alcohol was a stupid way of dealing with Paul's tale, Wayne knew. But the orthodox strategy of consoling his friend didn't seem right either: monotone discussions of how grief can affect us all differently, especially a tragedy without a perceivably end. Wayne could have even put him in contact with decent CBT therapists, or a few viable private ones. Yet the words didn't come, his tongue tied down by the memory of seeing something too. Something anomalous. It would happen usually on waking night shifts whilst doing handovers, or adding next day's staff to the whiteboard. Something in the corners of his vision. A boy in a Technics bomber jacket. Pale faced. Smiling. A fading, traceless effigy.

Like a polaroid in reverse.

Maybe Wayne should have opened up there and then outside the pub, confide in Paul that, yes, he isn't alone. But openly talking about ghosts? News travels fast. And if his team got wind of it, there'd be questions raised, no doubt. About his workload, his progression. His career.

"I can't let you drive home in that state," Paul says. "Listen: there's something else I have to show you, actually. I think it would help."

IT'S ONLY A FIVE-MINUTE WALK, but Wayne's unwilling legs and Paul's relentless optimism about the surprise in store, makes it feel like a pilgrimage walked on bare feet.

"This is going to blow your mind, mate," insists Paul, bringing a fist up to his head, and detonating his fingers. "Trust me, pal."

Yet for all the buildup, and promise of more booze and weed and valium, when they do eventually arrive, it's an anticlimax. Paul stops short in front of an end of terrace, Victorian townhouse. Its frontage that has been boarded up, the smoke-stained brickwork filtering a century of pollution. Mantels of once chalky white, now grey and tired.

"The hell is this place," says Wayne.

"My home of three years," says Paul, as he brandishes some keys, jingling them right in front of Wayne's eyeline. "Won at a property auction, thirty-five k. Not bad, when the local average is two hundred thousand."

Unlocking the front door, Wayne could sense why. The hall is a syrupy dark, filled with mounds of indistinguishable shapes. And a smell, something nostalgic. A deodorant? Paul presents an open palm, an over-the-top welcome.

"This isn't an elaborate stitchup, is it?"

Paul does a mock three finger Scout salute.

"Right," says Wayne under his breath, and flips on the torch of his phone. The shoulder-high shapes are actually stacks of old electronics, tube style TV units and beige PC tower cases, an assortment leagues above even the staunchest hoarders. Wayne twists and contorts his body through, finding refuge in the kitchen.

Paul follows close behind and turns on a bare light bulb, temporarily blinding them both. The space is almost devoid of tat, though stomach-churningly dirty. Paint peels off from the ceiling like strips of neglect. The fridge, stove, microwave, are all licked with a coating of nicotine.

"Sunshine Mick?" says Paul out of nowhere, chucking a teabag in a Dairy Milk mug. "Do you remember him? D'you remember that day?"

The silence of the room seems to push in against Wayne's head, a dull ache behind his eyes, alcohol yielding to adrenaline. Yes, how could he not? One of the main suspects in Laurence's disappearance, the social outcast that ran a small little arcade near Hanover Buildings, always sporting a pair of knock-off Rayban, and a frayed straw boater hat sandwiched on top of an unkempt, greying ponytail.

"That weirdo who owned the arcade? Used to put on puppet shows in the courtyard outside, yeah, I remember that misfit," says Wayne.

Paul flips the switch of the kettle. "And at closing time, he'd march round that dingy arcade turning off machines regardless of how much change you'd sunk in 'em. The bastard. And what about that prank you played on him, when he was on the verge of winning a world-besting high score on 1941? It was you who persuaded Laurence to do it, didn't you? To pull the plug. Now, Sunshine wasn't particularly strong, him and his chicken legs, but boy did he beat the crap out of Laurence that day."

The kettle boils. Wayne licks his teeth, his mouth suddenly dry. "We were kids. Shit happens. And I was the one who called the police from the phone box."

Paul shrugs. "Sunshine's little arcade went bust thanks to all his pictures in the local rags, and the guilt by association when Laurence disappeared. The prime suspect. You think he did it? Kidnapped Laurence and murdered him?"

"Fuck knows," says Wayne. Paul retrieves a rollie from behind his ear, lights up, and exhales a twinned stream of smoke through his nose. Wayne clears his throat, and says, "Look, this whole meeting. It was a bad idea, I'm sorry. My Dad, he—"

"This was Sunshine Mick's house."

That name again. Like a slap around the face. Wayne scrambles for a response, to block a tide of memories, of old neural pathways being wedged open with a screwdriver.

"Bollocks," says Wayne. A reflex, the only response he's got.

"You ain't seen nothing, yet. Just come and take a look. Five minutes. That's all."

Despite the twisting in his stomach, that tingling feeling of trespassing as a kid, the smile that Paul brandishes wins him a little more time. They start in the living room, and after Paul flicks the power on from a tampered fuse box, Wayne's jaw lowers like a drawbridge in defeat. He counts eight arcade cabinets lining the walls, each coin slot glowing cranberry red. There's Yie Ar Kung Fu, and TANK! TANK! TANK! and Splatterhouse all chattering away in a din of noise that makes Wayne's skin break out in goose pimples of wonder. A kitchen table in the centre is stacked high with PCBs spotted with dust bunnies, controllers, old Atari STs lying open as if someone had been tinkering with them that afternoon. There's old gaming posters rolled up by the hundred plus stacks of gaming magazines: Computer and Video Games, GamesMaster. Bags of old fifty pence pieces are strewn left, right, and centre.

Wayne lets out a laugh, picking up an old Mega Drive cartridge:

Golden Axe. It's like a shot of undiluted childhood. Like slipping into all those summer holidays in Great Yarmouth, spending every single coin he'd earnt washing cars on titles just like the one he was seeing now. There was even that arcade smell, of old carpet, plastic, and sweat masked by Lynx Java—the citrus tang unmistakable. Laurence's favourite.

Wayne goes to ask Paul if he can have a go, but he's already gone, hopping up the hallway stairs, his Reebok trainers stomping on creaking steps. As Wayne follows him, Paul cocks his head halfway up the stairs as if to say *this way* and carries on.

Dust scratches Wayne's throat like fiberglass by the time he reaches the first floor. A space littered with scrunched-up packets of noodles, a grimy sleeping bag. Traces of Paul's day-to-day activity.

"You must be sitting on a gold mine here," says Wayne, reaching Paul, standing at the bottom of another set of stairs. Only, Paul puts a finger to his mouth, and points.

Wayne stops still, staring at a date splashed across a wall at the top of a stairwell.

26/09/95.

It's painted in erratic, violent gestures. A white Dulux emulsion, probably. Cracked from age.

The numbers glue Wayne's Ben Sherman shoes to a groove in the threadbare carpet.

"Hey," says Paul, sensing Wayne's trepidation. "You've come this far."

Paul climbs the rest of the steps two at a time, and unlocks a door leading off somewhere, disappearing inside.

Not for the first time, Wayne thinks about ghosting him, hurrying back to his Golf, blasting his face with cold air con, and driving to somewhere far from Southampton, to a patch of starless night deep in the Wiltshire countryside, maybe. It's the same gut feeling he's gotten whenever the fatigue starts to play tricks on his mind, the anxiety constricting his chest, a python coiling between ribs. He can hear Paul imploring him from inside the room. His voice sounds strung out, as if it's skipping across a stretch of frozen waters.

"*Wayne.*"

A new voice, now. Yet it's clearer. Younger.

Charged with static.

There's a creeping recognition from the base of Wayne's dodgy back right up to his balding scalp. That it isn't Paul. And doesn't belong to the world of present day. A boy's voice. A quiver of hesitancy in its tone.

Wayne takes it one step at a time, clutching the handrail. *Just have a quick look*, he thinks. *It can't be what you think. It can't be who you think.*

"Hello?" says Wayne, "*Laurence?*"

There's a second of full fat silence, before Wayne bulldozes his way up the stairs, a bluff of cutting a path directly through his fear. Half falling through the door, Wayne scans the room only to find Paul and no one else. No arcade machines, either. Just pine bookcases punctuating the room like Scandinavian stellae, overloaded with vintage programming books, reams of old graph paper, silvered in places from layers of obsessive penciling. The walls are crucified with newspaper clippings. Seemingly every article ever printed about Laurence's case.

Central to everything is an old beech-veneered desk, plastered with faded Hero Turtle stickers, complete with a Commodore 64, monitor, joystick, acoustic coupler, an olive-green rotary telephone. And the floppy disk from Paul's photo.

"Here it is," says Paul, sitting down reverently at the computer, pulling out the disk from its cardboard sleeve. "*The* game Laurence was playing at the time he disappeared. Not a fake."

Paul smiles. He inserts the disk into the drive, boots up, and types LOAD "*",8,1 into the command prompt. The title screen forms in a wash of pixelated blocks. "Sunshine hand coded this beast," he says, "the only one in existence."

There are noises from the street below, crashing bottles from a bin somewhere, screeching foxes. The mundanity makes Wayne's head spin, normal life invading this space, this anachronism, a trespasser like he is. He thinks about leaving again, but the pulse of black and purple graphics arrests his eyes.

"Turns out Sunshine was a genius," Paul says. "Can you imagine writing code like this with no internet, no tutorials, no nothing. Only works when it's connected to the internet too—or some ancient back corridor of the web, anyway. Fucked if I know. I tried unplugging the modem, but it doesn't run."

The screen opens with the title: THRESHOLD, written in that faux-futuristic font so popular back in the day, a chrome fade reflecting the brown mountains of some Martian, desert terrain. Paul's face, washed in the monitor's glow, seems suddenly ten years younger, until the screen goes black, quickly followed by a slow-scrolling quote:

"Some I sent into the fire, unto the embrace of the flames, which was the last visible sign of their footsteps."

And then the game starts, the player dropped into gameplay without preamble. It's a format Wayne vaguely remembers: an isometric world in which the map reloads after entering every scene. The graphics depict a rundown Southampton, that isn't quite Southampton. Or not England at all. There are wrecked cars. Corpses in the streets. Smashed shop fronts. All rendered in a blocky style of 8-bit, outdated technology.

Within minutes, Paul's attempt is over, his onscreen sprite falling down an open manhole. "It's bolt hard, this game. Really is. I've only ever gotten to level fourteen out of seventy, and even then, I suspect it was luck." Paul unsticks the joystick's feet from the table and offers it up to Wayne like a chalice.

"Your turn," says Paul. "You were always the best of us. If anyone can complete it, you can."

Peeling off his jacket before sitting down, Wayne adjusts the gaming chair, and starts maneuvering the character around the map with a joystick far more cumbersome than he remembers. The onscreen character wields a battery-operated torch needing replacing every time the batteries drains, sometimes fast, sometimes slow. Wherever Wayne points the character, a portion of environment becomes illuminated in a pyramid of light.

"There's clues hidden around the world," says Paul. "Like a diary in a bedroom of an abandoned house. But every time you die, like when the torch loses charge, or you get chased and killed by the shadow man who dwells in the city, you have to start again. To win, you have to locate the remains of Chloe Launderer, and put her bones to rest in a family mausoleum. Chloe Launderer, get it? Laurence Holder?"

Wayne's first play goes horribly wrong, the torch's battery draining almost instantly. On his seventh life he finds the diary. On his eighth, the shadow man appears, a contorted stick figure in a boating hat that moves with ping pong-like rapidity. Wayne cries out as the figure tears up the screen, thanks in part to the accompanying sound effect: an ear-piercing trill as if the Commodore's sound chip is melting.

"Gets me every time that," says Paul, sitting down beside him with a tray of tea, a multipack of Twix bars, and a little resealable bag of white powder. Wayne hadn't even registered he'd gone. He checks the time: quarter past two in the morning.

"Listen," says Wayne, putting down the joystick. "I really should be making a move. It is fascinating, all this. But, the guy was a loner, an obsessed loner. The game's probably unbeatable. Anyway. Been good catching up, yeah?"

Paul is silent as Wayne stands and gathers up his jacket, his eyes set purposefully forward, not daring to make eye contact.

"It's not just any game," says Paul, quietly. "It's a means of finding Laurence."

Wayne lets out a sigh, hours in the making. "Laurence is dead, Paul. And we both need to let him go. Start by getting rid of all this crap. It's chaining you to the past. You believe you'll find him still, but there's despair in hope if held on too long. Renovate the house. Sell it. Go traveling. Backpacking in Laos, or somewhere. Anywhere but here. He was our friend. I'm sorry."

As Wayne traipses down the stairs, popping the corduroy collars of his rain mac, Paul hurries down after him, "But you swore you'd never give up."

"Fuck sake, man—"

"I can show you Laurence."

Wayne screws up his face in disbelief, processing the words that just came out of Paul's mouth.

"Yeah," continues Paul. "I've completed the game, I just wanted you to see. After the final boss, a set of numbers gets revealed. Co-ordinates. 50.9026° N. It's 2,6,0,9.5—the same bloody numbers. And Laurence's birthday: fourteenth of March, 1982. 1.4032° W, it's all there, mate. It's his location."

Wayne pinches the bridge of his nose, resisting the mental gymnastics. "So what if the numbers are co-ordinates? What does that prove?"

"Follow me right now, and I'll never bother you again with this. I fucking promise."

It's a long walk to the city centre. Made longer by Wayne's begrudging feet. About halfway, Wayne pops into a petrol station to buy some cigarettes, Lambert and Butler for old time's sake. Paying at the counter, he catches their fuzzy, monochrome image on a CCTV monitor, its timestamp a blur from years of burn-in. It has a dissociative effect: makes Wayne look like another bland, faceless goon of the rat race, another middle-aged professional filling up the tank with diesel. And Paul, oblivious to the image, choosing some prawn cocktail Pringles, someone who never outgrew munchies and getting stoned. It reminds Wayne of the last images of Laurence. Where he queued up at the bar of Riley's snooker hall in town, acting suspicious, or—as Wayne often ponders having endlessly rewatched the clip on YouTube—utterly tweaked out on speed.

By the time they reach the old Bargate shopping centre, it's pretty much all but dead, apart from the homeless people rammed up against shop fronts, life-size chrysalides. The once-bustling mall is now a shadow of its former self, infected with decay. The place where they used to hang out as teenagers. One of the last places that Wayne remembers seeing Laurence alive.

Paul hitches up his rucksack, without saying a word. Wayne had wondered what exactly he'd hastily packed, but felt disinclined to ask. The night had been weird enough. Wayne takes a long drag of a newly-lit cigarette and lets the tar steep in his lungs, sensing Paul's new business-like manner.

"Laurence is in *there?*"

Paul nods. "From day one. There's an access point on the roof."

Making their way to the back of the shopping centre, Paul wastes little time in scaling up bins and fire ladders and rope-thick cables like he'd done it a million times before.

"But I'm not good with heights," calls Wayne.

Paul doesn't answer. So, Wayne deliberately takes his time, each foot placement tested and retested, determined not to slip, until he joins Paul on the roof, his heart hammering from the sheer juvenile thrill of breaking and entering.

"What next?" asks Wayne, taking in the skyline. Seagulls caw overhead, a blast of wind lashing their backs. Paul offers a hand to signal patience, scanning his phone light over rusting air vents and patches of bubbling roofing membranes and smashed sky-light windows angled at forty-five degrees, a two-storey drop beneath them.

"Over there," says Paul, before scrambling over a series of vents and slipping into a small, dark opening.

Wayne puffs out his cheeks. Nods to himself.

Crouching down, virtually crawling, Wayne enters too. The opening leads to an antechamber filled with piping and cabling; an area never meant to be seen by the public. Paul doesn't seem to notice him, grabbing hold of some metal cladding and peering over the edge. It prompts Wayne to do the same, and it's only then he realises quite how far they've climbed.

The mall below is cavernous.

A space so big, the light of Paul's phone can't even attempt to pierce the layers of shadows that cushion the depths. Wayne can just about see a set of dilapidated escalators forty feet down, and despite himself, his curiosity is piqued. It's a place that he used to remember so vibrantly, with so much life, thrumming with consumerism. Now dead and scooped-out.

As they climb down a steel structure welded permanently in place, Paul mutters something like *easy does it, easy does* it—the first time he's offered up any concerns for safety. "Any slip now, mate," he says louder, "and we'll have a forty-foot freefall onto imported marble."

The adrenaline coursing through Wayne's body has rendered his hands like clamps, though, and soon, after taking a lot longer in his descent than Paul, Wayne sets foot on the concourse of the mall, heels clicking home. Glass and debris and old cheque books litter the ground. Close by, the handrails of the escalators are completely shorn off like giant liquorice strips, and beyond them, another drop of fifty feet or so straight down to the basement.

"Here," says Paul, pulling something out of his rucksack. "You should be the one."

Paul hands over a resealable bag with an old-school torch contained within. Bright red, and smeared with fingerprints, the gaps in its case grouted with old sweat. Before Wayne can switch it on, Paul grabs his hand, refusing to let go. "There's not much I can say to prepare you for this. But don't run. You could break your neck."

Wayne flicks on the torch. Its beam cuts into the space, an arc of pure incredulity. Where once there was abandonment, there now resides a pristine wonderland. The mall as it once was. Gleaming surfaces. Neon signs. Potted plants. Rows of spotlights punctuating immaculate mannequins. Every wall is painted in that homogenous swimming-centre-blue that only true Sotonians would doubtless remember. And shops long since bankrupted, open for business; Burton, Littlewoods, Our Price. Filled with merchandise. Brimming with cellophaned stock. The only thing missing is the people.

"What the actual fuck?" whispers Wayne, mouth dry as dust.

Paul tentatively shakes his head. "This is where Laurence lives, now."

"Yeah. But. Where is this?"

"It's when, not where. 1995. The threshold. I know, I know, it's messed up. You can lose your mind, if you think about it too hard. So don't. And don't dilly dally wither. We got to be quick. The batteries never last long."

After Wayne clicks his neck, he follows Paul, matching his cautious steps. They reach the escalators, and in the beam of the torch, the revolving metal steps and glistening handrail look as polished as ever. "Don't bother with them," Paul says. "I nicked a talking Barney from the Argos downstairs once, and sat it on there just to see. Thing got mangled. Shredded to bits. Something about being in two worlds at once, I guess."

They take the stairs instead, descending deeper into the aberration of time. The beam has an effect of a swimming pool in the darkness of the present: ripples of light jounce outwards, sounds scattering from the past to the present, twisting and echoing and gnawed. Wayne can't believe how calm his friend is. It's an effort for him not to hyperventilate. He concentrates on the talking therapies he's dished out to people in his care. Advice on agoraphobia, and dissociation. Advice fading from him like the blood from his cheeks. And the more he ventures inside the ad hoc labyrinth he's lit up, the more unease breeds between each shortened breath from the fever dream of shell suits and baggy jeans, forgotten VCR players, aftershaves, vintage football kits, and a Beatties shopfront crammed with pristine Monaco Scalextric sets and Tamiya Mini Cooper models and Playstation 1's selling for £399.99. Wayne pauses briefly there as if he's a kid again, cajoling his mum to buy shit she can't afford, for Christmases spent well below the breadline.

When they reach the basement level, Wayne stops altogether. He knows this is the spot now, the place where his friend was leading him to all along.

One of England's biggest amusement arcades.

"A bit farther," says Paul, taking a breather beside a life-size statue of Sonic. "promise."

Sega Park is the only place where there's noise. A dim mix of arcade machines, and a garbled version of Oasis' *Some Might Say* leaking through the speakers. Paul forges ahead, until, at the top of a set of stairs, carpeted in the grey and blue of Sega's livery, he thrusts a hand across Wayne's chest, ordering him to stop.

Without a word, he motions with a tilt of his head for Wayne to look below. At an arcade cabinet. 1941. The one on which a teenage boy is playing, silhouetted by a halo of electric white. Dressed in stonewashed jeans. A Spliffy coat. Hair gelled into place, a centre parting.

It's a sight that collapses Wayne.

His legs buckle underneath him, until he's kneeling, crumpled against a pane of glass etched with Sega logos. The torch in his hand has taken on a weight of a blackhole, its gravity coalescing from a lifetime's worth of guilt.

"It's impossible."

"Here," whispers Paul, gently taking the torch from Wayne. "Go on. Talk to him."

Wayne wipes his eyes, gathering himself. And using the cheat codes of reality, steps into the torch's beam. Into Sega Park. As it once was. It's like slipping into a preternatural dome, a silken place. He looks back towards Paul, but he can't be seen, just a point of blinding light, shimmering from his tears. A weird cinema projector throwing out defunct dimensions.

Go on. Paul's voice filters into the arcade, *I'm right behind you.*

Each step feels like an age, a sacrilege, but soon, Wayne is standing beside his long-lost friend, a fully-fledged legend.

"Laurence?" he says, sniffling back tears.

The boy turns to face him. A youthful face, preserved wrong. Like he's been bathed in formaldehyde, the skin beneath his eyes sagging and crinkled. Eyes sore to the point of bleeding tears. He tries to speak, but it's an unintelligible moan from a thirty-year vow of silence.

"It's alright, mate. It's okay. Listen, can I play?"

Wayne sidles up closer to him, hits the player two button.

Come on, Laurence. Paul's voice echoes around them, closer now, but still firmly residing in the real, derelict reality of Bargate. *Wayne's here. Let him play. You've paid enough for his coercion.*

There is something in Paul's voice that ices Wayne's heart. Before he can ask for reassurance, Paul angles the torch, and grabs Laurence's hood, wrenching him arse-backward into the present, the skin of his hands peeling clean from joystick and buttons.

"You got him?" says Wayne, spinning around, one hand on the machine, the other shielding his eyes from the torch. "Hey? You got him, yeah?"

Your turn, Wayne. Just keep playing, and don't mind HIM.

The torch snaps off, the arcade engulfing Wayne whole.

"Hey. *Paul?*"

Glancing around, Wayne stifles a cry, trapped in a private, mirror archive of Sega Park Southampton.

And there above, a figure stands at the top of the stairs they'd just descended, or rather hovers, fleeting between standing and flickering faster than the eye. Wayne isn't sure how long he's been there, but is undeniably sure it's Sunshine Mick from the boater hat alone. A paler version of him, at least. Bloated too, from the glimpses Wayne can identify. Veins wispy against pockmarked skin, hands clotted with white emulsion. Taller than any human should be. Mick's seething form ricochets to a stop by a pool table meters from Wayne, letting out a deep and rotted noise, stretching into a scream that cracks his eel-blue lips.

And Wayne understands.

Because even through that ear-piercing hiss, the meaning is clear: *keep playing*, it sings. *Beat my high score.*

DAMIEN B. RAPHAEL lives and works in Oxfordshire. His stories have appeared in The Ghastling. You can follow him on Instagram @damienbraphael.

"Threshold" is illustrated by Jenny Kiefer.

ACKNOWLEDGMENTS

AHH! That's What I Call Horror started as a group project among weird, horror writing friends and acquaintances. As a crew of about twenty, we collectively chose the theme of '90s horror and embarked on turning our stories into an anthology. For the first few months the group chat was filled with brainstorms, critique swapping, deadlines come and gone, writers come and gone (life, am I right?), and lots and lots of memes. After the stories were complete, "the '90s kids" nominated me, Chelsea Pumpkins, to take over as editor. And it's been a blast.

So, first and foremost, thank you to all the authors in this anthology for putting your faith and trust in me to carry our work over the finish line. I've come to love each of your '90s horror stories as my own, and I'm so grateful you chose to put them in my care. If you're proud of the book you're holding in your hand right now, then I've done my job. Thank you for making it fun, rewarding, and easy (most of the time).

The aesthetic design of this book is a perfect complement to its contents. Thank you, P.L. McMillan, for coordinating all the artistic efforts and for contributing your own inimitable talents to the interior illustrations, line breaks, and all kinds of merchandise. Thank you, Jenny Kiefer, for volunteering your time and hands to the other half of the interior illustrations. It's still my goal to get Devon Sawa to read this book for you. And thank you to our final (and most colorful) artist, Cassie Daley. The cover and matching swag are everything us '90s kids wanted and more. You truly brought our weird little dreams to life.

When I took this over, I had no idea what publishing a book really takes. I couldn't have made it this far without the generosity of those who've gone before me, and I have many friends to thank for chipping in their time, wisdom, and skills to help me get here. Thank you, Chris O'Halloran, for helping me copyedit. Thank you, Jolie Toomajan and Jessica Peter, for providing sensitivity reading for every story. Thank you, Bridget D. Brave, for drafting up the best anthology contract I've ever seen. Thank you, C.B. Jones, for your memes and schemes. Thank you, J.W. Donley, for all the video chats explaining the process of publishing to me. Thank you, Caleb Stephens, for all your sage marketing advice. Thank you, Patrick Barb, for drumming up the back cover copy. Thank you, Max Booth III, for kicking off our stories in style. Thank you again, P.L., for being my sounding board (*did she just say sounding?!*) through this whole endeavor. I promise I love your art, forever and always. And thank you, Carson Winter, for formatting the manuscript, tolerating me, and for the whole mad idea.

I was a reader before I was a writer, and as a writer my appreciation for readers has grown exponentially. Thank you to every single person who has given this book a chance. From blurbers to bloggers —whether the cover caught your eye, or I bullied you into buying a copy; whether you left it a Goodreads review or left it collecting dust on your nightstand—I sincerely appreciate you.

Finally, I've gotten more support from my family and friends than I could have hoped for. Thank you to everyone who's asked me about this project and listened to me ramble excitedly right past my welcome. Thank you to my parents for being the first to order a copy. And thank you so, so much to my husband who fed, encouraged, and cheered me along every step of the way. I love you.

CONTRIBUTORS

Chelsea Pumpkins
Editor
Who in the World is The Hat Man?

Most likely to turn the light on during Bloody Mary.

Max Booth III
Foreword

Biggest stack of Christopher Pike fan letters returned to sender.

S. E. Denton
Madame Crystal

Cutest Couple: S. E. & Gillian Anderson.

Bridget D. Brave
The Harvest Queen

Most likely to star on *Mr. Show*

Christopher O'Halloran
Between the Barbie and the Deep-Blue Ranger

Most likely to be a Dickies catalog model.

Caleb Stephens
The Grunge

Most consecutive bounces on a Pogo Bal.

Edith Lockwood
Nona's First and Last Album Drop

Most evocative Lunchables Pizza artist.

C. B. Jones
The One With the Mysterious Package

Most kills in *Goldeneye N64*.

Mathew Wend
Caution: Choking Hazard

Most likely to sit on a flagpole for Harvey Danger.

P. L. McMillan
Return to Gray Springs: Blockbuster Blues

Most reading pizza parties won; *Fear Street* series.

Carson Winter
Alive and Living (Pilot)

Loudest laugh on the *Boy Meets World* laugh track.

Patrick Barb
The End of the Horror Story

Most likely to wear out his *Mallrats* VHS.

J. W. Donley
The Final Away Game

Homecoming King with Queen, Gwen Stefani.

J. V. Gachs
About A Girl

Most likely to sing backup for Christina y los Subterráneos.

Damien B. Raphael
Threshold

Most likely to trade you his lunch milk for your Opal Fruits.

Jenny Kiefer
Artist

Biggest collection of HitClips.

Cassie Daley
Artist

Most likely to get Polly Pocket stuck up her nose.

COVER ARTIST

CASSIE DALEY is a writer and illustrator living in Northern California. Her first published short story, *Ready or Not*, debuted as a part of Fright Girl Summer, and is available to read online. Her nonfiction has been published by Unnerving Magazine, and her short fiction has appeared in several horror anthologies. Her first YA horror novella, BRUTAL HEARTS, was published in 2022. She is also the creator of THE BIG BOOK OF HORROR AUTHORS: A Coloring & Activity Book and ROSIE PAINTS WITH GHOSTS, an illustrated horror book for kids.

In addition to her writing, Cassie owns an online art shop and is a host on The PikeCast, a book podcast dedicated to reading and discussing the works of Christopher Pike. You can find Cassie on Twitter as @ctrlaltcassie, and you can find her portfolio and more at ctrlaltcassie.com.

STORY ILLUSTRATORS

P.L. McMillan is a writer whose works have been known to cause rifts in time and space itself... Well, not quite. But writing often makes her feel that powerful. With a passion for cosmic horror and sci-fi horror, P.L. McMillan sees every shadow as an entryway to a deeper look into the black heart of the world, meant to be discovered and explored. Infatuated with the works of Shirley Jackson, H.P. Lovecraft, and Ridley Scott, her dream is to create stories of adventure, of chills, of heartbreak, and thrills. P.L. McMillan lives in Colorado, with her large selection of teas, her husband, and her two chinchillas (Sherlock and Spuds) – all under the supervision of their black cat overlords, Poe and Zerg. Find her on her website: https://www.plmcmillan.com/ Or on Twitter @authorplm.

Jenny Kiefer is a horror author and occasional illustrator living in Louisville, Kentucky. Her debut novel THIS WRETCHED VALLEY is forthcoming from Quirk Books in 2024. She is the co-owner of Butcher Cabin Books, a horror-specific bookstore. Her words have appeared in Pseudopod, Howls from the Dark Ages, and Miracle Monocle.

CONTENT WARNINGS

Madame Crystal by S. E. Denton: domestic terrorism

The Harvest Queen by Bridget D. Brave: cannibalism, cults, coercion, child abuse

Who in the World is The Hat Man? by Chelsea Pumpkins: implied abuse, bullying

Between the Barbie and the Deep-Blue Ranger by Christopher O'Halloran: child death, vomit

The Grunge by Caleb Stephens: gore, body horror, bullying, homophobia, overdose, alcoholism/addiction

Nona's First and Last Album Drop by Edith Lockwood: implied grooming, implied child sexual abuse, gore

The One With the Mysterious Package by C. B. Jones: sex, violence

Caution: Choking Hazard by Mathew Wend: gore, vomit

Return to Gray Springs: Blockbuster Blues by P. L. McMillan: alcoholism/addiction

Alive and Living (Pilot) by Carson Winter: parricide

The End of the Horror Story by Patrick Barb: body horror, animal death, implied sexual violence

The Final Away Game by J. W. Donley: homophobia, gore, bullying

About A Girl by J. V. Gachs: implied abuse, body horror, Christianity

Threshold by Damien B. Raphael: alcohol and drug consumption, body horror

CPSIA information can be obtained
at www.ICGtesting.com
Printed in the USA
LVHW052246030223
738450LV00003B/5